LEGION

WILLIAM PETER BLATTY was born in New York City in 1928, the son of immigrants from the Lebanon. Educated at Georgetown University, he is the author of numerous books and screenplays, including *A Shot in the Dark* and *The Exorcist*, for which he won the Academy Award.

Legion transcends *The Exorcist* in terror, suspense and intensity.

WILLIAM PETER BLATTY

Legion

FONTANA/Collins

First published in Great Britain by
William Collins Sons & Co. Ltd 1983
A continental edition first issued
in Fontana Paperbacks 1984
This edition issued in Fontana Paperbacks 1984

Made and printed in Great Britain by
William Collins Sons & Co. Ltd, Glasgow

Acknowledgements
My thanks to my good friend, Jack Vizzard, for first
suggesting the theory of 'The Angel'; and to the
lovely Julie Jourdan, without whose encouragement and
support this novel could not have been written.

For Billy and Jennifer
with love
from their father

PART ONE

Jesus asked the man his name,
and he answered,
'Legion,
for we are many.'

Mark 5.9

SUNDAY, MARCH 15

Chapter One

He thought of death in its infinite groanings, of Aztecs ripping out living hearts and of cancer and three-year-olds buried alive and he wondered whether God was alien and cruel; but then remembered Beethoven and the dappling of things and the lark and 'Hurrah for Karamazov' and kindness. He stared at the sun coming up behind the Capitol, streaking the Potomac with orange light; and then down at the outrage, the horror at his feet. Something had gone wrong between man and his creator and the evidence was here on this boathouse dock.

'I think they've found it, Lieutenant.'

'Excuse me?'

'The hammer. They've found it.'

'The hammer. Oh, yes.'

Kinderman's thoughts found a grip on the world. He looked up and saw the crime lab crew on the dock. They were gathering with eyedropper, test tube and forceps; remembering with camera, sketchpad and chalk. Their voices were hushed, mere whispered fragments, and they moved without sound, grey figures in a dream. Nearby, the blue police dredgeboat's engines churned with the morning's completion of dread.

'Well, I guess we're almost finished here, Lieutenant.'

'Are we really? Is that so?'

Kinderman squinted against the cold. The search helicopter was skimming away, throbbing low above the mud-brown darkness of the waters with its lights blinking softly red and green. The detective watched it growing smaller. It dwindled in the dawn like a fading hope. He listened, inclining his head a little; then he shivered and his hands began to dig deeper into the pockets of his coat. The shrieking of the woman had grown more piercing. It clawed at his heart and the twisted forests silent on the banks of the icy river.

'Jesus.'

Kinderman looked at Stedman. The police pathologist was down on one knee beside a sheet of soiled canvas. Something lumpy lay under it. Stedman was staring at it, frowning in concentration. His body was motionless. Only his breath had life: it came frosty and then vanished in the hungry air. Abruptly he stood up and looked at Kinderman oddly. 'You know those cuts on the victim's left hand?'

'What about them?'

'Well, I think they've got a pattern.'

'Is that so?'

'Yes, I think so. A sign of the zodiac. I think Gemini.'

Kinderman's heart skipped a beat. He drew a breath. Then he looked at the river. A Georgetown University crew team scull slipped silent and slim behind the bulky stern of the dredge. It reappeared, and then vanished underneath Key Bridge. A strobe light flashed. Kinderman looked down at the canvas throwsheet. *No. It couldn't be*, he thought. *It couldn't be.*

The pathologist followed Kinderman's gaze. A hand blotched red from the freezing air pulled the folds of his coat collar tighter together. He regretted not wearing his scarf that day. He'd forgotten. He'd dressed in too much of a hurry. 'What a weird way to die,' he said softly. 'So unnatural.'

Kinderman's breathing was emphysematous; white vapour wisped at his lips. 'No death is natural,' he murmured.

Someone had created the world. *Made sense.* For why would an eye want to form? To see? And why should it see? In order to survive? And why should it survive? And why? And why? The child's question haunted the nebulae, a thought in search of its Maker that cornered reason in a dead end maze and made

Kinderman certain the materialistic universe was the greatest superstition of his age. He believed in wonders but not in the impossible: not in an infinite regression in contingencies, or that love and acts of will were reducible to neurons firing in the brain.

'How long has the Gemini been dead?' asked Stedman.

'Ten, twelve years,' answered Kinderman. 'Twelve.'

'Are we *certain* that he's dead?'

'He is dead.'

In a sense, thought Kinderman. *Partly*. Man was not a nerve net. Man had a soul. For how could matter reflect upon itself? And how was it Carl Jung had seen a ghost in his bed and confession of a sin could cure a bodily illness and the atoms of his body were continually changing, yet each morning he awakened and was still himself? Without an afterlife, what was the value of work? What was the point of evolution?

'He is dead on the bias,' Kinderman murmured.

'What was that, Lieutenant?'

'Nothing.'

Electrons travelled from point to point without ever traversing the space between. God had his mysteries. Yahweh: 'I shall be there as who I am shall I be there.' *Okay. Amen.* But it was all so confusing, such a mess. The creator made man to know right from wrong, to feel outrage at all that was monstrous and evil, yet the scheme of creation itself was outrageous, for the law of life was the law of feeding in a universe crammed from end to end with exploding stars and bloodied jaws. Avoid being food and there was always a chance you would die in a mudslide or in an earthquake or in your crib or you might be fed rat poison by your mother or fried in oil by Genghis Khan or be skinned alive or beheaded or suffocated just for the thrill of it, for the fun of it. Forty-three years on the force and he had seen it. Hadn't he seen it all? *And now this.* For a moment he attempted familiar escapes: imagining the universe and everything in it were merely thoughts in the mind of the creator; or that the world of external reality existed nowhere but in his head: that nothing outside of him actually suffered. Sometimes it worked. This time it didn't.

Kinderman studied the lump beneath the canvas. No, it wasn't this, he thought: not the evil that we choose or inflict. The horror was the evil in the fabric of creation. The songs of the whales were haunting and lovely but the lion ripped open the stomach of the wildebeest and the tiny ichneumenidae fed in the living bodies of caterpillars underneath the pretty lilacs and the lawns; the black-throated Honey Guide bird chattered gaily but it laid its eggs in alien nests, and when the baby Honey Guide hatched, it immediately killed its foster brethren with a hard, sharp hook near the tip of its beak, which it promptly shed upon completion of the slaughter. *What immortal hand or eye?* Kinderman grimaced at an awful recollection of a hospital psycho ward for children. In a room there were fifty beds with cages, each with a shrieking child inside. Among them was an eight-year-old whose bones had not grown since infancy. Could the glory and beauty of creation justify the pain of one such child? Ivan Karamazov deserved an answer.

'Elephants are dying of coronaries, Stedman.'

'Beg pardon?'

'In the jungle. They are dying of stress about their food and their water supply. They try to help one another. If one of them dies too far away, then the others take its bones to the burial ground.'

The pathologist blinked and clutched at the folds of his coat more tightly. He'd heard of these flights, these irrelevant sallies and that they'd been occurring with frequency lately; but this was the first he had personally witnessed. Rumours had been drifting and circling through the precinct that Kinderman, colourful or not, was getting senile and Stedman examined him now with an air of professional interest, seeing nothing unusual in the detective's manner of dress: the oversized, tattered grey tweed coat; the rumpled trousers, baggy and cuffed; the limp felt hat, in the band a feather plucked from some mottled, disreputable bird. *The man is a walking Thrift Shop*, he thought and his eye caught an eggstain here and there. But this much had always been Kinderman's style, he knew. Nothing unusual there. Nor in his physical being: the short, fat fingers were neatly manicured; the jowly cheeks gleamed of soap; and the moist brown eyes which drooped at the corners still seemed to be staring into times gone by. As ever, his manner and his delicate movements suggested an old world Viennese father perpetually engaged in the arranging of flowers.

'And at Princeton University,' Kinderman continued, 'they're doing experiments with chimpanzees. The chimp pulls a lever and out from this machine comes a nice banana. So far, so wonderful, correct? But now the good doctors build a little cage and they put a different chimp inside it. Then along comes the first chimp looking for his usual sturgeon and bagel, only this time when the lever gets pulled, the banana comes out, all right, but the chimp sees his pal in the cage is now screaming from electrical shock. After that, no matter how hungry or starving he is, the first chimp won't pull the lever whenever he sees another chimp in that cage. They tried it on fifty, a hundred chimps, and every time it was the same. All right, maybe some *goniff*, some smartass Dillinger type, some sadist would pull the lever; but ninety per cent of the time they wouldn't do it.'

'I didn't know that.'

Kinderman continued to stare at the canvas. Two Neanderthal skeletons discovered in France were examined and found to have lived for two years despite seriously incapacitating injuries. Clearly, he thought, the tribe had kept them alive. *And look at children*, he pondered. There was nothing keener, the detective knew, than a child's sense of justice, of what was fair, of how things should be. Where did that come from? *And when my Julie was three, you couldn't give her a cookie or a toy but she'd give it away to some other kid.* Later on she'd *learned* to hoard it for herself. It wasn't power that corrupted, he thought: it was the jostling and unfairness of the world of experience and a bag of 'M and M's' with short weight. Children came into this world with no baggage except for their innocence. Their goodness was innate. It wasn't learned and it wasn't enlightened self-interest. *What chimpanzee ever buttered up a buyer so she'd buy his entire Spring line of negligées? It's ridiculous. Really. Who ever heard of such a case?* And there lay the paradox. Physical evil and moral goodness intertwined like the strands of a double helix embedded in the DNA code of the cosmos. *But how can this be?* the detective wondered. Was there a Spoiler at large in the universe? A Satan? *No. It's dumb. God would give him such a dizzying klop on the head that he'd be spending his eternity explaining to the Sun how he'd met Arnold Schwarzenegger once and shook his hand.* Satan left the paradox intact, a bleeding wound of the mind that never healed.

Kinderman shifted his weight a little. God's love burned with a fierce dark heat but gave no light. Were there shadows in his nature? Was he brilliant and sensitive but bent? After all was said and done was the answer to the mystery no more than that God was really Leopold and Loeb? Or could it be that he was closer to being a putz than anyone heretofore had imagined, a Being of stupendous but limited power? The detective envisioned such a God in court pleading, 'Guilty with an explanation, Your Honour.' The theory had appeal. It was rational and obvious and certainly the simplest that suited all the facts. But Kinderman rejected it out of hand and subordinated logic to his intuition, as he had in so many of his homicide cases. 'I did not come into this world to sell William of Occam door-to-door,' he had often been heard to tell baffled associates or even, on one occasion, a computer. 'My hunch, my opinion,' he would always say. And he felt that way now about the problem of evil. Something whispered to his soul that the truth was staggering and somehow connected to Original Sin; but only by analogy and dimly.

Something was different. The detective looked up. The dredgeboat's engines had stopped. So had the shrieking of the woman. In the silence he could hear the river lapping at the dock. He turned and met Stedman's patient gaze. 'Point one, we can't go on meeting like this. Point two, have you ever tried putting your finger in a red hot frying pan and holding it there?'

'No, I haven't.'

'I've tried. You can't do it. It hurts too much. You read in the papers that somebody died in a hotel fire. "Thirty-two Lost in Mayflower Blaze" it says. But you never really know what it means. You can't appreciate, you can't imagine. Put your finger in a frying pan, you'll know.'

Stedman nodded mutely. Kinderman's eyelids drooped and he stared at the pathologist sullenly. *Look at him*, he thought; *he thinks I'm crazy. It's impossible to talk about things like this.*

'Was there anything else, Lieutenant?'

Yes. Shadrach, Meshach and Abednego. 'Then the king, being angry, commanded frying pans and brazen cauldrons to be made hot; and he commanded to be cut out the tongue of him that had spoken first and, the skin of his head being drawn off, to chop off also his hands and his feet. And now he commanded him, being yet alive, to be brought to the fire and fried in the frying pan.'

'No, nothing else.'

'Can we have the body now?'

'Not yet.'

Pain had its uses, Kinderman ruminated: And the brain could shut it off at any time. But how? *The Great Phantom in the Sky hasn't told us.* The secret Orphan Annie pain decoder rings, through some clerical mistake, had not been issued. *Heads will roll*, thought Kinderman bleakly.

'Stedman, go away. Get lost. Drink coffee.'

Kinderman watched him walk to the boathouse where soon he was joined by the crime lab team, by the Sketcher and the Evidence Man and the Measurer and the Master Taker of Notes. The Sketcher was shivering, rubbing his hands, and their manner was casual. One of them chuckled. Kinderman wondered what it was that had been said and he thought of Macbeth and the gradual numbing of the moral sense.

The Taker of Notes handed Stedman a ledger. The pathologist nodded and the crew walked away. Their steps crunched gravel along the path that led them quickly past an ambulance and waiting paramedics and soon they would be quipping and complaining of their wives on Georgetown's empty cobblestoned streets. They were hurrying, probably heading for breakfast, perhaps at the coy White Tower on 'M' Street. Kinderman glanced at his watch and then nodded. Yes. The White Tower. It was open all night. *Three eggs over easy, please,*

Louie. Lots of bacon, okay? And grill the roll. Heat had its uses. They rounded a corner and vanished from view. A laugh rang out.

Kinderman's gaze shifted back to the pathologist. Someone else was talking to him now, Sergeant Atkins, Kinderman's assistant. Young and frail, he wore a Navy peacoat over the jacket of his brown flannel suit, and a black woollen seaman's cap was pulled down over his ears, obscuring a trim and bristling crewcut. Stedman was handing him the ledger. Atkins nodded, walked away a few steps and sat down on the bench in front of the boathouse. He opened the ledger and studied its contents. Seated not far from him were the weeping mother and a nurse. The nurse had her arms around the woman, consoling her.

Now Stedman was alone and he stood there staring at the mother, unmoving. Kinderman observed his expression with interest. *So you feel something, Alan,* he thought; *all the years of mutilations and violent endings, and still there is something within you that feels. Very good. Me, too. We are part of the mystery. If death were like rain, only natural, why would we feel this way, Alan? You and I in particular? Why?* Kinderman ached to be home in his bed. The tiredness sank to the bones of his legs and then into the earth beneath him, heavy.

'Lieutenant?'

Kinderman turned and said, 'Yes?'

It was Atkins. 'It's me, sir,' he said.

'Yes, I see that it's you. I can see that.'

Kinderman pretended to eye him with distaste, casting dismal looks at the coat and the cap before meeting his gaze. His eyes were small and the colour of jade. They turned inward a little, and gave Atkins a perpetual look of meditation. He reminded Kinderman of a monk, the medieval kind, the kind that you saw in the movies, their expressions unsmiling and earnest and dumb. Dumb, Atkins was not, the Lieutenant knew. Thirty-two and a Vietnam naval veteran out of Catholic University, behind that deadpan mask he hid something bright and strong that hummed, something wonderful and fey that he hid not from deviousness, in Kinderman's opinion, but because of a certain gentility of soul. Although slight of build, he had once pulled a dope-crazed, knife-wielding giant from Kinderman's throat; and when Kinderman's daughter had been in that near-fatal automobile crash, Atkins had spent twelve days and nights in the visitors' room of her hospital ward. He had taken his vacation time to do it. Kinderman loved him. He was as loyal as a dog.

'I am also here, Martin Luther, and I'm listening. Kinderman, the Jewish sage, is all ears.' What was there to do now, otherwise? Cry? 'I am listening, you walking anachronism, Atkins. Tell me. Report the good news from Ghent. Any fingerprints?'

'Plenty. All over the oars. But they're smeared pretty badly, Lieutenant.'

'A shame.'

'Some cigarette butts,' offered Atkins hopefully. This was useful. They would check them for blood type. 'Some hair on the body.'

'This is good. Very good. It could help to identify the killer.'

'And there's this,' said Atkins. He held out a cellophane envelope. Kinderman delicately grasped it at the top and frowned as he held it up to his eyes. Inside it was something plastic and pink.

'What is it?'

'A barrette. For a woman's hair.'

Kinderman squinted, holding it closer. 'There's some printing on it.'

'Yes. It says, "Great Falls, Virginia".'

Kinderman lowered the bag and looked at Atkins. 'They sell them at the souvenir stand at Great Falls,' he said. 'My daughter Julie, she had one. That was years ago, Atkins. I bought it for her. Two of them, I bought. She had two.' He gave the envelope to Atkins and breathed, 'It's a child's.'

Atkins shrugged. He glanced towards the boathouse, pocketing the envelope in his coat. 'We have that woman here, Lieutenant.'

'Would you kindly remove that ridiculous cap? We're not doing Dick Powell in *Here Comes the Navy*, Atkins. Stop shelling Haiphong, it's all over.'

Dutifully, Atkins slipped off the cap and stuffed it in the other pocket of the peacoat. He shivered.

'Put it back,' said Kinderman quietly.

'I'm okay.'

'I'm not. The crewcut is worse. Put it back.'

Atkins hesitated, then Kinderman added, 'Come on, put it back. It's cold.'

Atkins fitted the cap back on. 'We have that woman here,' he repeated.

'We have who?'

'The old woman.'

The body was discovered on the boathouse dock that morning, Sunday, March 15, by Joseph Mannix, the boathouse manager, on his arrival to open for business: bait and tackle, and the rental of kayaks, canoes and rowboats. Mannix's statement was brief:

STATEMENT OF JOSEPH MANNIX

My name is Joe Mannix and – What?
(Interruption by investigating officer)

Yes. Yes, I've got you, I understand. My name is Joseph Francis Mannix and I live at 3618 Prospect Street in Georgetown, Washington, D.C. I own and manage the Potomac Boathouse. I got here at half-past five or so, that's when I usually open up and set out the bait and start the coffee. Customers show up as early as six, sometimes they're waiting for me when I get here. Today there was nobody. I picked up the paper from in front of the door and I – Oh. Oh, Jesus. Jesus.

(Interruption; witness composes himself)

I got here, I opened the door, I went in, I started the coffee. Then I came out to count the boats. Sometimes they rip them off. They cut the chain with a wire cutter. So I count them. Today they're all there. Then I turn to go

18

back in and see the kid's cart and this stack of papers and I
see – I see . . .

(The witness gestures towards the body of the victim; cannot
continue; investigating officer postpones further questioning.)

The victim was Thomas Joshua Kintry, a twelve-year-old
black and the son of Lucy Annabel Kintry, widowed, 38, and a
teacher of languages at Georgetown University. Thomas Kintry
had a newspaper route and delivered *The Washington Post*. He
would have made his delivery that morning at the boathouse at
approximately 5:00 a.m. Mannix's call to police headquarters
came in at 5:38 a.m. Identification of the victim was immediate
because of the nametag – with address and telephone number –
embroidered on his green plaid windbreaker: Thomas Kintry
was a mute. He'd had the paper route for only thirteen days, or
else Mannix would have recognized him. He didn't. But
Kinderman did: he had known the boy from police club work.

'The old lady,' Kinderman echoed dully. Then his eyebrows
gathered in a look of puzzlement and he stared away at the river.

'We've got her in the boathouse, Lieutenant.'

Kinderman turned his head and fixed Atkins with a penetrating look. 'She's warm?' he asked. 'Make sure that she's warm.'

'We've got a blanket around her and the fireplace going.'

'She should eat. Give her soup, hot soup.'

'She's had broth.'

'Broth is good, just be sure that it's hot.'

The dragnet had picked her up about fifty yards above the
boathouse, where she was standing on the grassy southerly
bank of the dried-out 'C&O' Canal, a now-disused waterway
where horsedrawn wooden barges once carried passengers up
and down its fifty mile length; although now it had been given
up mainly to joggers. Perhaps in her seventies, when the search
team picked her up the woman had been shivering, standing
with her arms tightly folded and staring all around her with
tears in her eyes as if lost and disoriented and frightened. But
she could not or would not answer questions and gave the
appearance of being either senile, stunned or catatonic. No one

knew what she'd been doing there. There were no habitations nearby. She wore cotton pyjamas with a small flower pattern underneath a blue woollen belted robe, and pale pink wool-lined slippers. The temperature outside was freezing.

Stedman reappeared. 'Are you through with the body yet, Lieutenant?'

Kinderman looked down at the bloodstained canvas. 'Is Thomas Kintry through with it?'

The sobbing came through to him again. He shook his head. 'Atkins, take Mrs Kintry home,' he breathed. 'And the nurse, take the nurse with you, too. Make her stay with her today, the whole day. I'll pay the overtime myself, never mind. Take her home.'

Atkins started to speak and was interrupted.

'Yes, yes, yes, the old lady. I remember. I'll see her.'

Atkins left to do Kinderman's bidding. And now Kinderman stooped to one knee, half wheezing, half groaning with the effort of bending. 'Thomas Kintry, forgive me,' he murmured softly, and then lifted off the drape and let his gaze brush lightly over the arms and the chest and the legs. *They're so thin, like a sparrow*, he thought. The boy had been an orphan and had once had pellagra. Lucy Kintry had adopted him when he was three. A new life. And now ended. The boy had been crucified, nailed through the wrists and feet to the flat end sections of kayak oars arranged in the form of a cross; and the same thick three-inch carpenters' ingots had been pounded through the top of his skull in a circle, penetrating dura and finally brain. Blood streaked down in twisted rivulets over eyes still wide in fright and into a mouth still gaping open in what must have been the mute boy's silent scream of unendurable pain and terror.

Kinderman examined the cuts on the palm of Kintry's left hand. It was true: they had a pattern – the sign of the Gemini. Then he looked at the other hand and saw that the index finger was missing. It had been severed. The detective felt a chill.

He replaced the canvas and heaved to his feet with a laboured breath. Then he stood looking down. *I will find your murderer, Thomas Kintry*, he thought.

Even if it were God.

'All right, Stedman, take a walk,' he said. 'Take the body and get out of my sight. You stink of formaldehyde and death.'

Stedman moved to get the ambulance team.

'No, no, wait a minute,' Kinderman called to him.

Stedman turned. The detective moved in to him and spoke to him softly. 'Wait until his mother is gone.'

Stedman nodded.

The dredge had docked and a sergeant of police in a fleece-lined black leather jacket jumped lightly to the dock and came over. He was carrying something wrapped in cloth and was about to speak when Kinderman stopped him. 'Wait a minute, hold it; not now; just a minute.'

The sergeant followed Kinderman's gaze. Atkins was talking to the nurse and Mrs Kintry. Mrs Kintry nodded and the women stood up. Kinderman had to look away as for a moment the mother stared over at the canvas. At her boy. He waited for a while and then asked, 'Are they gone?'

'Yes, they're getting in the car,' said Stedman.

'Yes, Sergeant,' said Kinderman, 'let's see it.'

The sergeant silently undid the brown cloth wrapping and disclosed what appeared to be a kitchen meat-pounding mallet; he was careful not to touch it with his hands.

Kinderman stared and then said, 'My wife has a thing like that. For the schnitzel. Only smaller.'

'It's a type used in restaurants,' Stedman observed. 'Or in large institutional kitchens. I saw them in the Army.'

Kinderman looked up at him. 'This could do it?' he asked.

Stedman nodded.

'Give it to Delyra,' Kinderman instructed the sergeant. 'I'm going inside to see the old lady.'

The boathouse interior was warm. Logs burned and crackled in a massive fireplace faced with large grey rounded stones and mounted on the walls there were crew racing shells.

'Could you tell us your name, please ma'am?'

She was sitting on a torn yellow naugahyde sofa in front of the fireplace, a policewoman close beside her as Kinderman stood

21

before them, wheezing, his hat held in front of him, clutched by the brim. The old woman didn't seem to see or hear him, and her vacant stare seemed fixed on something inward. The detective's eyes crinkled up in puzzlement. He sat down in a facing chair and placed his hat on some coverless, old magazines that lay torn and neglected on a small wooden table in between; the hat covered up an ad for whisky.

'Could you tell us your name, dear?'

No response. Kinderman's eyes threw a silent question to the policewoman, who immediately nodded and told him quietly, 'She's been doing that continually, except for when we gave her some food. And when I was brushing her hair,' she added. Kinderman's stare returned to the woman: she was making curious, rhythmic motions with her hands and arms. Then his eye fell on something he had missed before, something small and pink near his hat on the table. He picked it up and read the small print: 'Great Falls, Virginia.' The letter 'n' was missing in Virginia.

'I couldn't find the other one,' the policewoman said, 'so when I brushed her hair I left it off.'

'She was wearing this?'

'Yes.'

The detective felt a thrill of discovery and bafflement. The old woman was conceivably a witness to the crime. But what had she been doing on the dock at that hour? And in this cold? What had she been doing, for that matter, up above by the 'C&O' Canal where they had found her? It occurred to Kinderman immediately that this sickly old creature was senile and perhaps had been walking a dog. *A dog? Yes, maybe he ran off and she couldn't find him, that would account for the way she was crying.* A more terrible suspicion then occurred to him: the woman might have witnessed the murder and it might have unbalanced and traumatized her; temporarily, at least. He felt a mixture of pity, excitement and annoyance. They must get her to speak.

'Can't you tell us your name, please, ma'am?'

No response. In the silence, she continued her mysterious movements. Outside a cloud slipped past the sun and thin winter

22

sunlight fell like an unexpected grace through a nearby window. It softly illuminated the old woman's face and eyes and gave her a look of tender piety. Kinderman leaned forward a little; he thought he'd detected a pattern to the movements: her legs pressed together, the old woman would alternately move each hand to her thigh, make a slight, odd movement, and then draw the hand high into the air above her head where she finished with several minute and jerky pulls.

He continued to watch for a while, then stood up. 'Keep her in the holding ward, Jourdan, until we find out who she is.'

The policewoman nodded.

'You brushed her hair,' the detective told her. 'That was nice. Stay with her.'

'Yes.'

Kinderman turned and left the boathouse. He gave various instructions, closed his mind, and then drove home to a small, warm Tudor house on nearby Foxhall Road. It was only six years since he'd broken the habit of apartment living to please his wife, and he still called this mildly rustic area 'the country'.

He entered the house and called, 'Dumpling, I'm home. It's me, your hero, Inspector Clouseau.' He hung up his hat and coat on a coat-tree in the tiny hall, then unstrapped his revolver in its holster and locked it in the drawer of a small, dark chest beside the coat-tree. 'Mary?' No one answered. He smelled fresh coffee and shuffled toward the kitchen. Julie, his twenty-two-year-old daughter, doubtless was sleeping. But where was Mary? And Shirley, his mother-in-law?

The kitchen was colonial. Kinderman cast a glum eye at the copper pots and various utensils hanging from hooks affixed to the stove hood, trying to picture them hanging in somebody's kitchen in a Warsaw ghetto; then he sauntered heavily and slowly to the kitchen table. 'Maple,' he muttered aloud, for when alone he often talked to himself. 'What Jew would know maple from cheese? They wouldn't know, it's impossible, it's strange.' He saw a note on the table. He picked it up and read it.

Dearest Billy,

Don't get sore, but when the phone woke us up, Mom insisted we should go and visit Richmond, as a punishment, I guess, so I thought we'd better get an early start. She said Jews in the South should stick together. Who's in Richmond?

You had fun at your Police Encounter Group? I can't wait to get home and hear all about it. I fixed you the usual and put it in the fridge. Are you planning to be home this Sunday night, or as usual ice-skating on the Potomac with Omar Sharif and Catherine Deneuve?

> Kisses,
> Me

A small, fond smile warmed his eyes. He replaced the note, found the cream cheese, tomatoes, lox, pickle and an Almond Roca on a plate in the refrigerator. He sliced and toasted two bagels, poured coffee and sat down to it all at the table. Then he noticed the Sunday *Washington Post* on the chair to his left. He looked at the plate of food before him. His stomach was empty but he could not eat. He had lost his appetite.

For a time he sat drinking his coffee. He looked up. Outside a bird was singing. *In this weather? He ought to be put in an institution. He's sick, he needs help.* 'Me, too,' the detective muttered aloud. Then the bird fell silent and the only sound was the beat of the pendulum clock on the wall. He checked the time: it was 8:42. All the *goyim* would be going to church. Couldn't hurt. *Say a prayer for Thomas Kintry, please.* 'And William F. Kinderman,' he added aloud. *Yes. And one other.* He sipped at the coffee. What a twisted coincidence, he thought, that a death like Kintry's should occur on this day, this twelfth anniversary of a death just as shocking and violent and mysterious.

Kinderman looked up at the clock. Had it stopped? No. It was running. He shifted in his chair. He felt a strangeness in the room. What was it? *Nothing. You're tired.* He picked up the candy and unwrapped it and ate it. *Not as good without the pickle taste first*, he mourned.

He shook his head and stood up with a sigh. He put away the plate of food, rinsed out his coffee cup at the sink, and then left the kitchen and walked up the stairs toward the second floor. He thought he might nap for a while and allow his unconscious to work, to sort out clues he never knew he had seen; but at the top of the stairs he halted and muttered, 'Gemini.'

The Gemini? Impossible. That monster is dead, it couldn't be. And so why was the hair on the back of his hands prickling upward? he wondered. He held them up, the palms turned down. *Yes. They are standing on end. Why is that?*

He heard Julie waking up now and clumping to her bathroom, and he stood there for a while, baffled and uncertain. He ought to be doing something. But what? The usual lines of investigation and induction were precluded: they were looking for a maniac; and the lab would have nothing to report until tonight. Mannix, he sensed, had already been squeezed of what little he knew; and Kintry's mother was surely to be left alone at this time. Anyway, the boy had no unsavoury acquaintances or habits, that much Kinderman knew himself from his regular contact with him. The detective shook his head. He had to get out, to get moving, to pursue. He heard Julie's shower water running. He turned and walked back down the stairs to the foyer. He recovered his gun, put on his hat and coat and went out

Outside, he stood with his hand on the doorknob, troubled and thoughtful and undecided. The wind blew a styrofoam cup down the driveway and he listened to its thin and forlorn little impacts; then it was still. Abruptly he went to his car, got in it and drove away.

Without knowing how he'd gotten there, he found himself parked illegally on 33rd Street, close to the river. He got out of the car. Here and there he saw a *Washington Post* on a doorstep. He found the sight painful and glanced away. He locked the car.

He walked through a little park to a bridge that traversed the canal. He followed a towpath to the boathouse. Already, the curious had gathered and were milling about and chattering, although no one seemed to know just exactly what had happened. Kinderman went up to the boathouse doors. They were locked and a red-and-white sign said CLOSED. Kinderman glanced at the bench by the doors and then sat down, his breath coming raspingly as he drooped with his back against the boathouse.

He studied the people on the dock. He knew that psychotic killers frequently relished the attention that their violent deeds had drawn. He might be here in this group on the dock, perhaps asking, 'What happened? Do you know? Was someone murdered?' He looked for somebody smiling a little too fixedly, or with a tic or with the stare of the drugged; and most especially for anyone who'd heard what had happened but then lingered and asked the same questions of some newcomer. Kinderman's hand reached into an inside pocket of his coat; there was always a paperback book in there. He pulled out *Claudius, the God* and looked at its jacket with dismay. He wanted to pretend to be an old man who was passing his Sunday by the river; but the Robert Graves novel held the danger that he might unwittingly actually read it and perhaps allow the killer to elude his scrutiny. He'd already read it twice and knew well the danger of becoming engrossed in its pages again. He slipped it back inside the pocket and quickly extracted another book. He looked at the title. It was *Waiting for Godot*. He sighed with relief and turned to Act Two.

He stayed until noon, seeing no one suspicious. By eleven there was nobody else on the dock and the flow had stopped, but he'd waited the extra hour, hoping. Now he looked at his watch, and then at the boats that were chained to the dock. Something was nagging at him. What? He thought for a while but could not identify it. He put away *Godot* and left.

He discovered a parking ticket on the windshield of his car. He slipped it out from under the wiper blade and eyed it with disbelief. The car was an unmarked Chevrolet Camaro but it carried the plates of the District Police. He crumpled the ticket into his pocket, unlocked the car, got in and drove off. He had no clear idea of where to go and wound up at the precinct house in Georgetown. Once inside he approached the sergeant in charge of the desk.

'Who was giving parking tickets on 33rd near Canal this morning, Sergeant?'

The sergeant looked up at him. 'Robin Tennes.'

'I am thrilled to be alive in a time and a place where even a blind girl can be a policewoman,' Kinderman told him. He handed him the ticket and waddled away.

'Any news on the kid, Lieutenant?' the sergeant called out. He hadn't yet examined the ticket.

'No news, no news,' replied Kinderman. 'Nothing.'

He went upstairs and walked through the squad room, deflecting the questions of the curious until at last he was in his office. The space of one wall was taken up with a finely detailed map of the northwest.section of the city, while still another was covered by a blackboard. On the wall behind the desk, between two windows that faced toward the Capitol, hung a Snoopy poster, a gift from Thomas Kintry.

Kinderman sat behind his desk, his hat and coat still on, the coat buttoned. On the desk were a calendar pad, a paperback copy of the New Testament, and a clear plastic box containing Kleenex. He pulled out a tissue and wiped his nose, and then gazed at the photos set into the facings of the box: his wife and his daughter. Still wiping, he turned the box a little, disclosing a photo of a dark-haired priest; then Kinderman sat motionless, reading the inscription. 'Keep checking those Dominicans, Lieutenant.' The signature read, 'Damien'. The detective's glance flicked up to the smile on the rugged face, and then to the scar above the right eye. Abruptly, he crumpled the tissue in his hand, threw it into a wastebasket, and had reached to pick up a phone when Atkins walked in. Kinderman looked up as he was closing the door. 'Oh, it's you.' He released the phone and clasped his hands together in front of him, looking like a garment district Buddha. 'So soon?'

Atkins sauntered closer and sat on a chair in front of the desk. Slipping off his cap, his eyes shifted up to Kinderman's hat.

'Never mind the insolence,' Kinderman told him. 'I told you to stay with Mrs Kintry.'

'Her brother and sister came over. Some people from the school, the university. I thought I should come back.'

'And a good thing, Atkins. I have lots for you to do.' Kinderman waited while Atkins produced a little red notepad and a ballpoint pen. Then he continued: 'First, get hold of Francis Berry. He was chief investigator on the 'Gemini' Squad years back. He's still with San Francisco Homicide. I want everything he's got on the Gemini Killer. Everything. The whole entire file.'

'But the Gemini's been dead for twelve years.'

'Is that so? Really, Atkins? I had no idea. You mean all of those headlines in the papers were true? And the radio and television, Atkins? Astonishing. Really. I'm floored.'

Atkins was writing, a small, wry smile curving his mouth. The door cracked open and the head of the crime lab team looked in. 'Stop loitering in doorways, Ryan, come in here,' Kinderman told him. Ryan entered and closed the door behind him.

'Attend me, Ryan,' said Kinderman. 'Notice young Atkins. You are standing in the presence of majesty, a giant. No, really. A man should get his just recognition. Would you like to know the highlight of Atkins' career with us? Certainly. We shouldn't cover stars with an okra basket. Last week, for the nineteenth –'

'Twentieth,' Atkins corrected him, holding up his pen for emphasis.

'For the twentieth time, he brings in Mishkin, the notorious evildoer. His crime? His unvarying M.O.? He breaks into apartments and moves all the furniture around. He redecorates.' Kinderman shifted his remarks to Atkins. 'This time we send him to "Psycho", I swear it.'

'How does Homicide fit into this?' asked Ryan.

Atkins turned to him, expressionless. 'Mishkin leaves messages threatening death if he ever comes back and finds something out of place.'

Ryan blinked.

28

'Heroic work, Atkins. Homeric,' said Kinderman. 'Ryan, have you anything to tell me?'

'Not yet.'

'Then why are you wasting my time?'

'I just wondered what was new.'

'It's very cold out. Also, the sun came up this morning. Have you any more questions of the oracle, Ryan? Several kings from the East have been waiting their turn.'

Ryan looked disgusted and left the room. Kinderman followed him with his gaze and when the door had closed he looked at Atkins. 'He bought the whole thing about Mishkin.'

Atkins nodded.

'The man hears no music,' Kinderman sighed.

'He tries, sir.'

'Thank you, Mother Theresa.' Kinderman sneezed and reached for a Kleenex.

'God bless you.'

'Thank you, Atkins.' Kinderman wiped his nose and got rid of the tissue. 'So you're getting me the Gemini file.'

'Right, sir.'

'After that see if anyone has claimed the old lady.'

'Not yet, sir. I checked when I came in.'

'Call the *Washington Post*, the distribution department; get the name of Kintry's route boss and run it through the FBI computer. Find out if he's ever been in trouble with the law. At five in the morning in the freezing cold chances are that the killer wasn't out for a stroll and came across Kintry just by accident. Somebody knew that he'd be there.'

The clatter of a teletype machine began to seep through the floor from below. Kinderman glanced toward the sound. 'Who can think in this place?'

Atkins nodded.

Abruptly the teletype stopped. Kinderman sighed and looked up at his assistant. 'There's another possibility. Someone on Kintry's paper route might have killed him, someone he'd already delivered a paper to before he got to the boathouse. He could have killed him and then dragged him to the boathouse. It's possible. So all of those names should go into the computer.'

'Very well, sir.'

'One more thing. Almost half of Kintry's papers had yet to be delivered. Find out from the *Post* who called in and complained that they didn't get their paper. Then cross them off the list and whoever is left – whoever didn't call in – feed their names to the computer as well.'

Atkins stopped writing in his notepad. He looked up at the detective with surmise.

Kinderman nodded. 'Yes. Exactly. On Sunday, people always want their funnypapers, Atkins. So if someone didn't call and say they wanted their paper there could only be two reasons – either the subscriber is dead or he's the killer. It's a longshot. Couldn't hurt. You should check those names also with the FBI computer. Incidentally, do you believe there will come a day when computers will be able to think?'

'I doubt it.'

'Me, too. I once read some theologian was asked this question and he said that this problem would give him insomnia only when computers started to worry that maybe their parts were wearing out. My sentiments. Computers, good luck, God bless them, they're okay. But a thing made out of things cannot think about itself. Am I right? It's all *ka-ka* saying mind is really brain. Sure, my hand is in my pocket. Is my pocket my hand? Every wino on 'M' Street knows a thought is a thought and not some cells or *khazerei* going on in the brain. They know that jealousy is not some kind of game from Atari. Meantime, who is kidding who? If all those wonderful scientists in Japan could manufacture an artificial brain cell only one-fourth a cubic inch, for an artificial brain you'd need to keep it in a warehouse one and a half million cubic feet so you could hide it from your neighbour, Mrs Briskin, and assure her nothing funny's going on next door. Besides, I dream the future, Atkins. What computer that you know could do that?'

'You've eliminated Mannix?'

'I don't mean I dream the general, predictable future. I

dream what you never could guess. Not just me. Read *Experiment with Time*, J. W. Dunne. Also Jung the psychiatrist and Wolfgang Pauli, his bigshot quantum physicist buddy that they call now the father of the neutrino. You could buy a used car from such people, Atkins. As for Mannix, he's the father of seven, a saint, and I've known him for eighteen years. Forget it. What's peculiar – on my mind – is that Stedman didn't notice any sign that maybe Kintry first was hit on the head. With what was done to him, how could this be? He was conscious. My God, he was conscious.' Kinderman looked down and shook his head. 'We must be looking for more than one monster, Atkins. Someone had to hold him down. It had to be.'

The telephone rang. Kinderman looked at the buttons. The private line. He picked up the phone and said, 'Kinderman.'

'Bill?' It was his wife.

'Oh, it's you, honey. Tell me, how is Richmond? You're still there?'

'Yes, we just saw the Capitol Building. It's white.'

'How exciting.'

'How's your day, honey?'

'Wonderful, sweetheart. Three murders, four rapes and a suicide. Otherwise, my usual jolly time up here with the boys at Precinct Six. Sweetheart, when is the carp coming out of the tub?'

'I can't talk now.'

'Oh, I see. Then the Mother of the Gracchi is at hand. Mother Mystery. She's squeezed in the booth with you, right?'

'I can't talk. You're coming home tonight for dinner or not?'

'I think not, precious angel.'

'Then lunch? You don't eat right when I'm not there. We could start back now, we'd be home by two.'

'Thank you, darling, but today I have to cheer up Father Dyer.'

'What's the matter?'

'Every year on this day he gets blue.'

'Oh, it's today.'

'It's today.'

'I'd forgotten.'

Two policemen were dragging a suspect through the room. He was forcibly resisting and screaming imprecations. 'I didn't do it! Let go of me, you cocksucking fucks!'

'What's that?' asked Kinderman's wife.

'Only *goyim*, sweetheart. Never mind.' A detention room door slammed on the suspect. 'I'll take Dyer to a movie. We'll discuss. He'll enjoy.'

'Well, okay. I'll fix a plate up and put it in the oven, just in case.'

'You're a sweetheart. Oh, incidentally, lock the windows tonight.'

'What for?'

'It would make me feel better. Hugs and kisses, darling dumpling.'

'You, too.'

'Leave a note about the carp, would you sweetheart? I don't want to walk in there and see it.'

'Oh, *Bill*!'

'Bye, darling.'

'Bye.'

He hung up the phone and stood up. Atkins was staring at him. 'The carp is none of your business,' the detective told him. 'It should only concern you that something is rotten in the state of Denmark.' He moved toward the door. 'You have much to do, so kindly do it. As for me, from two until half-past four I'm at the Biograph. After that, I'm at "Clyde's" or back here. Let me know when there's something from the lab. Anything. Beep me. Goodbye, Lord Jim. Enjoy your luxury cruise on the *Patna*. Check for leaks.'

He walked through the doorway and into the world of men who die. Atkins watched him as he shuffled through the squad room waving off questions like beggars in a Bombay street. And then he was down the stairs and out of sight. Already Atkins missed him.

He got up from his chair and moved to the window. He looked out at the city's white marble monuments washed in sunlight, warm and real. He listened to the traffic. He felt uneasy. Some darkness was stirring that he could not comprehend; yet he sensed its movement. What was it? Kinderman had felt it. He could tell.

Atkins shook it off. He believed in the world and men and pitied both. Hoping for the best, he turned away and went to work.

Chapter Two

Joseph Dyer, a Jesuit priest, Irish, forty-five years of age and a teacher of religion at Georgetown University, had started his Sunday with the Mass of Christ, refreshing his faith and renewing its mystery, celebrating hope in the life to come and praying for mercy on all mankind. After Mass he walked down to the Jesuit Cemetery in the hollow of the campus grounds where he placed a few flowers in front of a tombstone marked DAMIEN KARRAS, S. J. Then he'd breakfasted heartily in the refectory, consuming gargantuan portions of everything: pancakes, pork chops, corn bread, sausages, bacon and eggs. He'd been sitting with the university president, Father Healy, a friend of many years.

'Joe, where do you put it?' marvelled Healy, watching the diminutive, freckled redhead building a pork chop and pancake sandwich. Dyer turned his fey, blue eyes on the president and said without expression, 'Clean living, *mon père*.' Then he'd reached for the milk and poured another glass.

Father Healy had shaken his head and sipped coffee, forgetting where he'd been in their discussion of Donne as a poet and a priest. 'Any plans today, Joe? You'll be around?'

'You want to show me your necktie collection or what?'

'I've got this speech for the American Bar Association next week. I'd like to kick it around.'

Healy watched with fascination as Dyer poured a lake of maple syrup on his plate.

'Yeah, I'll be here until a quarter of two, and then I've got to see a movie with a friend. Lieutenant Kinderman. You've met him.'

'With the face like a beagle? The cop?'

Dyer nodded, stuffing his mouth.

'He's an interesting guy,' observed the president.

'Every year on this day he gets down and depressed, so I have to cheer him up. He loves movies.'

'It's today?'

Dyer nodded, his mouth full again.

The president sipped at his coffee. 'I'd forgotten.'

Dyer and Kinderman met at the Biograph Cinema on 'M' Street and saw almost half of *The Maltese Falcon*, a pleasure interrupted when a man in the audience sat down next to Kinderman, made some perceptive and appreciative comments concerning the film, which Kinderman welcomed, and then stared at the screen while placing a hand on Kinderman's thigh, at which point Kinderman had turned to him, incredulous, breathing out, 'Honest to God, I don't believe you,' while snapping a handcuff around the man's wrist. There ensued a slight commotion while Kinderman led the man to the lobby, called for a squad car and then packed him inside it.

'Just give him a scare and then let him go,' the lieutenant instructed the policeman driver.

The man poked his head through the back seat window. 'I'm a personal friend of Senator Klureman.'

'I'm sure he'll be terribly sorry to hear that on the Six O'Clock News,' the detective responded. And then to the driver, '*Avanti*! Go!'

The squad car moved off. A small crowd had gathered. Kinderman looked around for Dyer and finally spotted him pressed in a doorway. He was looking up the street, and his hand held his coat lapels together at the throat so that the round Roman collar could not be seen. Kinderman approached him. 'What are you doing, founding an order called "Lurking Fathers"?'

'I was trying to make myself invisible.'

'You failed,' said Kinderman ingenuously. He reached out his hand and touched Dyer. 'Look at that. There's your arm.'

'Gee, it's sure a lot of fun going out with you, Lieutenant.'

'You're being ridiculous.'

'No kidding.'

'That pathetic putz,' the detective breathed mournfully. 'He ruined the movie for me.'

'You've already seen it ten times.'

'And another ten – even twenty – couldn't hurt.' Kinderman took the priest's arm and they walked. 'Let's go and have a bite at "The Tombs" or maybe "Clyde's" or "F. Scott's",' the detective cajoled. 'We can have a little *nosh* and discuss and critique.'

'Half a movie?'

'I remember the rest.'

Dyer halted them. 'Bill, you look tired. Tough case?'

'Nothing much.'

'You look down,' insisted Dyer.

'No, I'm fine. And you?'

'I'm fine.'

'You're lying.'

'You, too,' said Dyer.

'True.'

Dyer's gaze flicked over the detective's face with concern. His friend looked exhausted and deeply troubled. There was something very wrong. 'You really do look awfully tired,' he said. 'Why don't you go home and take a nap?'

Now he's worried about me, thought Kinderman. 'No, I can't go home,' he said.

'Why not?'

'The carp.'

'You know, I thought you said "Carp".'

'The carp,' repeated Kinderman.

'You said it again.'

Kinderman moved in closer to Dyer, his face but an inch away from the priest's and he fixed him with a grim and steady stare. 'My Mary's mother is visiting, *nu*? She who complains that I keep bad company and am somehow related to Al Capone; she who gives my wife Hannukah presents of "Chutz-pah" and "Kibbutz Number 5", these of course being per-fumes made in Israel – the best. Shirley. You now have a picture

36

of her? Good. Soon she is cooking us a carp. A tasty fish. I'm not against it. But because it's supposedly filled with impurities, Shirley has purchased this fish alive and for three days now it's been swimming in the bathtub. Even as we *speak* it is swimming in my bathrub. Up and down. Down and up. Cleaning out the impurities. I hate it. One further note: Father Joe, you are standing very close to me, right? Have you noticed? Yes. You have noticed that I haven't had a bath in several days. Three. The carp. So I never go home until the carp is asleep. I'm afraid that if I see it while it's swimming I'll kill it.'

Dyer broke away from him, laughing.

Better. Much better, thought Kinderman. 'Come on, now, is it "Clyde's" or "The Tombs" or "F. Scott's"?'

'"Billy Martin's".'

'Don't be difficult. I've already made a reservation at "Clyde's".'

'Clyde's.'

'You know, I thought you might say that.'

'I did.'

Together they walked off to forget the night.

Atkins blinked. He thought that perhaps he'd misunderstood, or perhaps had not explained himself clearly enough. He went through it again, this time holding the telephone closer to his mouth, and then again he heard the answers that he'd heard once before. 'Yes, I see. Yes, thank you. Thank you very much.' He hung up the phone and could feel himself squeezing his body together in the wooden chair behind his desk. In the tiny, windowless little office he could hear his own breathing. He angled the desk lamp away from his eyes, and then held his hand underneath its glow. The tips of his fingers were bloodless and white underneath his nails. Atkins was frightened.

'Could I maybe have a little more tomato for the burger?' Kinderman was clearing a space on the table for the order of French Fried potatoes that the dark-haired young waitress had brought them. 'Oh, thank you,' she said and then set down the plate between Kinderman and Dyer. 'Will three slices be enough?'

'Two is plenty.'

'More coffee?'

'No, I'm fine, thank you, Miss.' The detective looked over at Dyer. 'And you, Bruce Dern? A seventh cup?'

'No, thanks,' said Dyer, putting down his fork beside a plate on which rested a largely uneaten coconut-curry omelette. He reached for the cigarettes on the blue-and-white checkered tablecloth.

'I'll be back with the tomato,' said the waitress. She smiled and moved away toward the kitchen.

Kinderman stared at Dyer's plate. 'You're not eating. Are you sick?'

'Too spicy,' said the priest.

'Too spicy? I've seen you dip "Twinkies" in mustard. Here, my son, let the expert tell you what's spicy. Chef Milani to the rescue.' Kinderman picked up his fork and took a bite of Dyer's omelette. Then he put down the fork and stared without expression at Dyer's plate. 'You have ordered an archaeological find.'

'Getting back to the movie,' said Dyer. He exhaled his first drag of smoke.

'On my list of the ten greatest movies ever made,' declared Kinderman. 'What are your favourites, Father? Maybe name the top five.'

'My lips are sealed.'

'Not often enough.' Kinderman was salting the fried potatoes.

Dyer shrugged diffidently. 'Who can pick the five best of anything?'

'Atkins,' the detective immediately responded. 'He can tell you at the drop of a category: movies, fandangoes – whatever. Mention heretics, he'll give you a list of ten and in order of preference without hesitation. Atkins is a man of hurried decision. Never mind, he has taste and is usually right.'

'Oh, really? And so what are his favourite films?'

'The top five?'

'The top five.'

'*Casablanca.*'

'And what are the other four?'

'The same. He is absolutely crazy about that movie.'

The Jesuit nodded.

'He nods,' said Kinderman bleakly. '"God is a tennis shoe", the heretic tells him, and Torquemada nods and says, "Guard, let him go. There is much to be said on both sides." Really, Father, these rushes to judgement have to stop. That's what comes of all this singing and guitars in your ears.'

'You want my favourite movie?'

'Kindly hurry,' glowered Kinderman. 'Prominent reviewers are waiting for my call.'

'*It's a Wonderful Life,*' said Dyer. 'Are you happy?'

'Yes, an excellent choice,' said Kinderman. He beamed.

'I guess I've seen it twenty times,' the priest admitted with a smile.

'It couldn't hurt.'

'I sure do love it.'

'Yes, it's innocent and good. It fills the heart.'

'You said the same about *Eraserhead.*'

'Don't mention that obscenity,' Kinderman growled. 'Atkins calls it "Long Day's Journey into Goat".'

The waitress had come over and set down a dish of tomato slices. 'Here you are, sir.'

'Thank you,' the detective told her.

She looked at the omelette in front of Dyer. 'Something wrong with the omelette?'

'No, it's just sleeping,' said Dyer.

She laughed. 'Can I get you something else?'

'No, that's fine. I guess I just wasn't hungry.'

She gestured at the plate. 'Shall I take it?'

He nodded, and she took it away.

'Eat something, Gandhi,' said Kinderman, pushing the plate of potatoes toward Dyer. The priest ignored them and asked, 'How's Atkins? Haven't seen him since Christmas Eve Mass.'

'He is well and in June will be married.'

Dyer brightened. 'Oh, that's great.'

'He is marrying his childhood sweetheart. It's so nice. It's so sweet. Two little babes in the woods.'

'Where's the wedding going to be?'

'In a truck. Even now they are saving their money for furniture. The bride is employed at a supermarket checkout stand, God bless her, while Atkins, as usual, assists me in the daytime and by night robs "7–Eleven" stores. Incidentally, is it ethical for government employees to work two jobs, or am I just being finicky about this, Father? I welcome your spiritual advice.'

'I didn't think they kept very much cash in those stores.'

'Incidentally, how's your mother?'

Dyer had been stubbing out his cigarette. He stopped and looked at Kinderman oddly. 'Bill, she's dead.'

The detective looked aghast.

'She's been dead for a year and a half. I thought I told you.'

Kinderman shook his head. 'I didn't know.'

'Bill, I told you.'

'I'm so sorry.'

'I'm not. She was ninety-three and in pain and it was a blessing.' Dyer looked aside. The jukebox had come to life in the bar and he looked toward the sound. He saw students drinking beer from thick steins. 'I guess I'd had five or six false alarms,' he said, returning his gaze to Kinderman. 'A brother or a sister calling me over the years to say, "Joe, Mom's dying, you'd better get up here." This time it happened.'

'I'm so sorry. It must have been terrible.'

'No. No, it wasn't. When I got there they told me she was dead – my brother, my sister, the doctor. So I went in and read the Last Rites by her bed. And when I finished she opened her eyes and looked at me. I nearly jumped out of my socks. She said, "Joe, that was lovely, a dear, nice prayer. And now could you fix a little drink for me, son?" Well, Bill, all I could do was just tear downstairs to the kitchen, I was so damned excited. I poured her a scotch on the rocks, brought it up to her and she drank it. Then I took the empty glass from her hands, and she looked me in the eye and said, "Joe, I don't think I ever told you this, son – but you're a wonderful man." And then she died. But the thing that really got me –' He broke off, seeing Kinderman's eyes welling up. 'If you do your blubbering act, I'm leaving.'

Kinderman rubbed at his eye with a knuckle. 'I'm sorry. But it's sad to think that mothers are so fallible,' he said. 'Please continue.'

Dyer leaned his head across the table. 'The thing I can't forget – the thing that really struck me more than anything – was that here was this wasted ninety-three-year-old lady with her brain cells shot, her vision and her hearing half gone, and her body just a rag of what it was – but when she spoke to me, Bill – when she spoke to me, *all of her was there*.'

Kinderman nodded, looking down at his hands clasped together on the table. Black and unbidden, an image of Kintry nailed to the oars hit his mind like a bullet.

Dyer put a hand on Kinderman's wrist. 'Hey, come on. It's okay,' he said. '*She*'s okay.'

'It just seems to me the world is a homicide victim,' Kinderman answered him morosely. He lifted his drooping gaze to the priest. 'Would a God invent something like death? Plainly speaking it's a lousy idea. It isn't popular, Father. It isn't a hit. It's not a winner.'

'Don't be dumb. You wouldn't want to live forever,' said Dyer.

'Yes. I would.'

'You'd get bored,' said the priest.

'I have hobbies.'

The Jesuit laughed.

Encouraged, the detective leaned forward and continued. 'I think about the problem of evil.'

'Oh, that.'

'I must remember that. A very good saying. Yes, "Earthquake in India, Thousands Dead," says the headline. "Oh, *that*," I say. Saint Francis here is speaking to the birds, and in the meantime we have cancer and mongoloid babies, not to mention the gastrointestinal system and certain aesthetics related to our bodies Audrey Hepburn wouldn't like we should mention to her face. Can we have a good God with such nonsense going on? A God who goes blithely *shtravansing* through the cosmos like some omnipotent Billie Burke while children suffer and our loved ones lie on their waste and die? Your God on this question always takes the Fifth Amendment.'

'So why should the Mafia get all the breaks?'

'Enlightening words. Father, when are you preaching again? I would love to hear more of your insights.'

'Bill, the point is that right in the middle of this horror there's a creature called man who can *see* that it's horrible. So where do we come up with these notions like "evil" and "cruel" and "unjust"? You can't say a line looks a little bit crooked unless you've got a notion of a line that's straight.' The detective was trying to wave him off but the priest went on. 'We're a part of the world. If it's evil, we shouldn't be *thinking* that it's evil. We'd be thinking that the things we call evil are just natural. Fish don't feel wet in the water. They belong there, Bill. Men don't.'

'Yes, I read this in G. K. Chesterton, Father. In fact, that's how I know your Mister Big in the *velterrayn* isn't some kind of a Jekyll and Hyde. But this only compounds the great mystery, Father, the big detective story in the sky that from the Psalmists to Kafka has been making people crazy with trying to figure the whole thing out. Never mind. Lieutenant Kinderman is on the case. You know the Gnostics?'

'I'm a Bullets fan.'

'You are shameless. The Gnostics thought a "Deputy" created the world.'

'This is truly insufferable,' said Dyer.

'I'm just talking.'

'Next you'll tell me Saint Peter was a Catholic.'

'I'm just talking. So then God told this angel I mentioned, this Deputy, "Here – here's two dollars, go create for me the world, it's my brainstorm, my latest new idea." And the angel went and did it, only not being perfect we have now the current *khazerei* of which I speak.'

'Is that your theory?' asked Dyer.

'No, that wouldn't get God off the hook.'

'No kidding. What *is* your theory?'

Kinderman's manner grew furtive. 'Never mind. It's something new. Something startling. Something big.'

The waitress had come by and slipped their check on the table. 'There it is,' said Dyer, eyeing it.

Kinderman absently stirred his cold coffee and shifted his glance around the room as if watching for some eavesdropping secret agent. He leaned his head forward conspiratorially. 'My approach to the world,' he said guardedly, 'is as if it were the scene of a crime. You understand? I am putting together the clues. In the meantime, I have several "Wanted" posters. You'd be good enough to hang them on the campus? They're free. Your vow of poverty hangs heavy on your mind; I'm very sensitive to that. There's no charge.'

'You're not telling me your theory?'

'I will give you a hint,' said Kinderman. 'Clotting.'

Dyer's eyebrows knit together. 'Clotting?'

'When you cut yourself, your blood cannot clot without fourteen separate little operations going on inside your body, and in just a certain order; little platelets and these cute little corpuscles, whatever, going here, going there, doing this, doing that, and in just this certain way or you wind up looking foolish with your blood pouring out on the pastrami.'

'That's the hint?'

'Here's another: the autonomic system. Also, vines can find water from miles away.'

'I'm lost.'

'Stay put, we have picked up your signal.' Kinderman leaned his face closer to Dyer's. 'Things that supposedly have no consciousness are behaving as if they do.'

'Thank you, Professor Irwin Corey.'

Kinderman abruptly sat back and glowered. 'You are the

living proof of my thesis. You saw that horror movie called *Alien*?'

'Yes.'

'Your life story. In the meantime, never mind, I have learned my lesson. Never send Sherpa guides to lead a rock; it will only fall on top of them and give them a headache.'

'But that's all you're going to tell me about your theory?' protested Dyer. He picked up his coffee cup.

'That is all. My final word.'

Suddenly the cup fell out of Dyer's grasp. His eyes were unfocused. Kinderman grabbed at the cup and righted it, then picked up a napkin and blotted at the spillage before it ran over onto Dyer's lap.

'Father Joe, what's the matter?' asked Kinderman, alarmed. He began to get up, but Dyer waved him down. His manner seemed normal again.

'It's okay, it's okay,' said the priest.

'Are you sick? What's the matter?'

Dyer picked a cigarette out of his pack. He shook his head. 'No, it's nothing.' He lit up and then fanned out the match and tossed it lightly into an ashtray. 'I've been getting these dumb little dizzy spells lately.'

'Seen a doctor?'

'I did but he couldn't find a thing. It could be anything. An allergy. A virus.' Dyer shrugged. 'My brother Eddie had the same thing for years. It was emotional. Anyway, I'm checking in Tuesday for some tests.'

'Checking in?'

'Georgetown General. Father President insists. He's got a sneaking suspicion I'm allergic to exam papers, frankly, and he wants some scientific confirmation.'

Kinderman's wristwatch alarm began to buzz. He turned it off and checked the time. 'Half-past five,' he murmured. His expressionless gaze flicked up to Dyer. 'The carp is sleeping,' Kinderman intoned.

Dyer lowered his face into his hands and laughed.

Kinderman's beeper sounded. He plucked it from his belt

and turned it off. 'You'll excuse me a moment, Father Joe?' He was wheezing, pushing up from the table.

'Don't leave me with the check,' said Dyer.

The detective did not answer. He went to a telephone, called the Precinct and spoke to Atkins.

'Something peculiar here, Lieutenant.'

'Oh, really?'

Atkins related two developments. The first concerned subscribers on Kintry's route. No one had complained of not receiving a paper; all had received one, even those to whom Kintry would have delivered one after his stop at the Potomac Boathouse. All had received one after he was dead.

The second development concerned the old woman. Kinderman had ordered a routine comparison of her hair to strands of other hair that were found clutched tightly in Kintry's hand.

They matched.

Chapter Three

When she saw him through the window he'd been gone for only minutes but she gave a little gasp of delight and started running. She tore through the door with her arms outstretched to him, her laughing young face a fond radiance. 'Love of my life!' she cried out to him joyously. And in a moment, the sun was in his arms.

'Mornin', Doc. The same as usual?'

Amfortas did not hear it. His mind was in his heart.

'The same as usual, Doc?'

He came back. He was standing in a narrow little grocery and sandwich shop around the corner from Georgetown University. He looked around. The other customers had gone. Charlie Price, the old grocer behind the counter, was studying his face with a gentle look. 'Yes, Charlie, the same,' Amfortas said absently. His voice was dark and soft. He looked and saw Lucy, the grocer's daughter, resting in a chair by the storefront window. He wondered how his turn had come so quickly.

'One Chop Suey for the doctor,' murmured Price. The grocer bent over to the windowed compartments where the morning's fresh doughnuts and sweet rolls were stored and he extracted a large glazed bun filled with cinnamon and raisins and nuts. He stood up and slapped a square of wax paper around it and then placed it in a bag which he set on the counter. 'And one black coffee.' He shuffled toward the Silex and the styrofoam cups.

They had bicycled halfway around Bora Bora and suddenly he spurted swiftly ahead and around a sharp curve where he knew she couldn't see him. He braked and jumped off and quickly gathered up a clutch of the vivid red poppies growing wild by the road in blazing swarms like the love of angels massed before God; and when she rounded the corner he was waiting for her, standing in the middle of

the road with the burning flowers held out to her gaze. She braked in
surprise and looked at them, stunned; and then tears began to slip
from her eyes and down her face. 'I love you, Vincent.'

'You been working in the lab all night again, Doc?'

A paper bag was being folded and closed at the top. Amfortas looked up. His order was ready and waiting on the counter. 'Not all night. A few hours.'

The grocer examined the haggard face, met the umber eyes as dark as forests. What were they saying to him? Something. They shimmered with a silent, mysterious cry. More than grief. Something else. 'Don't push it,' said the grocer. 'You look tired.'

Amfortas nodded. He was fumbling at a pocket of the navy blue cardigan that he wore above his hospital whites. He slipped out a dollar and gave it to the grocer. 'Thanks, Charlie.'

'Just remember what I said.'

'I'll remember.'

Amfortas took the bag and in a moment the front door chime tinkled lightly and the doctor was out in the morning street. Tall and slender, his shoulders bent, for a time he stood pensively in front of the shop with his head angled downward. A hand held the bag up against his chest. The grocer moved over beside his daughter and together they watched him.

'All these years and I've never seen him smile,' murmured Lucy.

The grocer propped an arm on a shelf. 'Why should he?'

He was smiling but he said, 'I couldn't marry you, Ann.'

'Why not? Don't you love me?'

'But you're only twenty-two.'

'Is that bad?'

'I'm twice your age,' he said. 'Someday you'd be pushing me around in a wheelchair.'

She jumped from her seat with that merry laugh and she sat on his lap and put her arms around him. 'Oh, Vincent, I'll keep you young.'

Amfortas heard shouts and the pounding of feet and he looked toward Prospect Street on his right and at the landing of the sheer, stone flight of steps that plunged to 'M' Street far below and, a little beyond it, the river and the boathouse; for years they had been known as 'The Hitchcock Steps'. The Georgetown crew team was running up. It was part of their drill. Amfortas watched as they appeared at the landing and then jogged toward the campus and out of view. He stood until the vivid cries had dwindled, leaving him alone in the soundless corridor where the doings of men were blurred and all life had no purpose except to wait.

He felt the hot coffee on his palm through the bag. He turned from Prospect Street and walked slowly along 36th until he came to his squeezed two-storey frame house. It was just a few yards away from the grocery and was modest and very old. Across the street were a women's dormitory and a foreign service school; and a block to the left was Holy Trinity Church. Amfortas sat down on the white, scrubbed stoop and then opened the bag and took out the bun. She used to fetch it for him on Sundays.

'After death we go back to God,' he told her. She'd been speaking of the father she had lost the year before and he wanted to comfort her. 'We'll be part of Him then,' he said.

'As ourselves?'

'Maybe not. We might lose our identity.'

He saw her tearing up, the little face contorting as she tried not to cry.

'What's wrong?' he asked her.

'Losing you forever.'

Until that day, he had never feared death.

Church bells rang and a slim line of starlings arced up from Holy Trinity, veering and circling in a wild dance. People were beginning to come out of the church. Amfortas checked his watch. It was seven-fifteen. Somehow he'd missed his six-thirty Mass. He'd been going to it daily for the last three years. How could he have missed it? He stared at the bun in his hand for a moment, then slowly he dropped it back into the bag. He lifted his hands and placed his left thumb on his right-hand wrist and his first two left fingers on his right-hand palm. He then applied pressure with all three digits and began to move the fingers around on his palm. The right hand, grasping in a reflex action, groped and followed the movement of the fingers.

Amfortas stopped the manipulation. He stared at his hands.

When he thought of the world again, Amfortas checked the time. It was seven-twenty-five. He picked up the bag and the copy of the Sunday *Washington Post* that lay bulky and ink-smeared by the door. They never wrapped it. He went into the gloom of his empty house, set the bag and the paper on the small hall table, and then stepped outside again and locked up. He turned around on the terrace and looked at the sky. It was turning overcast and grey. Across the river, black clouds scudded swiftly toward the west and a stinging wind sprang up, shaking branches of the elders lining the streets. They were bare at this season. Amfortas slowly buttoned up the neck of his sweater, and with no other baggage but his pain and his loneliness, began walking toward a far horizon. He was ninety-three million miles from the sun.

Georgetown General Hospital was massive and fairly new. Its modern exterior sprawled between 'O' Street and Reservoir Road and fronted on the western side of 37th. Amfortas could walk there from his home in two minutes, and that morning he arrived at the fourth floor Neurology wing at precisely half-past seven. The Resident was waiting for him at the Charge Desk, and together they began to make the rounds, moving from room to room among the patients, with the Resident presenting each new case, while Amfortas asked questions of the patient. They discussed the diagnoses while moving through the hall.

402 was a thirty-six year old salesman manifesting symptoms of cerebral lesion; in particular, 'unilateral neglect'. He would carefully dress one half of his body, the side ipselateral to the lesion, while completely ignoring the other side. He would shave only one side of his face.

407 was an economist, male, fifty-four. His problems had begun six months before when he'd undergone a brain operation for epilepsy. The surgeon, given no other choice, had

removed certain portions of the temporal lobes.

A month before arriving at Georgetown General, the patient had walked into a Senate committee meeting and for nine straight, gruelling hours devised a new plan for revising the tax code based upon the problems the committee had set him only that morning. His judgement and marshalling of facts was astonishing, no less than his acquaintance with the present code, and it took six hours just to organize the details of the plan and set them down in an orderly manner. At the end of the meeting the economist summarized the plan in half an hour without ever referring to the newly made notes. Afterwards he went to an office and sat at his desk. He answered three letters; then he turned to his secretary and said, 'I've got a feeling that I should have attended a Senate meeting today.' From minute to minute, he could not form memories that were new.

411 was a girl, aged twenty, with a probable case of Cocci meningitis. The Resident was new and didn't notice the flinch when Amfortas was given the name of the disease.

In 420 was a fifty-one-year-old carpenter complaining of a 'phantom limb'. He'd lost an arm the year before and was continuing to suffer excruciating pain in a hand he did not have.

The disorder had evolved in the usual manner, with the carpenter at first having 'tingling feelings' and a sense of a definite shape to the hand. It seemed to move through space like an ordinary limb when he walked or sat down or stretched out on a bed. He would even reach for objects with it unthinkingly. And then came the terrible pain as the hand clenched up and refused to relax.

He submitted to a reconstruction operation as well as the removal of small neuromas, nodules of regenerated tissues of nerve. And at first there was relief. The sense of having the hand remained, but now he felt that he could flex it and move his fingers.

Then the pain came back, with the phantom hand in a very tight posture with the fingers pressed closely over the thumb and the wrist sharply flexed. No effort of will could move any part of it. At times, the sense of tenseness in the hand was unbearable; at others, the carpenter had explained, it felt as though a scalpel was being driven repeatedly deep into the site of the original wound. There were complaints of a boring sensation in the bones of the index finger. The feeling seemed to start at the tip of the finger, but then rose to the shoulder and the stump would begin to have clonic contractions.

The carpenter reported he was frequently nauseated when the pain was at its extreme. As the pain at last faded, the tenseness of the hand seemed to ease a bit, but never enough to permit it to be moved.

Amfortas asked the carpenter a question. 'Your greatest concern seems to be the tenseness in your hand. Would you tell me why?'

The carpenter asked him to clench his fingers over his thumb, flex his wrist, and then raise his arm into a hammerlock position and hold it there. The neurologist complied. But after some minutes, the pain proved too much and Amfortas ended the experiment.

The carpenter nodded his head. He said, 'Right. But you can take your hand down. I can't.'

They left the room silently.

Walking down the hallway, the Resident shrugged. 'I don't know. Can we help him?'

Amfortas recommended a novocaine injection in the upper thoracic sympathetic ganglia. 'That should relieve it for a while. A few months.' But no longer than that. He knew of no cure for the phantom limb.

Or the broken heart.

424 was a housewife. From the age of sixteen, she'd complained of abdominal pain so persistently, that finally, over the years, she had fourteen abdominal operations on her record. After these came a minor head injury that had her complaining of pain in the head so severe that subtemporal decompression was performed. Now her complaint was of agonizing pain in her limbs and back. At first she had refused to give her history. And now she lay constantly on her left side and cried out when the Resident made an effort to turn her over on her back. When

Amfortas leaned over and gently stroked the region of her sacrum, she screamed and violently trembled.

When they left her, Amfortas agreed with the Resident that she ought to be referred to Psychiatric with a finding of probable addiction to surgery.

And to pain.

425, another housewife, aged thirty, complained of chronic, throbbing headaches, with attendant anorexia and vomiting. The worst possibility was a lesion, but the pain was confined to one side of the head, as was also teichopsia, a temporary blindness caused by the appearance in the visual field of a luminous area that was bounded by zigzag lines. Ordinarily, teichopsia symptomized migraine. Moreover, the patient had come from a family that emphasized attainment and had rigid standards of behaviour that denied and punished any expression of aggressive feelings. That was usually the history of a classic migraine patient. The repressed hostility gradually built to unconscious rage, and the rage attacked the patient in the form of the disorder.

Another referral to Psychiatric.

427 was the last, a man of thirty-eight, with a possible lesion of the temporal lobe. He was one of the janitors of the hospital, and only the day before had been discovered in a basement storage room where he had placed a dozen or so electric light bulbs in a bucket of water and was rapidly bobbing them up and down. Afterwards, he couldn't remember what he'd done. This was an automatism, a so-called 'automatic action' characteristic of a psychomotor seizure. Such attacks could be seriously destructive, depending on the patient's unconscious emotions, though most often they were harmless and simply out of keeping. Always bizarre, such fugues were normally brief in duration, although in rare cases they had lasted many hours and were considered to be totally inexplicable, like the baffling case of a man who had flown a light aircraft from an airport in Virginia to Chicago, yet had never learned how to fly a plane and had no recollection of the event. Sometimes, violent assaults took place. A man later found to have a scarred temporal lobe in

association with hemangioma, killed his wife while in a state of epileptic furor.

The janitor's case was more the norm. His history was studded with uncinate seizures, auras of unpleasant tastes or smells: his description of a chocolate bar tasting 'metallic', and a smell of 'rotten flesh' without apparent source. There were also fugues of *déjà vu*, as well as its opposite, *jamais vu* – a sense of strangeness in familiar surroundings. These episodes were often preceded by a peculiar smacking of the lips. The consumption of alcohol often triggered them.

Further, there were visual hallucinations, among them micropsia, in which objects seemed smaller than they were; and levitation, a sensation of rising in the air, unsupported. The janitor had also had one brief episode of a phenomenon known as 'the double'. He had seen his three-dimensional likeness mimicking his every word and action.

The EEG had been especially ominous. Tumours of this nature, if such it was, worked slowly and insidiously for many months, putting upward pressure on the brain stem; but at last it would gather a sudden momentum and in a matter of weeks, if left unattended, compress and crush the medulla.

The result was death.

'Willie, give me your hand,' said Amfortas gently.

'Which one?' asked the janitor.

'Either. The left.'

The janitor complied.

The Resident was looking at Amfortas with an expression of mild pique. 'I've done that already,' he said with an edge.

'I want to do it again,' said Amfortas quietly.

He put his first two left-hand fingers on the janitor's palm, and his right-hand thumb on the janitor's wrist; and then he pressed and began to move the fingers around. The janitor's hand was grasping reflexively and followed the movement of the fingers.

Amfortas stopped and released the hand. 'Thanks, Willie.'

'All right, sir.'

'Don't you worry.'

'I won't, sir.'

By half-past nine, Amfortas and the Resident were standing by the coffee vending machine around the corner from the entrance to Psychiatric. They discussed their diagnoses, wrapping up the new cases. When they came to the janitor, the summing up was swift.

'I've ordered up a "CAT-scan", already,' said the Resident.

Amfortas nodded in agreement. Only then could they be certain that the lesion was there and probably close to its final stages. 'You might want to book an operating room, just in case.' Even now, timely surgery would save Willie's life.

When the Resident came to the girl with meningitis, Amfortas grew stiff and withdrawn, almost brusque. The Resident noticed the sudden transition, but research neurologists, he knew, had a wide reputation for being introverted, incommunicative and strange. He attributed the quirky manner to that; or perhaps the girl's youth and the possibility that nothing could be done to save her from serious crippling, or even a hideously painful death.

'How's your research coming, Vincent?'

The Resident had finished his coffee and was crumpling up his cup before he tossed it in the trash. Outside the hearing of the patients, the formalities were dropped.

Amfortas shrugged. A nurse wheeled a drug cart past them and he watched her. His indifference was beginning to annoy the young Resident. 'How long have you been at it?' he doggedly persisted, determined now to crack the odd barrier between them.

'Three years,' said Amfortas.

'Any breakthroughs?'

'No.'

Amfortas asked for updates on the ward's older cases. The Resident gave up.

At ten, Amfortas attended Grand Rounds, a full staff conference scheduled until noon. The Chief of Neurology delivered a lecture on multiple sclerosis. Like the interns and residents packed in the hallway, Amfortas couldn't hear it, although he was sitting at the conference table. He simply wasn't listening.

After the lecture came a discussion that soon was diverted into heated debate over inter-departmental politics, and when Amfortas said, 'Excuse me, just a minute,' and left, no one noticed that he never came back to the room. Grand Rounds closed out with the Chief of Neurology shouting, 'And I'm goddamn tired of the drunks on this service! Sober up or stay the hell off the ward, goddamnit!' This, all the interns and residents heard.

Amfortas had returned to Room 411. The girl with meningitis was sitting up, her gaze hypnotically glued to the television set that was mounted on the opposite wall. She was clicking through stations. When Amfortas entered, her eyes shifted down to him. She did not move her head. The disease had already caused her neck to be rigid. Moving it was painful.

'Hello, Doctor.'

Her finger pushed a button on the wireless control. The television picture sputtered out.

'No, that's all right, don't turn it off,' said Amfortas quickly.

She was looking at the empty screen. 'There's nothing on now. No good shows.'

He stood at the foot of the bed and observed her. She was pig-tailed and freckled. 'Are you comfortable?' he asked her.

She shrugged.

'What's wrong?' asked Amfortas.

'Bored.' Her eyes came back to him. She smiled. But he saw the dark sacs under her eyes. 'There's never anything good on TV in the daytime.'

'Are you sleeping well?' he asked her.

'No.'

He picked up her chart. Chloral hydrate had already been prescribed.

'They give me pills but they don't work,' said the girl.

Amfortas replaced the chart. When he looked at her again she had angled her body toward the window. She was staring out. 'Can't I keep the TV on at night? Without the sound?'

'I can get you some earphones,' said Amfortas. 'No one else will be able to hear it.'

'All the stations go off at two o'clock,' she said dully.

He asked her what she did.

'I play tennis.'

'Professionally?'

'Yes.'

'You give lessons?'

She didn't. She played on the tournament circuit.

'Are you ranked?'

She said, 'Yes. Number nine.'

'In the country?'

'In the world.'

'Forgive my ignorance,' he said. He felt cold. He couldn't tell if she had knowledge of what might be awaiting her. She continued to stare out the window. 'Well, I guess it's all memories now,' she said softly.

Amfortas felt a tightness in his stomach. She knew.

He pulled up a chair at the side of her bed and he asked her what tournaments she had won. She seemed to brighten at that, and he sat down. 'Oh, well, the French and the Italian. And the Clay Courts. The year I won the French there was nobody in it.'

'What about the Italian?' he asked her. 'Who did you beat in the finals?'

They talked about the game for another half hour.

When Amfortas checked the time and stood up to leave, the girl instantly withdrew and stared out through the window again. 'Sure, that's okay,' she murmured. He could hear the shields clanging down into place.

'Have you got any family in town?' he asked her.

'No.'

'Where are they?'

She angled her body away from the window and turned on the television set. 'They're all dead,' she said matter-of-factly. It was almost drowned out by the sound of the game show. As he left her, her eyes were still pinned to the set.

In the hall, he heard her crying.

Amfortas skipped lunch and worked in his office, finishing the paperwork on some cases. Two of them were epilepsies in which the seizures were triggered bizarrely. In the first case – a woman in her middle thirties – the onset was induced by the sound of music; and the girl of eleven in the second case had only to look at her hand.

All the other workups dealt with forms of aphasia:

A patient who repeated everything said to her.

A patient who was able to write, but completely unable to read back what he had written.

A patient unable to recognize a person from facial features alone, the recognition requiring hearing of the voice, or the noting of a characteristic feature, such as a mole or a striking hair colour.

The aphasias were connected to lesions of the brain.

Amfortas sipped coffee and tried to concentrate. He couldn't. He set down his pen and stared at a photograph propped on his desk. A golden young girl.

The door to his office flew open and Freeman Temple, the Chief of Psychiatry, bounded in with jaunty, lithe steps, springing upward on his toes a little as he walked. He careered to a chair near the desk and flopped down. 'Boy, have I got a girl for you!' he said gaily. He stretched out his legs and crossed them comfortably, tossing a fanned-out match on the floor. 'I swear to God,' he continued, 'you'd love her. She's got legs running all the way up to her ass. And tits? Jesus, one of them's big as a watermelon, and the other one's *really* big! It also happens she loves Mozart. Vince, you've *gotta* take her out!'

Amfortas observed him without expression. Temple was short and in his fifties, but his face had a puckish, youthful look with a constant merriment about it. Yet his eyes were like wheatfields stirring in the breeze, and at times had a deadly, calculating look. Amfortas neither trusted him nor liked him. When Temple wasn't bragging of his amorous conquests, he adverted to his boxing matches in college, and he tried to get everyone to call him 'Duke'. 'That's what they called me at Stanford,' he would say. 'They called me "Duke".' He would tell all the prettier nurses that he always avoided a fight because 'under the law, my hands are considered to be lethal weapons.' When he drank, he was insufferable and the boyish charm turned into meanness. He was drunk right now, Amfortas suspected; or high on amphetamine; or both.

'I've been dating her girlfriend,' Temple rushed headlong. 'She's married, but hell. So what? What's the difference? Anyway, the one for you is single. Want her number?'

Amfortas picked up his pen and looked down at his papers. On one, he made a note. 'No, thanks. I haven't dated in years,' he said quietly.

Abruptly, the psychiatrist seemed to sober and he stared at Amfortas with a hard, cold squint. 'I know that,' he said evenly.

Amfortas continued to work.

'What's the problem? Are you impotent?' Temple demanded. 'That happens a lot in your situation. I can cure it with hypnosis. I can cure *anything* with hypnosis. I'm good. I'm really, really good. I'm the best.'

Amfortas continued to ignore him. He made a correction on a paper.

'The goddam EEG's broken down. Can you believe it?'

Amfortas was silent and continued to write.

'Okay, what the hell's this?'

Amfortas looked up and saw Temple reaching into a pocket. He extracted a folded sheet of memo paper and tossed it onto the desk. Amfortas picked it up and unfolded it. When he read it, he saw, in what appeared to be his writing, the cryptic statement, 'The life is less able.'

'What the hell does that mean?' repeated Temple. His manner had now grown openly hostile.

'I don't know,' said Amfortas.

'You don't *know*?'

'I didn't write it.'

Temple bolted from his chair and to the desk. 'Christ, you gave it to me yesterday in front of the Charge Desk! I was busy and just stuck it in my pocket. What's it mean?'

Amfortas put the note aside and continued with his work. 'I didn't write it,' he repeated.

'Are you *crazy*?' Temple grabbed up the note and held it out before Amfortas. 'That's your writing! See those circles there over the 'i's? Incidentally, those circles are a sign of disturbance.'

Amfortas erased a word and wrote over it.

The white-haired psychiatrist's face turned crimson. He sprang to the door and yanked it open. 'You'd better make an appointment with me,' he snorted. 'You're a goddam hostile, angry man and you're fucking crazier than a loon!' Temple slammed the door behind him.

For a time, Amfortas stared at the note. Then he went back to work. He had to finish this week.

In the afternoon, Amfortas gave a lecture at the Georgetown University Medical School. He reviewed the case of a woman who from birth had been unable to feel any pain. As a child she had bitten off the tip of her tongue while chewing food, and had suffered third-degree burns after kneeling for minutes atop a hot radiator to look out of a window at a sunset. When later examined by a psychologist, she reported not feeling pain when her body was subjected to strong electric shock, to hot water at extremely high temperatures, or to an ice bath that was greatly prolonged. Equally abnormal was the fact that she showed no changes in blood pressure, heart rate, or respiration when these stimuli were applied. She could not remember ever sneezing or coughing; the gag reflex could be elicited only with great difficulty; and corneal reflexes that protect the eyes were totally absent. A variety of stimuli, such as inserting a stick up through the nostrils, pinching tendons, or injections of histamine under the skin – normally considered forms of torture – also failed to produce any pain.

The woman eventually developed serious medical problems; pathological changes in her knees, hip and spine. She underwent several orthopaedic operations. Her surgeon attributed her problems to the lack of protection to her joints that was usually given by sensation of pain. She had failed to shift her weight when standing; to turn over in her sleep; or to avoid certain postures which produce inflammation of the joints.

She died at age twenty-nine of massive infections which could not be controlled.

There were no questions.

At 3:35, Amfortas was back in his office. He locked the door and sat down and waited. He knew he couldn't work just now. Not now.

Occasionally, someone would rap at the door and he waited for the footsteps to go away. Once there was a rattling of the doorknob, then pounding, and he knew it was Temple even before he could hear his low growl through the wood of the door. 'You crazy bastard, I know that you're in there. Let me in so I can help you.' Amfortas kept silent and he heard no movement for a time on the other side of the door. Then he heard a guarded, soft, 'Big tits'. And another silence. He imagined that Temple had his ear to the door. At last he heard his springing footsteps creaking away on double-thick soles. Amfortas continued to mark the time.

At twenty to five he telephoned a friend at another hospital, a neurologist on their staff. When he reached him, he said, 'Eddie, this is Vincent. Has my CAT-scan result come in?'

'Yes, it has. I was just about to call you.'

There was a silence.

'Is it positive?' Amfortas asked at last.

Another silence. Then, 'Yes.' It was almost inaudible.

'I'll take care of it. Goodbye, Ed.'

'Vince?'

But Amfortas was already hanging up.

He took a sheet of department stationery from a right-hand drawer of his desk, and then carefully composed a letter addressed to the Chief of Neurology.

Dear Jim:

This is difficult to say, and I'm sorry, but I need to be

relieved from my regular duties effective this Tuesday evening, March 17. I need all the time I can get for my research. Tom Soames is very competent, and my patients are secure in his hands until you can find a replacement for me. By Tuesday, my reports on old patients will be finished, and Tom and I agree on the new ones seen today. After Tuesday, I'll try to be around for consultation, but I really can't promise. In any case, you'll find me in the lab or at home.

I know this is sudden and will cause you some problems. Again, I'm very sorry. And I know you'll respect my desire not to say any more about my decision. I'll have my desk cleaned out by week's end. The ward's been terrific. So have you. Thanks.

> Regretfully,
> Vincent Amfortas.

Amfortas left his office, put the letter in the Chief of Neurology's box, and walked out of the hospital. It was almost half-past five, and he quickened his steps towards Holy Trinity. He could make the evening Mass.

The church was crowded and he stood in the back and followed the Mass with an agonizing hope. The broken bodies he had treated through the years had imbued him with a sense of man's frailty and aloneness. Men were tiny candle flames apart and adrift in a void that was endless and terrifying and black. This perception brought humanity into his embrace. Yet God eluded him. He'd found His cryptic traces in the brain, but the God of the brain only beckoned him towards Him, and when he came close He held him out at arm's length; and at the last, there was nothing to embrace but his faith. It hugged the candle flames together in a oneness that soared and illumined the night.

'O Lord, I have loved the beauty of thy house . . .'

Here was all that could matter, for nothing else did.

Amfortas glanced over at the lines for confession. They were long. He decided to go the next day. He would make it a general, he thought: a confession of the sins of all his life. There would be time at the Morning Mass, he thought. There was rarely a line at that hour.

'*And may it become for us an everlasting healing . . .*'

'Amen,' prayed Amfortas firmly.

He had made up his mind.

He unlocked the front door and walked into the house. In the hall he picked up the bag and the *Post* and then carried them into the little living room, where he turned on all the lamps. The house was a rental, fully furnished in a cheap, drab mock-colonial style. The living room railroaded into a kitchen and a tiny breakfast nook. Upstairs were a bedroom and a den. It was all that Amfortas needed or wanted.

He eased himself down in an overstuffed chair. He looked around him. The room was, as usual, untidy. Disarray had never bothered him before. But now he felt an odd impulse to straighten it up; to organize and clean the entire house. It was something like the feeling before a long trip; or cleaning out his desk.

He put it off until tomorrow. He felt weary.

He stared at a tape recorder on a shelf. It was connected to an amplifier. There were earphones. Too tired for that as well, he decided. He didn't have the energy for it now. He looked down at the *Washington Post* on his lap, and in an instant the headache was tearing at his brain. He gasped and his hands flew up to his temples. He stood up and the newspaper scattered to the floor.

He lurched upstairs and into his bedroom. He fumbled for the lamp and turned it on. By the bed he kept a medical bag and he opened it, removing a swab, a disposable syringe and an amber-coloured vial filled with a fluid. He sat down on his bed, unbuckled his pants and pushed them down, exposing his thighs. And in moments, he'd injected six milligrams of Decadron, a steroid, in the muscle of his leg; the Dilaudid wasn't enough any more.

Amfortas fell back on the bed and waited. The amber-coloured vial was clutched in his hand. His heart and his head pounded out different rhythms, but then after a while they melted into one. Amfortas lost track of the time.

He sat up. His trousers were still at his knees. He pulled them up, and as he did, his eye caught the green-and-white ceramic on his bedstand, a fluffy duck in little girl's clothing. A legend read, 'HONK IF YOU THINK I'M ADORABLE'. For a moment he stared at it sadly. He buckled his belt and walked downstairs.

He went into the living room and gathered up the Sunday *Washington Post*. He thought to read it while the frozen dinner was heating. When he turned on the overhead kitchen light, he stopped in his tracks. On the breakfast nook table were the remains of a morning meal and a copy of the Sunday *Washington Post*. The paper was disarrayed and in sections.

Someone had been reading it.

Chapter Four

DIVISION OF CONSOLIDATED LABORATORY SERVICES
Bureau of Forensic Science

LABORATORY REPORT
March 15, 1982

TO: Alan Stedman, MD   cc: Dr Francis Caponegro

Your case # 50   FS LAB # 77-N-025

Victim(s): Kintry, Thomas   Examiner: Samuel Hirschberg, Ph.D.
       Joshua   Laboratory: Bethesda

Age: 12

Race: B   Sex: M   Date Received: March 15, 1982

Suspect(s): None

Evidence Submitted By: Dr Alan Stedman

One bottle of blood and one bottle of urine for alcohol and drug screen.

RESULTS OF EXAMINATION:

BLOOD: 0.06% ethanol weight/volume.

URINE: 0.08% ethanol weight/volume.

BLOOD AND URINE: Negative for significant quantities of cyanide and fluoride; negative for barbiturates, carbamates, hydantoins, glutarimides, and other sedative-hypnotic drugs. Negative for amphetamines, antihistamines, phencyclidines, benzodiazepines. Negative for natural and synthetic narcotics and analgesics. Negative for tricyclic antidepressants and carbon monoxide. Negative for heavy metals. Positive finding: succinylcholine chloride, 18 milligrams.

Samuel Hirschberg, Ph.D.
Toxicologist

Chapter Five

—⟨✦⟩—

'There is a doctrine written in secret that man is a prisoner who has no right to open the door and run away; this is a mystery which I do not quite understand. Yet I too believe that the gods are our guardians, and that we men are a possession of theirs.'

Kinderman thought of the passage from Plato. How could he help it? It haunted this case. 'What's the meaning of it?' Kinderman asked the others. 'How can this be?'

They sat around a desk in the middle of the squad room, Kinderman, Atkins, Stedman and Ryan. Kinderman needed the activity around him, the steadying bustle of a world where there was order and the floor would not vanish from beneath his feet. He needed the light.

'Well, of course it's not a positive identification,' said Ryan. He scratched at a muscle in his forearm. Like Stedman and Atkins, he was working in his shirtsleeves; the room was overheated. Ryan shrugged. 'Hair can never give you that, we all know that. Still . . .'

'Yes, still,' echoed Kinderman. 'Still . . .'

The medulla of the hairs were identical in thickness; and the shape and size and number per unit length of the overlapping scales of the cuticles were exactly the same in both the samples. The hairs that had been taken from Kintry's hand had fresh, round roots, implying a struggle.

Kinderman shook his head. 'It couldn't be,' he said. 'It's *farblundjet*.'

He looked down at a photo they had taken of the woman, and then into the cup of tea in his hand. He poked at the lemon slice with a finger, bobbing and stirring it around a little. He still wore his coat. 'What killed him?' he asked.

'Shock,' answered Stedman. 'And slow asphyxiation.'

Everyone stared. 'He was injected with a drug called succinylcholine. Ten milligrams for each fifty pounds of body weight causes instant paralysis,' he said. 'Kintry had almost twenty milligrams in him. He wouldn't have been able to move or cry out; and after ten minutes or so he couldn't breathe. The drug attacks the respiratory system.'

A cone of silence descended upon them, cutting them apart from the rest of the room, from the busy, loud chattering of men and machines. Kinderman heard them, but the sounds were muted and far away, like forgotten prayers.

'What is it used for,' Kinderman asked, 'this – what did you call it?'

'Succinylcholine.'

'You love to say that, don't you, Stedman.'

'It's basically a muscle relaxant,' said Stedman. 'It's used for anaesthesia. You mainly find it used in electroshock therapy.'

Kinderman nodded.

'I might point out,' the pathologist added, 'that the drug leaves almost no margin for error. To get the effect that he wanted the killer had to know what he was doing.'

'So a doctor,' said Kinderman. 'An anaesthetist maybe. Who knows? Someone medically qualified, right? And with access to the drug, this whatever. Incidentally, did we find a hypodermic syringe at the scene of the crime, or as usual, only some Crackerjack prizes that the rich kids are constantly throwing away?'

'We didn't find a syringe,' Ryan answered him stoically.

'It figures,' Kinderman sighed. The search of the crime scene had yielded them little. True, the mallet bore the marks of impacting on the nails; but only smeared fingerprints had been found, and blood antigen tests of the saliva on the cigarette butts showed the user had blood type 'O'. 'O' was the most common of them all. Kinderman saw Stedman checking his wristwatch. 'Stedman, go home,' he said. 'You, too, Ryan. Go away. Go on. Go home to your family and talk about Jews.'

Parting amenities were exchanged and Ryan and Stedman

escaped into the streets with nothing more on their minds now but dinner and the traffic. Watching them, the squad room came to life again for Kinderman, as though it had been touched by their ordinary thoughts; he heard telephones ringing, men shouting; then they passed through the door and the sounds were gone.

Atkins watched as Kinderman sipped at his tea, deep in thought; saw him reach inside his cup, extract the lemon slice, squeeze it, and then let it drop back into the cup. 'This thing about the newspapers, Atkins,' he brooded. He looked up and met Atkins' steady gaze.

'It's got to be an error, Lieutenant. It must be. There's some explanation. I'll check at the *Post* again tomorrow.'

Kinderman looked down at his tea and shook his head. 'It's no use. You'll find nothing. It makes my mind cold. Something terrible is laughing at us, Atkins. You'll find nothing.' He sipped at the tea and then murmured, 'Succinylcholine chloride. Just enough.'

'What about the old woman, Lieutenant?' No one had claimed her as yet. No traces of blood had been found on her clothing.

Kinderman looked at him, suddenly animated. 'Do you know about the Hunting Wasp, Atkins? No, you don't. It isn't known. It isn't common. But this wasp is incredible. A mystery. To begin with, its lifespan is only two months. A short time. Never mind though, as long as it's healthy. All right, it comes out of its egg. It's a baby, it's cute, a little wasp. In a month it's fullgrown and has eggs of its own. And now all of a sudden the eggs need food, but a special kind and *only* one kind: a live insect, Atkins, let's say a cicada; yes, cicadas would be good. We'll say cicadas. Now the Hunting Wasp figures this out. Who knows how? It's a mystery. Forget it. Never mind. But the food must be alive; putrefaction would be fatal to the egg and to the grub; and a live and *normal* cicada would crush the egg or even eat it. So the wasp can't drop a net on a bunch of cicadas and then give them to the eggs and say, "Here, eat your dinner". You thought life was easy for Hunting Wasps, Atkins?

67

Just flying and stinging all day, jaunty jolly? No, it isn't so easy. Not at all. They have problems. But if the wasp can just *paralyse* the cicada, this problem is solved and there's dinner on the table. But to do this, it has to figure out exactly *where* to sting the cicada, which would take total knowledge of cicada anatomy, Atkins – they're all covered with this armour, these scales – and it has to figure out exactly how much venom to inject, or else our friend the cicada flies away or is dead. All this medical-surgical knowledge it needs. Don't feel blue, Atkins. Really. It's all okay. All the Hunting Wasps everywhere, even as we sit here, they're all singing, "Don't Cry for Me, Argentina" and they're paralysing insects all over the country. Isn't that amazing? How can this be?'

'Well, it's instinct,' said Atkins, knowing what Kinderman wanted to hear.

Kinderman glared. 'Atkins, never say "instinct" and I give you my word, I will never say "parameters". Can we find a way of living?'

'What about "instinctive"?'

'*Also* verboten. "Instinct". What is instinct? Does a name explain? Someone tells you that the sun didn't rise today in Cuba and you answer, "Never mind, today is Sun-Shall-Not-Rise-In-Cuba-Day?" That explains it? Give a label and it's curtains now for miracles, correct? Let me tell you, I am also not impressed by words like "gravity". Okay. That's a whole other *tsimmis* altogether. In the meantime, the Hunting Wasp, Atkins. It's amazing. It's a part of my theory.'

'Your theory on the case?' Atkins asked him.

'I don't know. It could be. Maybe not. I'm just talking. No, another case, Atkins. Something bigger.' He gestured globally. 'It's all connected. As regards the old lady, in the meantime . . .' His voice trailed away and a distant thunder rumbled faintly. He stared at a window where a light fall of rain was beginning to splatter in hesitant touches. Atkins shifted in his chair. 'The old lady,' breathed Kinderman, his eyes dreamy. 'She is leading us into her mystery, Atkins. I hesitate to follow her. I do.'

He continued staring inwardly for a time. Then abruptly he crumpled his empty cup and tossed it away. It thudded in the wastebasket near the desk. He stood up. 'Go and visit your sweetheart, Atkins. Chew bubble gum and drink lemonade. Make fudge. As for me, I am leaving. Adieu.' But for a moment he stood there, looking around.

'Lieutenant, you're wearing it,' said Atkins.

Kinderman felt at the brim of his hat. 'Yes, I am. This is true. Good point. Well taken.'

Kinderman continued to brood by the desk. 'Never trust in the facts,' he wheezed. 'Facts hate us. They stink. They hate men and they hate the truth.' Abruptly he turned and waddled away.

In a moment he was back and ransacking pockets of his coat for books. 'One more thing,' he said to Atkins. The sergeant stood up. 'Just a minute.' Kinderman riffled through the books, and then he murmured, 'Aha!' and from the pages of a work by Teilhard de Chardin, he extracted a note that was written on the back of a Hershey Bar wrapper. He held it to his chest. 'Don't look,' he said sternly.

'I'm not looking,' said Atkins.

'Well, don't.' Kinderman guardedly held the note and began to read: '"Another source of conviction in the existence of God, connected with the reason and not with feelings, is the extreme difficulty or rather impossibility of conceiving this immense and wonderful universe as the result of blind chance or necessity."' Kinderman breasted the note and looked up. 'Who wrote that, Atkins?'

'You.'

'The test for lieutenant is not till next year. Guess again.'

'I don't know.'

'Charles Darwin,' said Kinderman. 'In *The Origin of Species*.' And with that, he stuffed the note in his pocket and left.

And again came back. 'Something else,' he told Atkins. He stood with his nose an inch away from the sergeant's, hands stuffed deep in the pockets of his coat. 'What does Lucifer mean?'

'Light Bearer.'

'And what is the stuff of the universe?'

'Energy.'

'What is energy's commonest form?'

'Light.'

'I know.' And with that, the detective walked away, listing slowly through the squad room and down the stairs.

He didn't come back.

Policewoman Jourdan sat in shadow in a corner of a room in the Holding Ward. The old woman was bathed in the eerie rays of an amber nightlight above her bed. She lay motionless and silent, arms at her sides, and her eyes stared blankly into her dreams. Jourdan could hear her regular breathing; that and the patter of rain against a window. The policewoman shifted in her chair, getting comfortable. She drowsily closed her eyes. And then suddenly opened them. An odd sound was in the room. Something brittle and crackling. It was faint. Uneasy, Jourdan scanned the room, and didn't know that she was frightened until she instinctively sighed with relief on discovering the sound had been caused by ice cubes shifting in a glass beside the bed.

She saw the door pushing open. It was Kinderman. He quietly entered the room. 'Take a break,' he told Jourdan.

With a feeling of gratitude, she left.

Kinderman stared at the woman for a time. He took off his hat. 'Are you feeling all right, dear?' he asked her gently. The old woman said nothing. Then abruptly her arms came up and her hands made the patterned, mysterious movements that Kinderman had seen in the Potomac Boathouse. Kinderman carefully picked up a chair and then put it down softly beside the bed. He smelled disinfectant. He sat in the chair and started watching intently. The movements had a meaning. What was their meaning? The hands were casting shadows on the opposite wall, black spidery hieroglyphs, like a code. Kinderman studied the woman's face. It had a look of sanctity about it; and in her eyes was something curiously like longing.

For almost an hour Kinderman sat in the strange half-light with the sound of the rain and his breathing and his thoughts. Once he brooded on the quarks and the whispers of physics that matter was not things, but merely processes in a world of shifting shadows and illusions; a world in which neutrinos were said to be ghosts, and electrons were able to go backwards in time. Look directly at the faintest stars and they vanish, he thought; their light strikes only cones in the eye; but look beside them and you see them: their light hits the rods. Kinderman sensed that in this strange new universe, he must look to the side to solve his case. He rejected the old woman's involvement in the murder; and yet in some way that he could not explain, she somehow embodied it. This instinct was puzzling, yet strong, whenever he looked away from the facts.

When the old woman's movements had finally stopped, the detective stood up and looked down at the bed. He held his hat by the brim in both hands, and said, 'Goodnight, Miss. I'm sorry to have troubled you.' With that, he walked out of the room.

Jourdan was nervously smoking a cigarette in the hall. The detective approached her and studied her face. She seemed uneasy.

'Has she spoken?' he asked her.

She exhaled smoke and shook her head. 'No. No, she hasn't.'

'She ate?'

'Yes, some oatmeal. Hot soup.' She flicked an ash that was not there.

'You seem troubled,' said Kinderman.

'I dunno. It just got a little creepy in there. No reason. Just a feeling.' She shrugged. 'I dunno.'

'You're very tired. Please go home,' the detective told her. 'There are nurses . . .'

'All the same, I hate to leave her. She's so pathetic.' She flicked another ash and her eyes were slightly darting. 'Yeah, I guess I'm pretty beat, though. You really think I should?'

'You've been wonderful. Go home now.'

Jourdan looked relieved. 'Thanks, Lieutenant. Goodnight.' She turned and walked away quickly. Kinderman watched her.

She felt it too, he thought; *the same thing. But what? What's the problem? The old lady didn't do it.*

Kinderman watched an old scrubwoman working. On her head was a soiled bandana. She was mopping up the floor. *That's a scrubwoman mopping*, he thought; *that's all*. Again in touch with normality, he went home. He ached for his bed.

Mary was waiting for him in the kitchen. She was sitting at the little maple table, dressed in a pale blue woollen robe. She had a sturdy face and mischievous eyes. 'Hello, Bill. You look tired,' she said.

'I am turning into an eyelid.'

He kissed her on the forehead and sat.

'Are you hungry' she asked him.

'Not a lot.'

'There's some brisket.'

'Not the carp?'

She giggled.

'And so how was your day?' she asked.

'Good times, as usual, gambling.'

Mary knew about Kintry. She'd heard it on the news. But they'd agreed, years before, that Kinderman's work was never to enter the peace of their house, at least not as a subject of conversation. The late night calls could not be helped.

'So what's new? How was Richmond?' he asked.

She made a face. 'We had a late breakfast there, some basted eggs and bacon, and they brought it with grits, and Mama said right out loud at the counter, "These Jews are crazy."'

'And where is she, our venerable *mavin* of the river bottoms?'

'Sleeping.'

'Thank God.'

'Bill, be nice. She can hear you.'

'In her sleep? Yes, of course, love. The Phantom of the Tub is ever vigilant. She knows I might do something really crazy to that fish. Mary, when are we eating the carp? I'm very serious.'

'Tomorrow.'

'So tonight there's no bath again, *nu*?'

'You can shower.'

72

'I want a bath with lots of bubbles. Would the carp mind some bubbles? I'm willing to negotiate a rapprochement. Incidentally, where's Julie?'

'At dance class.'

'Dance class at night?'

'Bill, it's only eight o'clock.'

'She should dance in the daytime. It's better.'

'Better how?'

'It's more light out. It's better. She can see the pointed shoes. Only *goyim* dance well in the dark. Jews stumble. They don't like it.'

'Bill, I've got a little news you're not going to be crazy about.'

'So the carp had quintuplets.'

'Close. Julie wants to change her last name to "Febré".'

The detective looked numb. 'You're not serious.'

'I am.'

'No, you're joking.'

'She says it might be better for her image as a dancer.'

Kinderman said tonelessly, 'Julie Febré.'

'So why not?'

He said, 'Jews are *fermischt*, not Febré. Is this what comes of all this packaging we see in our culture? Next comes Doctor Bernie Feinerman to spritz up her nose so it matches her name; and after that comes the Bible and the Book of Febré and in the Ark there will be nothing that looks like a gnu, only clean cut looking animals named Melody or Tab, all Wasps from Dubuque. The remains of the Ark some day they'll find in the Hamptons. We should only thank God that the Pharaoh isn't here, that *goniff*, he'd be laughing in our faces this minute.'

She said, 'Things could be worse.'

He said, 'Maybe.'

'Does the Ark stop at Richmond?'

He was staring into space. 'The Psalms of Lance,' he said. 'I'm drowning.' He sighed and let his head droop down to his chest.

'Honey, please go to bed,' said Mary. 'You're exhausted.'

73

He nodded. 'Yes, I'm tired.' He stood up and came over and kissed her cheek. 'Goodnight, dumpling.'

'Goodnight, Bill. I love you.'

'I love you, too.'

He went upstairs and was asleep within minutes.

He dreamed. At first he was flying over countrysides that were brightly coloured and vivid; then soon there were villages, and then cities that were strange, and yet ordinary, at once. They looked just as they should, but were somehow alien, and he knew that he could never describe them. As in any other dream, he had no sense of his body; and yet he felt vigorous and strong. And the dream was lucid: he knew he was asleep in his bed and dreaming, and had total recollection of the day's events.

Abruptly he was standing inside a titanic building made of stone. Its walls were smooth and of a soft rose colour, and they vaulted to a ceiling of breathtaking height. He had the feeling of being in a vast cathedral. An immense expanse was filled with beds of the kind found in hospitals, narrow and white, and there were hundreds of people, possibly more, engaged in various quiet activities. Some were either sitting or lying on their beds, while still others walked around in pyjamas or robes. Most were reading or talking, though a group of five of them near Kinderman were gathered at a table and a radio transmitter of some sort. Their faces were intent and Kinderman could hear one saying, 'Can you hear me?' Odd beings walked around, winged men like angels wearing the uniforms of doctors. They moved among the beds and the columns of sunlight that were shafting through circular, stained-glass windows. They seemed to be dispensing medication, or engaging in quiet conversation. The general atmosphere was of peace.

Kinderman walked along rows of beds that stretched as far as he could see. Nobody noticed him except, perhaps, for an angel who turned his head and stared at him pleasantly as he passed, and then returned to his work.

Kinderman saw his brother, Max. He'd been a rabbinical student for years until his death in 1950. As in ordinary dreams, where the dead are never perceived as such, Kinderman walked to Max unhurriedly and sat down with him on the bed. 'I'm glad to see you, Max,' he said. Then he added, 'Now *both* of us are dreaming.'

His brother gravely shook his head and answered, 'No, Bill; *I'm* not dreaming.' And Kinderman remembered that he was dead. Along with this sudden realization came an absolute certainty that Max was not an illusion.

Kinderman peppered him with questions about the here-after. 'Are these people all dead?' he asked.

Max nodded. 'What a mystery,' he said.

'Where are we?' asked Kinderman.

Max shrugged. 'I don't know. We're not sure. But we come here first.'

'It looks like a hospital,' Kinderman observed.

'Yes, all of us are treated here,' said Max.

'Do you know where you go after this?'

Max said, 'No.'

They continued to talk, and finally Kinderman asked him bluntly, 'Does God exist, Max?'

'Not in the dream world, Bill,' Max answered.

'Which is the dream world, Max? Is it this one?'

'It's the world where we meditate ourselves.'

When Kinderman pressed him to explain his answer, Max's statements grew vague and diffuse. At one point he said, 'We have two souls,' then again he grew dubious and uncertain, and the dream began melting around the edges, growing more flat and insubstantial, until finally Max was a phantom talking gibberish.

Kinderman awakened and lifted his head. Through a crack in the drapes in front of a window, he saw the cobalt light of dawn. He let his head drop back on the pillow and thought of the dream. What did it mean? 'Doctor angels,' he murmured aloud. Mary shifted beside him in her sleep. He quietly eased himself out of the bed and went into the bathroom. He fumbled for the light switch, and when he had found it, he closed the door and turned on the light. He lifted the toilet seat and urinated.

As he did, he glanced over at the bathtub. He saw the carp lazily finning around, and he looked away and shook his head. '*Momzer*,' he muttered. He flushed the toilet, lifted his robe off a hook on the door, turned off the light and went downstairs.

He made some tea and sat at the table, lost in thought. Was the dream of the future? An augur of his death? He shook his head. No, his dreams of the future had a certain texture. This one didn't have it. This one was unlike any dream he'd ever had. It affected him profoundly. '"Not in the dream world",' he murmured. '"Two souls". "It's the world where we meditate ourselves".' Was the dream his unconscious providing him with clues to the problem of pain? he wondered. *Maybe*. He remembered 'Visions', an essay by Jung describing the psychiatrist's brush with death. He had been hospitalized and in a coma when he suddenly felt himself out of his body and floating many miles above the planet. As he was about to enter a temple floating in space, the form of his doctor shimmered up to him in its archetypal form, that of a basileus of Kos. The doctor upbraided him and demanded he return to his body so that he could finish his work on earth. An instant later, Jung was awake in his hospital bed. His first emotion was concern for his doctor, because he had appeared in his archetypal form; and indeed, his doctor fell ill weeks later and soon was dead; but the dominant emotions Jung had felt – and continued to feel for the next six months – were depression and rage at being back in a body and a world and a universe that he now perceived as 'boxes'. Was that the answer? wondered Kinderman. Was the three-dimensional universe an artificial construction designed to be entered for the working out of specific problems that could be solved in no other way? Was the problem of evil in the world by design? Did the soul put on a body as men put on diving suits in order to enter the ocean and work in the depths of an alien world? Did we *choose* the pain that we innocently suffered?

Kinderman wondered if it were possible for a man to be a man without pain; or at least the *possibility* of pain. Would he not be no more than a chess-playing panda bear? Could there be honour or courage or kindness? A God who was good could not help but intervene upon hearing the cry of one suffering child. Yet He didn't. He looked on. But was that because man had *asked* Him to look on? Because man had deliberately chosen the crucible in order to be able to be man, before time began and the fiery firmaments had been flung?

A hospital. Doctor angels. *'Yes, we're all being treated here.'* Of course, thought Kinderman. *It fits. After life, comes a week at The Golden Door. Maybe also some Florida. Couldn't hurt.*

Kinderman fondled his thoughts for a while, and decided that the theory of the dream collapsed when confronted by the suffering of the higher animals. The wildebeest certainly hadn't chosen the pain, and the loyalest dog had no life to come. *But there is something there*, he thought; *it's close.* It needed a final, startling leap to make it all make sense and preserve God's goodness. He was certain he was close to tracking it down.

Footsteps on the staircase, quick and light. Kinderman looked aside and grimaced. The footsteps padded up to the table. He looked up. Mary's mother stood above him. She was eighty and short and her silvery hair was done up in a bun. Kinderman examined her. Never before had he seen a bathrobe that was black. 'I didn't know you were up,' she said inscrutably. Her entire face was pursed.

'I'm up,' said Kinderman. 'It's a fact.'

She seemed to be thinking that over for a while. Then she padded to the stove, and said, 'I'll make you some tea.'

'I have some.'

'Have more.'

Abruptly she came over and felt at his cup, and then gave him a look such as God had given Cain upon receiving the news. 'It's cold,' she said. 'I'll make hot.'

Kinderman looked at his watch. Almost seven. What had happened to the time? he wondered. 'How was Richmond?' he asked.

'All *schvartzers*. Don't ever force me to go there again.' She slapped a kettle on the stove and started mumbling in Yiddish. A phone on the breakfast counter chimed. 'Never mind, I'll get

77

it,' said Mary's mother. She moved swiftly and picked up the phone. She said, '*Nu?*'

Kinderman watched her as she listened, and then held the receiver out with a scowl. 'It's for you. Some more of your gangster friends.'

Kinderman sighed. He stood up and took the phone. 'Kinderman,' he said wearily.

He listened. His expression turned numb. 'I'll be there right away,' he said. He hung up.

At the 6:30 Mass at Holy Trinity, a Catholic priest had been murdered. He'd been decapitated in the box while in the act of hearing someone's confession.

No one at the scene had any notion who had done it.

MONDAY, MARCH 16

Chapter Six

The existence of life on earth was dependent on a certain pressure of the atmosphere. This pressure, in turn, was dependent on the constant operation of physical forces which in turn were dependent upon the earth's position in space, which in turn was dependent upon a certain constitution of the universe. And what caused that? wondered Kinderman.

'Lieutenant?'

'I am with you, Horatio Hornblower. What is your present situation?'

'No one saw anything unusual at all,' said Atkins. 'Can we let the parishioners go?'

Kinderman was seated in a pew near the crime scene, one of the confessionals at the back. They had closed the door of the confessor's box, but the blood still seeped into the aisle, where it branched into separate pools, indifferently, while the crime lab crew moved around it. All the doors of Holy Trinity Church had been locked and a uniformed officer guarded each entry. The pastor of the church had been allowed to come in, and Kinderman saw him listening to Stedman. They were standing near the left side altar of the church in front of a statue of the Virgin Mary. The old priest nodded now and then, and was biting down on his lower lip. His face had a look of stifled grief. 'Yes, all right, let them go,' the detective told Atkins. 'Hold the four who were witnesses. I have a thought.'

Atkins nodded, then looked for a prominence from which to

announce the dismissal of the scattering of worshippers still in the church. He decided on the choir loft and headed in that direction.

Kinderman retreated into his thoughts. Was the universe eternal? *Could be. Who knows?* An immortal dentist could fill cavities forever. But what was it that sustained the universe *now*? Was the universe the cause of its own constitution? Would it matter if the links in the chain of causation were extended indefinitely? *Wouldn't help*, the detective concluded. He envisioned a freight train carrying dresses to Abraham and Strauss from the small munitions plant near Cleveland where he'd always imagined they were manufactured. Each freight car was moved by the one in front of it. No car could move of itself. Proceeding to infinity in cars would not give to any car what it lacked, which was motion. Zero times infinity equalled zero. The train could not move unless pulled by an engine, something that was totally different from a car.

Prime Mover Unmoved. First Cause Uncaused. Was that a contradiction? Kinderman wondered. If everything had to have a cause, why not God? The detective was merely going through an exercise, and he answered himself immediately that the principle of causality derived from observation of the material universe, a particular kind of stuff. Was that stuff the only garment on the rack of possibility? Why not another kind of stuff altogether, a stuff outside of time and of space and of matter? The tea kettle thinks it is all there is?

'I was thinking, Lieutenant.'

Kinderman turned to look up at Ryan. 'Do you want I should call United Press or should we keep this miracle here in the church?'

'We ought to have some prints from those sliding panels inside the confessional box.'

'Why else have we called this meeting? Look for prints on the outside part of the panels, and also the inside part as well, in particular those little metal pulls that they have.'

'All you'd get from inside is the prints of the priest,' said Ryan. 'What's the point?'

'I am padding the job. The department has put me on an hourly wage. Keep an eye on your plumber and you wouldn't now be asking me ridiculous questions.'

Ryan stood his ground. 'I can't see what the prints of the priest would have to do with it.'

'Take it on faith, then. This is the place.'

'Okay,' said Ryan. He walked away, and with him went Kinderman's respite from the sense of sickness, the feeling of despair welling up within him. He returned to the struggle to regroup his beliefs. *Yes, this is the place*, he thought. *And the time.* He heard the shuffling of parishioners leaving the church and walking out into the ordinary daylight streets. *An American astronaut lands on Mars*, he thought, *and on its surface he discovers a camera.* How would he explain its presence there? He might think that his landing had not been the first, he guessed. *Not the Russians. It's a Nikon. Too expensive.* But perhaps there'd been a landing by some other nation, or even, conceivably, alien beings who had first made a visit to the planet Earth and taken the camera aboard for study. He might think that his Government had lied to him, had sent other Americans before him. He might even conclude that he was hallucinating, or dreaming the entire event. But the one thing he wouldn't do, Kinderman knew, was to think that since Mars had been bombarded by meteorites and churned by volcanic eruptions, it was reasonable that over many billions of years almost any imaginable arrangement of its materials could have happened, and the camera was one of those chance combinations. *They would tell him he was totally* meshugge *from exposure to some kind of cosmic ray, and then put him away in a special home with a bagful of matzohs and a Space Cadet badge.* Shutter, lens, shutter speed regulator, diaphragm, automatic focus, automatic exposure. Could such a device come about by chance?

In the human eye, there were tens of millions of electrical connections that could handle two million simultaneous messages, yet see the light of just one quantum.

A human eye is found on Mars.

The human brain, three pounds of tissue, held more than a

81

hundred billion brain cells and 500 trillion synaptic connections. It dreamed and wrote music and Einstein's equations, it created the language and the geometry and the engines that probed the stars; and cradled a mother asleep through a storm while it woke her at the faintest cry from her child. A computer that could handle all of its functions would cover the surface of the earth.

A human brain is found on Mars.

The brain could detect one unit of mercaptan amid 50 billion units of air and if the human ear were any more sensitive, it would hear air molecules colliding. Blood cells lined up one at a time when faced with the constriction of a tiny vein, and the cells of the heart beat at different rhythms until they came in contact with another cell. When they touched, they begin to beat as one.

A human body is found on Mars.

The hundreds of millions of years of evolution from paramecium to man didn't solve the mystery, thought Kinderman. The mystery was evolution itself.

The fundamental tendency of matter was toward a total disorganization; toward a final state of utter randomness from which the universe would never recover. Each moment, its connections were coming unthreaded and it flung itself headlong into the void in a reckless scattering of itself, impatient for the death of its cooling suns. And yet here was evolution, Kinderman marvelled, a hurricane piling up straws into haystacks, bundles of ever-increasing complexity that denied the very nature of their stuff. Evolution was a theorem written on a leaf that was floating against the direction of the river. A Designer was at work. *So what else? It's as plain as can be. When a man hears hoofbeats in Cental Park, he shouldn't be looking around for zebras.*

'We've cleared the church, Lieutenant.'

Kinderman's gaze flicked up at Atkins, then he stared at the confessional box with the body of the priest still inside it. 'Have we now, Atkins? Have we really?'

Ryan was dusting the exterior panels and Kinderman watched him for a time, his eyelids gradually beginning to droop. 'Get the inside parts,' he said. 'Don't forget.'

'I won't forget,' muttered Ryan.

'Wonderful.'

Kinderman heaved himself up with a sigh and then followed Atkins to another confessional at the back and to the right of the doors. Sitting in the back two pews of the church were the people whom Atkins had detained. Kinderman paused to look them over. Richard Coleman, a lawyer in his forties, worked in the Attorney General's office. Susan Volpe, an attractive twenty-year-old, was a student at Georgetown College. George Paterno was the football coach at Bullis Prep in Maryland. He was short and strongly built and Kinderman gauged him to be in his thirties. Beside him sat a well-dressed man in his fifties. He was Richard McCooey, a Georgetown graduate, and owner of the '1789' restaurant a short block away from the church. Kinderman knew him, for he also owned 'The Tombs', a popular *Ratskeller* where the detective had often met with a friend who had died many years before.

'One or two more questions, please,' said Kinderman. 'It will only take a minute. I'll hurry. First, Mister Paterno. Would you kindly step back inside the box?'

The confessional was divided into three distinct sections. In a middle compartment equipped with a door, a confessor sat in the darkness, with a small amount of light seeping in through a grill at the top of the door. The other two compartments, one on each side of the confessor, were equipped with kneelers and, again, a door. There was a sliding panel on each side. When a penitent was making his confession, the priest had the panel in the open position. That confession finished, he slid the panel shut and then opened the panel on the other side, where the other penitent was waiting.

At approximately 6:35 that morning, a man in his twenties, as yet unidentified, but described as having pale green eyes, a shaven head, and as wearing a heavy blue turtleneck sweater, exited the penitent's box on the left after making a fairly long confession, and his place was then taken by George Paterno. At that time, the deceased, Father Kenneth Bermingham, once the president of Georgetown University, had turned to confess a man on the right, also still unidentified, but described as wearing white cloth trousers and a black woollen windbreaker with a hood. After six or seven minutes, this man emerged, and his place was taken by an elderly man with a shopping bag. Then after a period of time described as 'long', the old man emerged, apparently without having made confession, inas much as Paterno's turn for confession should have come before his; yet Paterno wasn't seen to come out of the box. The old man's place had been taken by McCooey and both he and Paterno then waited in the darkness, with McCooey asserting he assumed that the priest was busy with Paterno, while Paterno's story was that he'd assumed that the man in the windbreaker hadn't finished. Whatever the truth of their averrals, neither Volpe's nor Coleman's turn ever came. It was Coleman who had noticed the blood flowing out from under the door.

'Mister Paterno?'

Paterno was kneeling in the left hand penitent's box. The colour was gradually coming back to what appeared to be a dark and olive complexion. He stared back at Kinderman and blinked.

'While you were in the box,' the detective continued, 'the man in the windbreaker was on the other side, and then after that, the elderly man, and then Mister McCooey. And you said you heard the panel sliding shut and into place on the opposite side at some point. Do you remember that?'

'Yes.'

'And you said that you presumed that the man in the windbreaker was finished.'

'Yes.'

'Did you hear the panel sliding again? Like maybe the priest had forgotten something that he wanted to tell him?'

'No, I didn't.'

Kinderman nodded, then he closed Paterno's door and stepped into the confessor's box and sat. 'I will close the panel on your side,' he told Paterno. 'After that, listen carefully, please.' He closed the panel on Paterno's side, and then slowly slid open the panel on the other. He opened Paterno's panel again. 'Did you hear something?'

'No.'

Kinderman considered this answer thoughtfully. When Paterno started to get up, he said, 'Stay where you are, please, Mister Paterno.'

Kinderman stepped out of the confessor's compartment and knelt in the penitent's box on the right. He slid the panel open and looked over at Paterno. 'Close your panel and then listen once again,' he instructed. Paterno closed his panel. Kinderman reached inside the confessor's box, found the pull on the back of the panel, and slid the panel closed as far as he could before his wrist got in the way and he could close it no further. At that point, he released the metal pull and, using the pressure of his fingertips against the facing of the panel on his side, he slid the panel the rest of the way, until it closed with a muffled thud.

Kinderman got up and walked over to the penitent's box on the left, where he opened the door and looked down at Paterno. 'Did you hear something?' Kinderman asked him.

'Yes. You shut the panel.'

'Did it sound just the same as when you waited for the priest to come over to your side?'

'Yes, exactly the same.'

'*Exactly* the same?'

'Yes, exactly.

'Please describe it.'

'Describe it?

'Yes, describe it. What did it sound like?'

Paterno looked hesitant. Then he said. 'Well, it slides for a way and then stops; and then it slides again until it's closed.'

'So a little hesitation in the sliding?'

'Just exactly the way you just did it.'

'And how can you be certain it was shut all the way?'

'There was a thud at the end. It was loud.'

'You mean louder than normally?'

'It was loud.'

'More than usual?'

'Yes. Very loud.'

'I see. And didn't you wonder why your turn didn't come right after that?'

'Did I wonder?'

'Why your turn didn't come.'

'I guess I did.'

'And when did you hear this sound? How long before the body was found?'

'I can't remember.'

'Five minutes?'

'I don't know.'

'Ten minutes?'

'I don't know.'

'Was it longer than ten minutes?'

'I'm not sure.'

Kinderman digested this for a while. Then he asked, 'Were there any other sounds while you were in there?'

'You mean talking?'

'Whatever.'

'No, I didn't hear talking.'

'Do you hear that at times in the confessional?'

'Sometimes. Only if it's loud, though, like sometimes the Act of Contrition at the end.'

'But you didn't hear it this time?'

'No.'

'No talking whatever?'

'No talking whatever.'

'No murmuring?'

'No.'

'Thank you. Now you may go back to your seat.'

Averting his gaze from Kinderman, Paterno got up quickly from the kneeler, and then sat down again with the others. Kinderman faced them. The attorney was glancing at his watch. The detective addressed him. 'The old man with the shopping bag, Mister Coleman.'

The attorney said, 'Yes?'

'How long would you say he was in the confessional?'

'Maybe seven, eight minutes or so. Maybe more.'

'Did he stay in the church when he finished his confession?'

'I don't know.'

'And what about you, Miss Volpe. Did you notice?'

The girl was still shaken and she stared at him blankly.

'Miss Volpe?'

She startled and then she said, 'Yes?'

'The old man with the shopping bag, Miss Volpe. After his confession, did he stay in the church or did he leave?'

She stared at him glassily for a moment, then she answered, 'I might have seen him leave. I'm not sure.'

'You're not sure.'

'No, I'm not.'

'But you think he might have left.'

'Yes, he might have.'

'Was there anything odd about his behaviour?'

'Odd?'

'Mister Coleman, was there anything odd?'

'He just seemed a little senile,' said Coleman. 'I figured that's what took him so long.'

'You said his age was in the seventies?'

'He was up there. He was walking pretty feebly.'

'Walking? Walking where?'

'To his pew.'

'Then he stayed in the church,' said Kinderman.

'No, I didn't say that,' said Coleman. 'He went to his pew and perhaps said his penance. After that he might have left.'

'I am properly corrected, Counsellor. Thank you.'

'Quite all right.' There was a glint of satisfaction in the lawyer's eyes.

'And what about the man with the shaven head and the man in the windbreaker?' Kinderman added. 'Can anyone tell me whether they stayed in the church or left?'

There were no replies.

Kinderman turned his gaze to the girl. 'Miss Volpe, the man who was wearing the windbreaker – did he seem in any way unusual?'

'No,' said Volpe. 'I mean – I didn't notice him all that much.'

'He didn't seem annoyed?'

'He was calm. Just ordinary.'

'Just ordinary.'

'That's right. He was smacking his lips a little, that's all.'

'He was smacking his lips a little?'

'Well, yes.'

Kinderman thought about this for a while. Then he said, 'That's all. Thank you for your time. Sergeant Atkins, let them out. Then come back. It's important.'

Atkins led the witnesses to the officer at the door. He was there in eight steps, but Kinderman watched him with an anxious concern, as if Atkins were journeying to Mozambique and might not come back.

Atkins returned and stood facing him. 'Yes, sir?'

'One more thing about evolution. They keep saying that it's chance, all chance, and that it's simple. Billions of fish kept flopping up on the shore, and then one day a smart one looks around and says, "Wonderful. Miami Beach. The Fontainebleu. I think I'll stick around here and breathe." So help me God, so goes the legend of the Piltdown Carp. But it's all a *schmeckle*. If the fish breathes the air, he drops dead, no survivors, and the playboy life is over. So okay, that's the fable in the popular mind. You want it better? Scientific? I am here to oblige. The real story is this mackerel who came in from the cold doesn't stay on the shore. He just takes a little breath, a little whiff, a little try-out, then he's back in the ocean in Intensive Care and playing his banjo and singing songs about his jolly times on land. He keeps doing this, and maybe he can breathe a little longer. Also definitely possible; maybe not. But after all this practice, he lays some eggs, and when he dies he leaves a will saying how his little children should try breathing on the land, and he signs it, "Do this for your father. Love,

Bernie." And they do it. And on and on it goes, maybe hundreds of millions of years they keep trying, each generation getting better and better because all of this practice is getting in their genes. And then finally one of them, skinny, with glasses, always reading, never playing in the gym with the boys, he breathes the air and keeps on breathing, and soon he's doing Nautilus three times a week in De Funiack Springs and going bowling with the *schvartzers*. Of course, needless to say, all his children have no trouble breathing air all the time, their only problem is walking and maybe throwing up. And that's the story from the scientists' mouths to your credulity. So okay, I'm oversimplifying. They don't? Any *schlump* who says "vertebrate" today is automatically considered a genius. Also "phylum". This will get you in the Cosmos Club for free. Science gives us many facts, but only very little knowledge. As regarding this theory about the fish, it has one little problem, God forbid this should deter them even though this problem makes the whole thing impossible, since it happens all this practice breathing air is going no place at absolutely maximum speed. Every fish starts all over again from the beginning, and from only one lifetime nothing changes in the genes. The big slogan for fish is, "One Day at a Time".

'I'm not saying I'm against evolution. It's okay. Here's the story on reptiles, however, think this over. They come up on dry land and they lay their eggs. So far it's a breeze, is that right? A piece of cake. But the little baby reptile in the egg needs water, or it dries up in the egg and never gets to be born. On top of that, it needs food, a whole lot, in fact, because it hatches as a grown-up, a great big person. In the meantime, don't worry. You need it? You've got it. Because now inside the egg a lot of egg yolk appears and says, "I'm here". This is the food. And the white of the egg is making do as the water. But the egg white needs a whole special casing around it, or the whole thing evaporates and says to you, "I'm leaving". So a shell made of leathery stuff comes along, and the reptile is smiling. Too soon. It's not so easy. Because of this shell, now the embryo cannot get rid of its waste. So we need now a bladder. Is this making you nauseous a little? I'll hurry. Also, there is needed now some kind of *draedle*, some tool the little embryo uses to get out of its hard, tough shell. There's even more, but that's enough, now, I'll stop, it's sufficient. Because, Atkins, all these changes in the egg of the reptile have to happen all at once! Are you hearing? *All at once*! If even *one* of them is missing, it's all over, and the embryos are keeping their appointments in Samarra. You cannot have the egg yolk come along and then keep it on hold another million years until the casing or the bladder comes along jaunty jolly saying, "Sorry I'm late, the rabbi talked too long." You get the answering service. Every change would be *derhangenet* right on the spot before the other one ever got to make its appearance. In the meantime, we have reptiles now up to our *tokis*. Talk to people in Okee Fenokee, they'll tell you. But how could this possibly come to be? All the changes in the embryo happened all at once by incredible coincidence? This notion only morons would embrace, I guarantee you. In the meantime, as regards this murder, the killer is also the killer of Kintry. Without the use of an instantly paralysing agent, we could have no murder here today. There would have been an outcry. It couldn't have been done. Point two, we have now five people as suspects: McCooey, Paterno, the man with the shopping bag, the man with the shaven head and the man in white pants and the black woollen windbreaker. However, these are savage, unspeakable crimes, and we are looking for a psycho with medical knowledge. McCooey I know and he is tolerably sane within certain limits, although in his bedroom he has to keep out where he can always see them every item of clothing that he owns. He hasn't any medical knowledge that I know of. The same with Paterno. Just to keep the record straight and absolutely on the *emiss*, get a medical history on him from Bullis. In the meantime, the killer wouldn't hang around, so McCooey and Paterno are absolutely out. It's one of the others. Point three, the old man by himself could have done it. Decapitation with a wire or a shears takes little strength. A sharp knife would do it also, something like a scalpel. The old man was in the box for a very long time and his reported senility might have been pretended. He was also the last one to see the priest. This is scenario number one. But the man in the windbreaker also could have done it. He would slide the panel shut so the man with the shopping bag doesn't see that the priest is dead. The old man, in the meantime, is waiting but he leaves without ever seeing the priest. It could be he gets gas, or he maybe gets tired; and if he is senile, as Coleman would have us believe, he might imagine that he actually made his confession, when in fact he was napping in the dark. This is scenario number two. In scenario three, the killer is the man with the shaven head. He kills the priest, slides the panel back shut, and leaves the box. But the man in the windbreaker saw the priest next, which would mean he was alive. It could happen like this: The man in the windbreaker is waiting while the shaven head is committing the murder. It could be that the man in the windbreaker now is getting antsy with all of this waiting and decides to leave without making his confession. He might think he was missing too much of the Mass. Any reason is possible,' Kinderman concluded. 'The rest is silence.'

The recitation concerning the murder had come out in a rapid, deadly cadence. Atkins suspected that Kinderman's digressions masked the working of his mind on some other level, and perhaps were even needed for that level to function. The sergeant nodded. He felt a curiosity about the questions that Kinderman had earlier put to Paterno concerning the sliding sounds of the panels. He knew better than to ask.

'You have the prints for me, Ryan?' asked Kinderman.

Atkins looked around. Ryan was joining them from behind him.

'Yeah, we've got the whole bunch,' said Ryan.

Kinderman eyed him expressionlessly and said, 'One clear set will be sufficient.'

'Well, we've got it.'

'From the inside and the outside, of course.'

'Not the inside.'

'I am going to read you your rights. Listen carefully,' Kinderman told him.

'How the hell can we get at them with the corpse in the box?'

There it was. The words had been spoken. Stedman had finished with the body long before. All the photos had been taken. Only Kinderman's own examination remained. He had delayed it. He'd known the dead priest. Another case long ago had brought him in touch with him, and now and then, across the years, he would see him with Dyer, who had been his assistant. Once they'd had a beer together in "The Tombs". Kinderman had liked him.

'You are right,' the detective told Ryan. 'Thank you for your timely reminder. I don't know what I would do without you, frankly.' Ryan turned away and flopped down at the end of a pew. He folded his arms and looked sour.

Kinderman walked to the other confessional at the back. He looked down at the floor. The blood had been removed, and the smooth grey tiles glistened with mop strokes. They were still wet. For a time, the detective stood there, breathing; then abruptly he looked up and pulled open the confessional box. Father Bermingham was seated on the chair in the compartment. The blood was on everything, and the dead priest's eyes were opened wide and staring out in terror. Kinderman had to look down to see them. Upright and facing out, the head was resting on Bermingham's lap. His hands had been arranged as if he were holding it for display.

Kinderman breathed a few times before he moved, carefully lifting the priest's left hand. He examined the palm and saw the Gemini marking. He lowered the hand and let it go, and then examined the other one. The right index finger was missing.

Kinderman carefully lowered the hand, and stared at the little black crucifix hanging on the wall behind the chair. For a time he stood motionless like that. Abruptly he turned away from the compartment. Atkins was there. Kinderman's hands slipped into the pockets of his coat, and he stared at the floor. 'Get him out,' he said quietly. 'Tell Stedman. Get him out and get the prints.' He walked away slowly towards the front of the church.

Atkins watched him. So bulky a man, he thought, and yet he

looked so forlorn. He saw Kinderman stop near the front of the church where he slowly sat down in one of the pews. Atkins turned away and went to find Stedman.

Kinderman clasped his hands on his lap and stared down at them broodingly. He felt abandoned. *Design and causality*, he thought. *God exists. I know. Very nice.* But what could He possibly be thinking of? Why didn't he simply intervene? *Free will. Okay. We should keep it.* But was there simply no limit to the tolerance of God? He remembered a line from G. K. Chesterton: 'When the playwright comes on stage, the play is over.' *So then let it be over. Who needs it? It stinks.* His mind drifted back to the possibility that God was a being of limited power. *Why not?* Such an answer was simple and direct. Yet Kinderman couldn't help strongly resisting it. *God a yokel? A putz? It couldn't be.* The leap of his mind from God to perfection had no transition. It was a motionless identity.

The detective shook his head. He found the notion of a God who was less than all-powerful every bit as frightening as none at all. Perhaps even more. Death was an ending, at least, without a God. But who knew what a God who was flawed might do? If less than all-powerful, why wouldn't He also be less than all-good, like the vain and capricious, cruel God of Job? With all of eternity at His disposal, what fiendish new tortures might He not devise?

A limited God? Kinderman brushed away the thought. God the Father of the orbits and the spinning nebulae and the shepherding moons of Saturn; the Author of the gravity and the brain, the Lurker in the genes and the subatomic particles: He couldn't handle cancer and some crab grass?

He looked up at the crucifix over the altar, and slowly his expression grew hard and demanding. *What's your part in this monkey business? Will you answer? Do you want to call a lawyer? Shall I read you your rights? Take it easy. I'm your friend. I can get you protection. Just answer me a few little questions. All right?*

The detective's face began to soften, and he looked at the crucifix with a meekness and a quiet wonder in his eyes. *Who are* you? God's son? No, you know I don't believe that. I just asked to be polite. You don't mind my being frank a little bit? It couldn't hurt. If it gets a little sensitive, maybe too forward, you could rattle all the windows here a little, I'll shut up. Just the windows. That's enough. I don't need any buildings to fall on my head. I already have Ryan. You've noticed? This affliction Job somehow missed out on. Who slipped up in that department? Never mind, I don't want to start trouble. In the meantime, I don't know who you are, but you are Someone. Who could miss it? You are Someone. That is clear as a brook. I don't need to have proof that you did all those miracles. Who cares? It doesn't matter. I know. Do you know how I know? From what you said. When I read, 'Love your enemy', I tingle, I go crazy, and inside of my chest I can feel something floating, something that feels like it was there the whole time. It's as if my very being for just those few moments consisted of the total recognition of a truth. And then I know that you are Someone. No one from the earth could ever say what you said. No one could even make it up. Who could imagine it? The words knock you down.

Something else, something little that I thought I might share with you. Would you mind? What's to mind? I'm just talking. On the boat, when the disciples see you standing on the shore and then they realize that it's you and that you've risen from the dead? Peter's standing on the deck in the total altogether. So why not? He's a fisherman, he's young, he should enjoy. But right away he can't wait for the boat to go in, he's so excited, so beside himself with joy that it's you. So he grabs the nearest garment – Do you remember this? – but he doesn't even want to take the time to pull it on. He just ties it around and jumps off the boat and then starts swimming like crazy for the shore. Is that something? Whenever I think of it, I glow! It isn't some goyischer holy picture full of reverence and stiffness and probably lies; it isn't some image being peddled, some myth. I can't believe it didn't happen. It's so human, so surprising, and so real all at once. Peter must have loved you very much.

So do I. Does that startle you? Well, it's true. That you ever existed is a thought that gives me shelter; that men could make you up is a thought that gives me hope; and the thought that you might exist even now would give me safety and a gladness that I could not contain. I would like to touch your face and make you smile. It couldn't hurt.

So much for tea time and pleasantries. Who are you? What is it that you want from us? To suffer like you did on the cross? Well, we're doing it. Please don't go sleepless with worrying about this problem. We are all in good shape on that score. We're doing fine. That is mainly what I wanted to tell you in the first place. Also, Father Bermingham, your friend, sends regards.

TUESDAY, MARCH 17

Chapter Seven

The detective arrived at his office at nine. Atkins was waiting for him. The lab results were in.

Kinderman sat at his desk and pushed aside a scattering of books with turned-down pages to make a space for the typed reports. He then went through them. The use of succinylcholine in the murder of the priest was confirmed. There were also prints that had been taken from the metal pull on the righthand panel of the confessional, and from the wood around it as well. They matched other prints from the front of the panel, the part that faced out to the penitent's side. They were not the priest's.

The information from the *Washington Post* had not changed. Atkins had a rundown on Paterno, but Kinderman waved it aside. 'No interest,' he said. 'It's the shopping bag or the windbreaker. Please don't confuse me with the facts this time of day. Where is Ryan?'

'He's off,' replied Atkins.

'This is true.'

Kinderman sighed and leaned back in his chair. Then he stared at the Kleenex box on his desk. He seemed lost in thought. 'Thalidomide cures leprosy,' he said absently. Abruptly he leaned forward towards Atkins. 'Have you any idea why the speed of light should be the top-limiting speed in the universe?' he asked.

'No,' answered Atkins. 'Why?'

'I don't know,' said Kinderman. He shrugged. 'I was just asking. In the meantime, as long as we're not on the subject, do you know what your church says the nature of an angel is?'

'Pure love,' answered Atkins.

'Exactly. Even a fallen angel, they say. Why didn't you tell me that before?'

'You never asked me.'

'I have to think of every single question?'

The detective snatched a green-coloured book from its forest, and he quickly opened it at its marker, a folded waxed paper that had once held a pickle. 'I had to come across it by accident,' he said. 'It's in here, in this book called *Satan* by your *lantzmen*, the Carmelite Fathers.' He began to read: '"An angel's knowledge is perfect. Because of it, the fire of an angel's love is not built up slowly; it has no stages of mere smouldering; rather the angel is immediately a holocaust, a roaring conflagration, aflame with a love that will never lessen."' Kinderman tossed the book back into the pile. 'It says also that this situation never changes, fallen angel, shmallen angel, whatever. And so what is all this press we are getting about devils always *shmutzing* up and down and all around making trouble? It's a joke. It couldn't be. Not according to your church, unless the Carmelites already are too long in the desert playing Scrabble with the lizards and telling them jokes.' He had started to search for another book.

'What's the meaning of the fingerprints?' Atkins asked him.

'Aha!' Kinderman had found what he wanted, and he opened the book to a turned-down page. 'We can learn a little something from the birds,' he said.

'We can learn a little something from the birds?' repeated Atkins.

Kinderman glared. 'Atkins, what did I just this minute say? Now pay attention. Listen here to what this says about the titlark.'

'The titlark?'

Kinderman looked up at him inscrutably. 'Atkins, please do not do this again.'

'No, I won't.'

'No, you won't. Now I will tell you how the titlark –'
Kinderman waited – 'How the titlark comes to building its nest.
It's incredible.' He looked down at the book and began to read:
'"The titlark uses four different building materials: moss,
spider's silk, lichens and feathers. First it finds a branch that
forks the right way. Then moss is collected and placed on the
fork. Most of the moss falls off, but the bird persists until some
pieces have stuck. Then it switches to spider's silk, which it
rubs on the moss until it sticks, and then it's stretched and used
for binding. These activities continue until a platform has taken
shape. And now the bird switches back to moss and starts
constructing the cup around it, first by sidewise weaving, and
then later by vertical weaving, which it does in a sitting
position, steadily rotating its body. When the cup begins to take
shape, new action patterns begin: breast-pressing and tram-
pling with the feet. Then when the cup is one-third complete,
the bird starts collecting lichens that are to cover just the outside
of the nest by using a number of acrobatic manoeuvres. When
the cup is two-thirds complete, the building routine is changed
in such a way as to leave a neat entrance hole at the most
convenient point of approach. Then the wall around the hole is
strengthened, the dome of the nest completed, and now the
furnishing with feathers begins."' Kinderman put down the
book. 'So you thought it was simple, Atkins, building nests?
Some kind of dry-wall prefabricated duplex in Phoenix? Look
what's happening. The bird must have some notion of what the
nest should look like, and besides that some idea that a little
moss here, a little lichen there, these are steps in the direction of
some pattern that's ideal. Is this intelligence? The titlark has a
brain like a lima bean. What is it that's directing these amazing
goings-on? You think Ryan could build such a nest? Never
mind. In the meantime, as a sidelight, a quiet little jab, where
on earth is this "carrot and stick reinforcement" the Behaviourists are telling us is needed for this bird to carry out these
operations, thirteen different types of construction jobs? B. F.
Skinner did a very good thing: in World War Two he trained
pigeons to be kamikaze pilots. This is *emiss*. You could even

look it up in some book. They had these cute little bombs strapped under their tummies, but as it happens they kept getting lost all the time and making these bombing runs on Philadelphia. So much for the lack of free will in man. As regards these fingerprints, they mean nothing: they are only confirming what I already knew. The killer has to slide the panel shut so the next in line won't see the priest dead. He does it also to make us suspect someone else. That's the meaning of the very loud sound when Paterno heard the panel sliding shut. The killer wanted to convince whoever else was around that he'd made his confession and the priest was still alive on account of they could hear the priest closing the panel. This is also the meaning of the hesitation in the sound of the sliding as reported by Paterno. A slide, a hesitation, and then it slams shut. The killer couldn't slide it all the way from inside, so he finishes the job from his side of the panel. The prints are the killer's. This eliminates the man with the shaven head. He was on the left. The prints and funny sounds all occurred on the right. The killer is the elderly man with the shopping bag, or the man in the black woollen windbreaker.' Kinderman stood up and went for his coat. 'I am going for a visit with Dyer at the hospital. Go and see the old lady, Atkins. See if she is talking yet. Has the Gemini file come in?'

'No, it hasn't.'

'Give a call. Also bring in the witnesses from the church and get composite sketches of the suspects. *Avanti*. I will see you by the waters of Babylon; I feel I may be ready for some serious lamenting.' He paused at the door. 'Is my hat on my head?'

'Yes, it is.'

'This is nothing if not a convenience.'

He went through the door and then came back. 'A subject for discussion on some other occasion: who would wear white cloth pants in the winter? A thought. Adieu. Remember me.' He went through the door again and was gone. Atkins wondered where to begin.

Kinderman made two stops while en route to Georgetown

General Hospital. He arrived at the Information Desk with a sack full of White Tower hamburgers. Cradled in an arm was a large stuffed teddy bear dressed in pale blue shorts and a T-shirt. 'Oh, Miss,' said Kinderman.

The girl at the desk flicked a glance at the T-shirt on the bear. On its chest was the inscription: 'If wearer is found depressed, administer chocolate immediately.'

'That's cute,' the girl smiled. 'For a little boy or for a girl?'

'For a little boy,' said Kinderman.

'His name, please?'

'Father Joseph Dyer.'

'Did I hear you correctly, sir? You said "Father"?'

'Yes, I did. Father Dyer.'

The girl threw a look at the bear and then at Kinderman, and then checked through her patient listings. 'Neurology, Room 417, Fourth floor. Take a right when you exit the elevator.'

'Thank you so much. You're very kind.'

When Kinderman arrived at Dyer's room, the priest was in bed. He was wearing his reading glasses and was comfortably sitting up, engrossed in a newspaper that he held in front of his face. Did he know? wondered Kinderman. Perhaps not. Dyer had checked in about the time that the murder was taking place. The detective hoped that they'd kept him busy and mildly sedated through the day. He knew he could tell from the Jesuit's unguarded demeanour and expression and, wanting to know what he had to prepare for, Kinderman gingerly moved to the bedside. Dyer didn't notice him standing there and Kinderman examined his face. The signs were good. But the priest was preoccupied with the paper. Would he read about the murder? worried the detective. He glanced at the paper, looking for the headline, and suddenly froze.

'Well, are you going to sit down or just stand there breathing your germs all over me?' said Dyer.

'What are you reading?' asked Kinderman bloodlessly.

'So it's *Women's Wear Daily*. So what?' The Jesuit's glance flicked over to the bear. 'Is that for me?'

'I just found it in the street. I thought it would suit you.'

'Oh.'

'Don't you like it?'

'I don't know about the colour,' said Dyer sullenly. Then he had a fit of coughing.

'Oh, I see. We are doing *Anastasia* today. I thought you told me that there's nothing really wrong with you,' said Kinderman.

'You never can tell,' said Dyer gloomily.

Kinderman relaxed. He understood now that Dyer was in perfect health, and still knew nothing about the murder. He thrust the bear and the bag into Dyer's hands. 'Here, take them,' he said. He found a chair, pulled it up beside the bed and sat down. 'I can't believe you're reading *Women's Wear Daily*,' he said.

'I have to know what's going on,' said Dyer. 'I can't give spiritual advice in a vacuum.'

'Don't you think you should be reading from your Office or something? The Spiritual Exercises, maybe?'

'It doesn't give you all the fashions,' the priest said blandly.

'Eat the burgers,' said Kinderman.

'I'm not hungry.'

'Eat half. They're White Tower.'

'Where'd the other half come from?'

'Space, your native country.'

Dyer began to open the bag. 'Well, maybe one.'

A short, stout nurse waddled into the room. Her eyes had the toughness of a veteran. She was carrying a rubber tourniquet and a hypodermic syringe. She moved towards Dyer. 'Come to take a little blood from you, Father.'

'Again?'

The nurse stopped short. 'What's "again"?' she asked the priest.

'Someone took it already ten minutes ago.'

'Are you kidding me, Father?'

Dyer pointed to the small, round piece of tape on his inner left forearm. 'There's the hole,' he said.

The nurse looked. 'There it sure as hell is,' she said grimly.

She turned and walked belligerently out of the room, and then bawled down the hall, *'Who stuck this guy?'*

Dyer stared through the open door. 'I just love all this attention,' he commented glumly.

'Yes, it's nice here,' said Kinderman. 'Peaceful. When comes the air raid drill?'

'Oh, I almost forgot,' said Dyer. He reached inside the drawer of a bedside table and extracted a cartoon torn out of the pages of a magazine. He handed it to Kinderman. 'I've been saving this for you,' he told him.

Kinderman stared. The cartoon depicted a mustached fisherman standing beside a gigantic carp. The caption read, 'Ernest Hemingway, while fishing in the Rockies, catches a carp over five feet long and then decides not to write about it.'

Kinderman looked up at Dyer. The detective's expression was severe. He said, 'Where did you get this?'

'Our Sunday Messenger,' said Dyer. 'You know, I'm beginning to feel a little better?' He took out a burger and began to eat. He said, 'Mmm, thanks Bill. This is great. Is the carp still in the tub, by the way?'

'He was executed last night.' The detective watched Dyer going after a second burger. 'Mary's mother wept openly at the table. As for me, I took a bath.'

'I could tell,' said Dyer.

'You're enjoying your burgers, Father? It's Lent.'

'I'm exempted from fasting,' said Dyer. 'I'm sick.'

'In the streets of Calcutta the children are starving.'

'They don't eat cows,' said Dyer.

'I give up. Most Jews, they pick a priest to be a friend, it's always someone like Teilhard de Chardin. What do *I* get? A priest who knows the latest from Giorgio's and treats people like Rubik's Cube, always twisting them around in his hands to make colours. Who needs it? No, really, you're a pain in the *tokis*.'

'Want a burger?' Dyer offered him the bag.

'Yes, I think I would like one.' Watching Dyer had made Kinderman hungry. He reached inside the bag and took out a burger. 'It's the pickle that makes me so crazy,' he said. 'It's what makes it.' He took a big bite and then looked up to see a doctor walking into the room.

'Good morning, Vincent,' said Dyer.

Amfortas nodded and stopped at the foot of the bed. He picked up Dyer's chart and studied it.

'This is my friend, Lieutenant Kinderman,' said Dyer. 'Meet Doctor Amfortas, Bill.'

'Pleased to meet you,' said Kinderman.

Amfortas didn't seem to hear them. He was writing something down on the chart.

'Someone told me I'd be out of here tomorrow,' said Dyer.

Amfortas nodded and replaced the chart.

'I was starting to like it here,' said Dyer.

'Yes, the nurses are so sweet,' added Kinderman.

For the first time since he'd entered the room, Amfortas looked at the detective directly. His face remained melancholy and grave, but deep in the sad, dark eyes something stirred. *What is he thinking?* the detective wondered. *Do I read a little smile behind those eyes?*

The contact was momentary, and Amfortas turned away and left the room. He turned left in the hallway and vanished from view.

'A laugh riot this doctor,' commented Kinderman. 'Since when is Milton Berle in the practice of medicine?'

'Poor guy,' said Dyer.

'Poor guy? What's wrong with him? Have you befriended him?'

'He lost his wife.'

'Oh, I see.'

'He's just never gotten over it.'

'Divorce?'

'No, she died.'

'Oh, I'm sorry. It was recent?'

'Three years,' said Dyer.

'That's a very long time ago,' said Kinderman.

'I know. But she died of meningitis.'

'Oh.'

'There's an awful lot of anger inside him. He treated her himself, but he just couldn't save her, or even do much about the pain. It just tore him apart. He's quitting the ward tonight. He wants to spend all his time on his research work. He started on it after she died.'

'What kind of research, exactly?' asked Kinderman.

'Pain,' said the priest. 'He studies pain.'

Kinderman considered this fact with interest. 'You seem to know a lot about him,' he said.

'Yes, he really opened up to me yesterday.'

'He talks?'

'Well, you know how it is with the Roman collar. It acts like a magnet for troubled souls.'

'Am I to draw some kind of personal inference from this?'

'If the gumshoe fits, then wear it.'

'Is he Catholic?'

'Who?'

'Toulouse Lautrec. Who else would I be talking about but the doctor?'

'Well, you're frequently oblique.'

'This is standard procedure when approaching some nut. Is Amfortas a Catholic or not?'

'He's a Catholic. He's been going to daily Mass for years.'

'What Mass?'

'The 6:30 a.m. at Holy Trinity. Incidentally, I've been thinking about your problem.'

'What problem?'

'The problem of evil,' said Dyer.

'This is *my* problem only?' said Kinderman, astounded. 'What do they teach you in your schools? You're all weaving theological baskets at Ostrich Seminary for the Blind? This is *everybody*'s problem.'

'I understand,' said Dyer.

'This is new.'

'You'd better start being nice to me.'

'The bear is only garbage then, I gather.'

'The bear has moved me deeply and profoundly. Can I talk?'

'It's so dangerous,' Kinderman replied. Then he sighed and picked up the copy of the newspaper. He opened to a page and began to read. 'Go ahead, you have my keenest attention,' he said.

'Well, I was thinking,' said Dyer, 'being here in the hospital and all.'

'Being here in the hospital with not a thing wrong with you,' Kinderman corrected him.

Dyer ignored it. 'I started thinking about things that I've heard about surgery.'

'These people have almost no clothes on,' said Kinderman, absorbed in the *Women's Wear Daily*.

'They say that when you're under the anaesthesia,' said Dyer, 'your unconscious is aware of everything. It hears the doctors and the nurses talking about you. It feels the pain of the knife.' Kinderman looked up from the paper and eyed him. 'But when you wake up from the anaesthesia, it's as if it never happened,' said Dyer. 'So maybe when we all go back to God, that's how it will be with all the pain of the world.'

'This is true,' said Kinderman.

'You agree with me?' Dyer looked astonished.

'I mean about the unconscious,' Kinderman explained. 'Some psychologists, all biggies, great names from the past, they made all these experiments and found out that inside us there's a second consciousness, this thing we now know as the unconscious. Alfred Binet, he was one of them. Listen! Once Binet does this: he gets a girl and then hypnotizes her, right? He tells her that from then she won't be able to see him or hear him or know what he's doing in any way. He puts a pencil in her hand and some paper in front of her. Someone else in the room starts talking to the girl and asking her lots of questions. Binet, in the meantime, is asking her questions at the very same time; and while she's talking with the first psychologist, the girl is at the *same time* writing down answers to the questions from Binet! Is that amazing? Something else. Binet at one point sticks a pin in her hand. The girl feels nothing, she continues to talk to the first psychologist. But in the meantime, the pencil is moving and writing the words, "Please don't hurt me." Isn't that something? Anyway, it's true what you said about the surgery. Someone is feeling all this cutting and pasting. But who is it?' He suddenly remembered his dream and the cryptic statement uttered by Max: '*Two souls*'.

'The unconscious,' Kinderman brooded. 'What is it? *Who* is it? What has it to do with the collective unconscious? It's all part of my theory, you understand.'

Dyer looked away and made a gesture of impatience. 'Oh, *that* again,' he muttered.

'Yes, you're eaten up with jealousy that Kinderman the mastermind, the Jewish Mister Moto in your midst, is on the verge of now cracking this problem of evil,' said Kinderman. His eyebrows bushed together. 'My giant brain is like a sturgeon surrounded by minnows.'

Dyer's head came around. 'Don't you think that's a little unseemly?'

'No, not.'

'Well, then why don't you tell me your theory? Let's hear it and be done with it,' said Dyer. 'Cheech and Chong have been waiting in the hall, their turn is next.'

'It's too huge for you to grasp,' said Kinderman sulkily.

'So what's wrong with just Original Sin?'

'Little babies are responsible for something done by Adam?'

'It's a mystery,' said Dyer.

'It's a joke. I'll admit I played around with such a notion,' said Kinderman. He leaned forward and his eyes began to sparkle. 'If the sin was that scientists blew up the earth many millions of years ago with something like cobalt bombs, we would have from this *tsimmis* atomic mutations. Maybe this creates the viruses that make sickness, maybe even messes up the whole physical environment so that now there comes earthquakes and natural catastrophes. As for men, they get altogether crazy and *fermischt* and they turn into monsters from the horrible mutations; they start eating meat, like the animals as well, and all this going to the bathroom and liking rock and roll. They can't help it. It's genetic. Even God cannot help it. The sin is a condition that's passed through the genes.'

'What if every man born was really once a part of Adam?' asked Dyer. 'I mean physically – actually one of the cells of his body?'

Kinderman's look became abruptly suspicious. 'So it's not all Sunday catechism class with you, Father. All these bingo games are making you a little bit adventurous. Where did you come up with this idea?'

'What about it?' asked Dyer.

'You're thinking. But this notion doesn't work.'

'Why not?'

'It's too Jewish. It makes God a little peevish, already. It's the same with what I said about the genes. Let's face it, God could stop this foolish nonsense whenever He pleases. He could start things all over again from the beginning. He couldn't say, "Adam, wash your face, it's almost dinner" and forget the whole thing? He couldn't fix up the genes? The gospel tells you to forgive and forget, but God can't? The hereafter is Sicily? Puzo should hear about this. We'll have "Godfather Four" in two seconds.'

'So, okay, what's your theory, then?' Dyer insisted.

The detective looked crafty. 'I'm still working on it, Father. My unconscious is *schmeckling* it together.'

Dyer turned and plopped his head against the pillows, exasperated. 'This is boring,' he said. His eyes were on the blank TV.

'I'll give another little hint,' offered Kinderman.

'I wish they'd come and fix that stupid thing.'

'Stop insulting me and listen to the hint.'

Dyer yawned.

'It's from your gospels,' Kinderman continued. '"What you do unto the least of these, my little ones, you do unto Me",' he quoted.

'They could at least have a Space Invaders game around this place.'

'Space Invaders?' echoed Kinderman dully.

Dyer turned to him and asked, 'Could you get me a paper from the gift shop?'

'What, the *National Enquirer*, the *Globe*, or the *Star*?'

'I think the *Star* comes out Wednesdays. Isn't that right?'

'I rush to find any common ground between our planets.'

Dyer looked offended. 'So what's wrong with those papers? Mickey Rooney saw a ghost that resembled Abe Lincoln. Where else can you find out about these things?'

The detective looked up and reached into his pockets. 'Here, I have a few books you might enjoy,' he told the priest. He extracted some paperbacks and Dyer looked over the titles. 'Non-fiction,' he said grumpily. 'Boring. Can't you bring me up a novel?'

Kinderman wearily stood up. 'I'll bring a novel,' he said. He walked to the foot of the bed and picked up the chart. 'What kind? A big historical?'

'*Scruples*,' said Dyer. 'I'm up to chapter three, but I forgot to bring it with me.'

Kinderman eyed him without expression, then replaced the chart. He turned and walked slowly towards the door. 'After lunch,' he told Dyer. 'You shouldn't excite yourself before lunch. I am also going to eat.'

'After scarfing down three hamburgers?'

'Two. But who's counting.'

'If they haven't got *Scruples*, get *Princess Daisy*,' Dyer called after him.

Kinderman exited shaking his head.

He walked down the hallway a little and then stopped. He saw Amfortas standing at the Charge Desk. He was writing on a clipboard. Kinderman approached him, assuming an expression of tragic concern. 'Doctor Amfortas?' the detective said gravely. The neurologist looked up. *Those eyes*, thought Kinderman. *What a mystery is in them!* 'It's about Father Dyer,' said the detective.

'He's all right,' said Amfortas quietly. He returned his attention to the clipboard.

'Yes, I know that,' said Kinderman. 'It's something else. Something terribly important. We're both friends of Father Dyer, but with this I can't help him. Only you.'

The urgent tone drew the doctor's gaze. The haggard dark eyes looked worried. 'What is it?' asked Amfortas.

Kinderman glanced around, looking guarded. 'I can't tell you here,' he said. 'Could we go someplace else and have a talk?' He looked at his watch. 'Maybe lunch,' he said.

'That's a meal I never take,' said Amfortas.

'Then watch me. Please. It's important.'

Amfortas probed his eyes for a time. 'Well, all right,' he said at last. 'But can't we do it in my office?'

'I'm hungry.'

'Let me go and get a jacket.'

Amfortas went away and when he returned he was wearing his navy blue cardigan sweater. 'All right,' he told Kinderman.

Kinderman stared at the sweater. 'You'll freeze,' he said. 'Get a jacket.'

'This will do.'

'No, no, get something warmer. I can see now the headline. "Neurologist Felled By Freezing Cold. Unknown Fat Man Sought For Questioning." Get a jacket, please. A windbreaker, maybe. Something warmer. I would feel too guilty. As it is, you're not exactly the picture of health.'

'This is fine,' said Amfortas softly. 'But thank you. I appreciate your concern.'

Kinderman looked crestfallen. 'Very well,' he said. 'I warned you.'

'Where are we going? It will have to be close.'

'"The Tombs",' said Kinderman. 'Come on.' He linked up an arm with that of the neurologist and walked him towards the elevators. 'It will do you some good. You need a little fresh air on your cheeks. A little *nosh* would also not make you thinner. Your mother, does she know about this meal-skipping nonsense? Never mind. You're stubborn. I can tell. I wish her luck.' The detective flicked a glance of appraisal at the doctor.

Was he smiling? Who knew? *He is tough, a tough case*, thought Kinderman.

On the walk to The Tombs, the detective asked questions about Dyer's condition. Amfortas seemed preoccupied and answered with brief, terse statements, or with nodding or shaking of his head. What came through was the likelihood that the symptoms described by Dyer, although sometimes a warning of a tumour in the brain, were in this case most likely due to strain and overwork.

'Overwork?' the detective exclaimed with incredulity, as they were walking down the steps of "The Tombs". 'Strain? Who would guess it. The man is more relaxed than a boiled noodle.'

"The Tombs" was red and white checkered tablecloths and a dark oak spherical bar where the beer came in large, thick steins made of glass. The walls were festooned with prints and lithos of Georgetown's past. The room was not crowded yet. It was just a few minutes before noon. Kinderman saw a quiet booth. 'Over there,' he said. They went over and sat down.

'I'm so hungry,' said Kinderman.

Amfortas said nothing. His head was bowed. He looked down at his hands, which were clasped before him on the table.

'You'll eat something, Doctor?'

Amfortas shook his head. 'What about Dyer?' he asked. 'What was it you wanted to tell me?'

Kinderman leaned forward, his expression and his manner vaguely portentous. 'Don't fix his TV,' he said.

Amfortas looked up, expressionless. 'I beg your pardon?'

'Don't fix his TV. He'll find out.'

'Find out what?'

'You didn't hear about the murder of the priest?'

'Yes, I heard,' said Amfortas.

'This priest was a friend of Father Dyer's. If you fix the TV he'll find out on the news. Also, don't bring him newspapers, Doctor. Tell the nurses.'

'That's what you brought me here to tell me?'

'Don't be hard-hearted,' said Kinderman. 'Father Dyer has a delicate soul. And a man in a hospital in any case shouldn't be getting such news as that.'

'But he already knows,' said Amfortas.

The detective looked mildly staggered. 'He knows?'

'We discussed it,' said Amfortas.

The detective looked away with an air of recognition and resignation. 'How very like him,' he nodded. 'He didn't want to worry me with his *angst*, so he puts on a show like he's blissfully ignorant.'

'Why did you bring me here, Lieutenant?'

The detective turned his head. Amfortas was staring at him intently. His gaze was disconcerting. 'Why did I bring you here?' said Kinderman. His eyes were blank and bulging as he struggled to hold the doctor's stare, and his cheeks were beginning to redden rapidly.

'Yes, why? Surely not about a television set,' said Amfortas.

'I lied,' the detective blurted out. Now his face was flushed and he looked away and began to shake his head and smile. 'I am so transparent,' he chuckled. 'I don't know how to keep a straight face.' He turned back to Amfortas and raised his hands above his head. 'Yes, guilty. I am shameless. I lied. I couldn't help myself, Doctor. Strange forces overcame me. I offered them cookies and told them, "Go away!" but they knew I was weak and held on and said, "Lie, or for lunch you get quiche and a slice of warm melon!"'

'The taco might have been more effective,' said Amfortas.

Kinderman lowered his arms in amazement. The neurologist's face had remained unreadable, and his stare was still flat and unblinking. But had he made a joke? 'Yes, also the taco,' said Kinderman numbly.

'What is it that you want?' Amfortas asked him.

'You'll forgive me? I wanted to pick your mind.'

'What about?'

'Pain. It drives me crazy. Father Dyer said you work in this field, that you're an expert. Do you mind? I used a ruse so we could talk about this subject a little. In the meantime, I'm embarrassed and I owe you an apology, Doctor. I'm forgiven? Maybe sentence suspended?'

'You have a recurring pain?' said Amfortas.

'Yes, a man named Ryan. But this is not the point now, it isn't the subject.'

Amfortas remained a dark presence. 'What is?' he asked quietly.

Before the detective could answer, a waiter appeared with menus. He was young, a student at the college. He was wearing a bright green tie and vest. 'Both for lunch?' he enquired politely. He was offering the menus, but Amfortas declined with a gesture of his hand. 'Not for me,' he said softly. 'A cup of black coffee, please. That's all.'

'No lunch for me either,' said the detective. 'Maybe some tea with a slice of lemon, please. And some cookies. You have the little round ones with the ginger and the nuts?'

'Yes, we do, sir.'

'Some of those. Incidentally, what is doing with the shirt and the vest?'

'Saint Patrick's Day,' said the student. 'Nothing else for you gentlemen?'

'You have today a little chicken soup?'

'With noodles.'

'With whatever. Bring it also for me, please.'

The waiter nodded and went to fill the order.

Kinderman stared at another table where he saw a stein that was filled with green beer. 'It's all a craziness,' he muttered. 'A man runs around chasing snakes like some looney, and instead of a nice padded cell in some rest home, the Catholics are making him a saint.' He turned back to Amfortas. 'Little garden snakes, they're harmless, they don't even eat potatoes. This is rational behaviour, Doctor?'

'I thought you were so hungry,' said Amfortas.

'Can't you leave a man a little shred of dignity?' asked Kinderman. 'All right, it was another big lie. I always do it. I'm a totally incorrigible liar and the shame of my precinct. You're happy now, Doctor? Use my brain for experiments and find out why this happens, then at least I'll have some peace when I die, I'll know the answer. This problem has been driving me crazy all my life!'

In the doctor's eyes there was a ghost of a smile. 'You were mentioning pain,' he said.

'A truth. Look, you know that I'm a homicide detective.'

'Yes.'

'I see a great deal of pain that's inflicted on the innocent,' the detective said heavily.

'Why does this concern you?'

'You're a Catholic. You should know, you'll understand,' said Kinderman. 'My questions have to do with God's goodness and the ways that little innocent children can die. At the end, does God save them from horrible pain? Is it like in that movie, *Here Comes Mr Jordan*, where the angel pulls the hero from the crashing plane just before it hits the ground? I hear rumours of such doings. Could it possibly be true? For example, there's a car crash. In the car there are children, they're not seriously injured, but the car is on fire and the children are trapped inside, they can't get out. They were burned alive, we read later in the papers. It's horrible. But what are they feeling, Doctor? I heard somewhere that the skin goes to sleep. Could this be true?'

'You're a very strange homicide cop,' said Amfortas. He was looking directly into Kinderman's eyes.

The detective shrugged. 'I'm getting old. I have to think about these things a little bit. It couldn't hurt. In the meantime, what's the answer to my question?'

Amfortas looked down at the table. 'No one knows,' he said softly. 'The dead don't tell us. Any number of things could be happening,' he said. 'Smoke inhalation might kill before the flames. Or immediate heart attack, or shock. Moreover, the blood tends to rush to vital organs in an effort to protect them. That accounts for reports of the skin turning numb.' He shrugged. 'I don't know. We can only guess.'

'So what happens if all these things *don't* happen?' asked the detective.

'It's all speculation,' Amfortas reminded him.

'Please, Doctor, speculate. It's eating me up.'

The waiter arrived with their order. He was setting down the soup in front of the detective, but Kinderman held him off with a gesture. 'No, give it to the doctor,' he said, and when Amfortas was about to decline, he interrupted him with, 'Don't make me call your mother. It's got vitamins and things only mentioned in the Torah. Don't be stubborn. You should eat it, it's full of strange goodness.'

Amfortas gave up and let the waiter set it down.

'Oh, is Mister McCooey around?' asked Kinderman.

'Yes, he's upstairs, I believe,' said the waiter.

'Would you ask if I could see him for a moment? If he's busy, never mind. It's not important.'

'Yes, I'll ask him. What's your name, sir?'

'William F. Kinderman. He knows me. If he's busy, it's okay.'

'I'll give him the message.' The waiter went away.

Amfortas was staring down at the soup. 'From the first sensation until death takes twenty seconds. When the nerve endings burn, they cease to function and the pain is all over. How long before that happens is also a guess. But no more than ten seconds. In the meantime, the pain is the most hideous imaginable. You're fully conscious and acutely aware of it. Your adrenalin is pumping.'

Kinderman was shaking his head, staring down. 'How could God let such horror go on? It's such a mystery.' He looked up. 'Don't you think about such things? Does it anger you?'

Amfortas hesitated, then he met the detective's gaze. *This man is burning with wanting to tell me something*, thought Kinderman. *What is his secret?* He thought he read pain and a longing to share it. 'I may have misled you, I think,' said Amfortas. 'I was trying to work within your assumptions. One thing I didn't mention is that when pain gets too unbearable, the nervous system overloads. It shuts down and the pain is over.'

'Oh, I see.'

'Pain is strange,' said Amfortas broodingly. 'About two per

cent of the people relieved of a long-standing pain develop serious mental disturbance as soon as that pain is taken away. There have also been experiments with dogs,' he continued, 'with rather peculiar implications.' Amfortas proceeded to describe for the detective a series of experiments in 1957 in which Scottish terriers were raised in isolation cages from infancy to maturity, so that they were deprived of environmental stimuli, including even the most minor of knocks and scrapes that might cause them discomfort. When fully grown, painful stimuli were applied, but the dogs did not respond in a normal manner. Many of them poked their noses into a flaming match, withdrew reflexively, and then immediately sniffed at the flame again. When the flame was inadvertently snuffed out, the dogs would continue to react as before to a second, or even a third, flaming match. Others did not sniff at the match at all, but made no effort to avoid its flame when experimenters touched their noses with it any number of times. And the dogs did not react to repeated pinpricks. In contrast the litter-mates of these dogs, which had been raised in an ordinary environment recognized possible harm so quickly that experimenters found themselves unable to touch them with the flame or the pin more than once. 'Pain is very mysterious,' concluded Amfortas.

'Tell me frankly, Doctor, couldn't God have thought of some other way to protect us? Some other kind of warning system to tell us our bodies were in trouble?'

'You mean like an automatic reflex?'

'I mean something like a bell that goes off in our heads.'

'Then what happens when you sever an artery?' said Amfortas. 'Would you put on the tourniquet right away, or put up with the bell while you finished your seven no-trump redoubled? And what if you're a child? No, it just wouldn't work.'

'Then why couldn't our bodies have been made impervious to injury?'

'Good question.'

'It is?'

'Yes, I think so,' said Amfortas.

'It makes me crazy,' said the detective. He shrugged. 'So what is it that you do in your laboratory, Doctor?'

'Try to learn how to shut off pain when we don't need it.'

Kinderman waited, but the neurologist said no more. 'Eat your soup,' the detective gently prodded him. 'It's getting cold. Like the love of God.'

Amfortas took a spoonful, and then put the spoon down. It made a fragile little pewtery sound against the plate. 'I'm not hungry,' he said. He looked at his watch. 'I just remembered something,' he said. 'I ought to be going.' Then he looked up at Kinderman and stared at him dully.

'It's a wonder you believe in God at all,' said Kinderman, 'what with all your knowledge of the workings of the brain.'

'Mister Kinderman?' the waiter was back. 'Mister McCooey looked terribly busy up there. I thought I hadn't ought to bother him.'

The detective looked blocked. 'No, interrupt him,' he said.

'But you said it wasn't really important.'

'It isn't. Interrupt him all the same. I'm crotchety. I never make sense. I'm old.'

'Well, okay, sir.' The waiter looked doubtful, but he walked towards the steps that led upstairs. Kinderman returned his attention to Amfortas. 'Don't you think it's all neurons, all this stuff we call a soul?'

Amfortas checked his watch. 'I just remembered something,' he said. 'I ought to be going.'

Kinderman looked puzzled. *Am I crazy? He just did that already.* 'Where were you?' he asked.

'I beg your pardon?' said Amfortas.

'Never mind. Listen, stay a little while. I have still some more things on my mind. They torment me. Won't you stay another minute? Besides, it's impolite to go now. I haven't finished with my tea. Is this civilized? Witch doctors wouldn't even do this. They would stay and enlarge shrunken heads to pass the time while the senile old white man kept talking and drooling. This is manners. Am I being too forward on this subject? Tell me frankly. People tell me all the time that I'm oblique and I'm

116

trying to correct this, although possibly too much. Is this true? Be honest!'

A pleasant expression came over Amfortas. He relaxed and said, 'What is it I can help you with, Lieutenant?'

'It's this brain versus mind *khazerei*,' said Kinderman. 'For years I've been meaning to consult some neurologist about it, but I'm terribly shy about meeting new people. In the meantime, here you are. My cup of matzoh soup runneth over. Meantime, tell me, are the things we call feelings and thoughts nothing more than some neurons that are firing in the brain?'

'You mean, are they the very same *fact* as those neurons?'

'Yes.'

'What do *you* think?' asked Amfortas.

Kinderman looked overly wise and nodded. 'I think they're the same,' he said almost sternly.

'Why is that?'

'Why not?' the detective countered. 'Who needs to reach out for this thing called a soul when the brain is clearly doing all these things? Am I right?'

Amfortas leaned forward a little. Some nerve had been touched. He spoke warmly. 'Suppose that you're looking at the sky,' he said intently. 'You see a great homogenous expanse. Is that the very same fact as a pattern of electrical discharges that run between wires in the brain? You look at a grapefruit. It produces a circular image in your sense field. But the cortical projection of this circle in your occipital lobe isn't circular. It occupies a space that's ellipsoidal. So how can these things be the very same fact? When you think of the universe, how do you contain it in your brain? Or for that matter, the objects in this room? They're shaped differently than anything in your brain, so how can they become those things in your brain? There are several other mysteries you ought to consider. One is the "executive" connected with thought. Every second you're bombarded with hundreds, maybe thousands, of sense impressions, but you filter out all but those immediately necessary to accomplish your ends of the moment, and those countless decisions are made every second and in less than a *fraction* of a second. What's making that decision? What's making the *decision* to make that decision? Here's one other thing to think about, Lieutenant: the brains of schizophrenics are often better structurally put together than the brains of people *without* mental problems; and some people with most of their brain removed continue to function as themselves.'

'But what about this scientist with his electrodes,' said Kinderman. 'He touches a certain brain cell and the person hears a voice from long ago, or he experiences a certain emotion.'

'That's Wilder Penfield,' the neurologist responded. 'But his subjects always said that whatever he produced in them with the electrodes weren't a part of them; it was something being *done* to them.'

'I am astounded,' said the detective, 'to be hearing such notions from a man of science.'

'Wilder Penfield doesn't think the mind is brain,' said Amfortas. 'And neither does Sir John Eccles. He's a British physiologist who won the Nobel Prize for his brain studies.'

Kinderman's eyebrows rose. 'Is that so?'

'Yes, that is so. And if mind is brain, then the brain has some capacities totally unnecessary for the physical survival of the body. I mean things like wonder and self-awareness. And some of us go so far as to believe that consciousness itself isn't centred in the brain. There's some reason to suspect that the whole human body, including the brain, as well as the external world itself, are all spatially situated inside consciousness. And one final thought for you, Lieutenant. It's a couplet.'

'I love them.'

'I love this one in particular,' said Amfortas. '"If the mass of the brain were the mass of the mind, the bear would be shooting at my behind".' And with this, the neurologist bent to his soup and began to eat it hungrily.

From the corner of his eye, the detective saw McCooey approaching the table. 'My sentiments exactly,' he said to Amfortas.

'What?' Amfortas stared over his spoon.

'I was playing devil's advocate a little. I agree with you, mind is not brain. I am certain.'

'You're a very strange man,' said Amfortas.

'Yes, you said that already.'

'You wanted to see me, Lieutenant?'

Kinderman looked up at McCooey. He was wearing his rimless glasses and looked studious. He still wore the colours of his school: a navy blue blazer and grey flannel pants. 'Richard McCooey, meet Doctor Amfortas,' said Kinderman, gesturing toward the doctor. McCooey reached down and shook hands. 'Pleased to meet you,' he said.

'Same here.'

McCooey turned back to the detective. 'What is it?' He glanced at his watch.

'It's the tea,' said Kinderman.

'The tea?'

'What kind are you using these days?'

'It's Lipton's. Same as always.'

'It tastes somehow different.'

'Is that what you wanted to see me about?'

'Oh, I could talk about a hundred trivialities and whatnots, but I know you're a very busy man. I'll let you go.'

McCooey glanced coolly around at the table. 'What did you order?' he asked. His expression was prim, if not stiff.

'This is it,' the detective told him.

McCooey eyed him without expression. 'This is a table for six.'

'We're just leaving.'

McCooey turned away without a word and left.

Kinderman looked at Amfortas. The neurologist had finished the soup. 'Very good,' said Kinderman. 'Your mother will get a good report.'

'Have you any other questions?' Amfortas asked him. He felt at his coffee cup. It was cool.

'Succinylcholine chloride,' said Kinderman. 'You use it at your hospital?'

'Yes. I mean, not me personally. But it's used in electroshock therapy. Why do you ask?'

'If someone in the hospital wanted to steal some, could he do it?'

'Yes.'

'How?'

'He could lift it off a drug cart when no one was looking. Why are you asking?'

Kinderman again deflected his question. 'Then someone who is *not* from the hospital could do it?'

'If he knew what to look for. He would have to know the schedules for when the drug is needed and when it's delivered.'

'Do you work in psychiatric at times?'

'At times. Is this what you brought me here to ask, Lieutenant?' Amfortas was drilling the detective with his eyes.

'No, it isn't,' said Kinderman. 'Honest. God's truth. But as long as we were here –' He let it trail off. 'If I asked at the hospital, they would naturally want to look good and insist that it couldn't be done. You understand? As we were speaking, I realized you would tell me the truth.'

'That's very kind of you, Lieutenant. Thank you. You're a very nice man.'

Kinderman felt something reaching out from him. 'Likewise and ditto by me,' he acknowledged. Then he smiled with recollection. 'You know "ditto"? It's a word that I love. It really is. It reminds me of *Here Comes Mister Jordan*. Joe Pendleton said it all the time.'

'Yes, I remember.'

'Do you like that movie?'

'Yes.'

'So do I. I am a patron of *schmaltz*, I'll admit it. But such sweetness and innocence, these days – well, it's gone. What a life,' sighed Kinderman.

'It's a preparation for death.'

Once again Amfortas had surprised the detective. He appraised him warmly now. 'This is true,' said Kinderman. 'We must speak some other time of these things.' The detective searched the tragic eyes. They were brimming with something.

What? What was it? 'You're through with your coffee?' asked Kinderman.

'Yes.'

'I'll stay behind and get the check. You were kind to spend this time, but I know you're very busy.' Kinderman reached out his hand. Amfortas took it and squeezed it firmly, then he stood up to go. For a moment he lingered, staring quietly at Kinderman. 'The succinylcholine,' he said at last. 'It's the murder. Is that right?'

'Yes, that's right.'

Amfortas nodded, then he walked away. Kinderman watched him threading through the tables until at last he was up the steps and gone. The detective sighed. He called for the waiter, paid the check, and walked up three flights to McCooey's office. He found him there talking to an accountant. McCooey looked up at him, inscrutable behind his glasses. 'Is it something to do with the catsup?' he said tonelessly.

Kinderman beckoned to him. McCooey stood up and came over. 'The man at my table,' Kinderman said. 'You got a good look at his face?'

'Pretty good.'

'You've never seen him before?'

'I don't know. I see thousands of people in my stores every year.'

'You didn't see him in the line for confession yesterday?'

'Oh.'

'Did you see him?'

'I don't think so.'

'Are you sure?'

McCooey thought. Then he bit his lower lip and shook his head. 'When you're waiting for confession, you tend not to look at the other people. You're mostly looking down and reviewing your sins. If I saw him, I sure don't remember it,' he said.

'But you did see the man in the windbreaker.'

'Yes. I just don't know if that was him.'

'Could you swear that it wasn't?'

'No. But I really don't think so.'

'You don't.'

'No, I don't. I really doubt it.'

Kinderman left McCooey's office and walked to the hospital. Once there, he walked into the gift shop and scrutinized the paperback books. He found *Scruples* and he plucked it from the shelf with a shake of his head. He turned to a page at random and read it. *He will devour this immediately*, he concluded, and he looked for something else to tide the Jesuit over until his release. He eyed *The Hite Report on Men*, but then selected a Gothic romance instead.

Kinderman walked to the counter with the books. The clerk eyed the titles. 'I'm sure she's going to love these,' she said.

'Yes, I'm sure.'

Kinderman looked for some comical trinket to add to the treasure. The counter was crammed with them. Then something caught his attention. He stared, unblinking.

'Something else for you today?' asked the clerk.

The detective didn't hear her. He picked up a plastic packet from a box. It held a set of pink barrettes, each bearing the marking, 'Great Falls, Virginia'.

Chapter Eight

Georgetown General's psychiatric department was housed in a sprawling wing beside Neurology and was divided into two main sections. One was the Disturbed Ward. Here were quartered patients who were prone to fits of violence, such as paranoids and active catatonics. Among the maze of hallways and patients' rooms in this ward, there were also padded cells. Security was tight. The other section was the so-called 'Open Ward'. Here the patients were harmless to themselves and to others. Most patients were aged and were there because of varying stages of senility. There were also depressives and schizophrenics, as well as alcoholics, post-stroke victims, and victims of Alzheimer's disease, which produced a state of premature senility. Among the cases there were also a handful of patients who were long-term passive catatonics. Totally withdrawn from their environment, they spent their days in immobility, often with a fixed, bizarre expression on their faces. They sometimes roused themselves to speech and were extremely suggestible, taking orders which they followed to the letter. In the Open Ward, security was non-existent. The patients, in fact, were permitted to check out for the day or even for a number of days. This required only the signing of an Order Form by one of the doctors, or more often, the nurse on duty, or even the social worker, at times.

'Who signed her out?' asked Kinderman.

'Nurse Allerton. As it happens, she's on duty right now. She'll be here in just a second,' said Temple.

They were sitting in his office, a narrow little cubbyhole just around the corner from the nurse's station in the Open Ward. Kinderman gazed around at the walls. They were covered with degrees and photographs of Temple. Two of the photos saw him posed in a boxer's crouch. He looked young, nineteen or twenty, and he wore the gloves and T-shirt and headgear of collegiate boxers. His stare was menacing. All the other photos showed Temple with his arm around a pretty woman, each one different from all the others, and in each he was smiling into the camera. Kinderman dropped his gaze to the desk, where he saw a chipped, green sculpture of Excalibur, the sword of Arthurian legend. Imprinted on its base were the words 'To Be Drawn In Case of Emergency'. Tacked against the side of the desk was the motto, 'An Alcoholic Is Someone Who Drinks More Than His Doctor'. Cigarette ash was on scattered papers. Kinderman's gaze flicked over to Temple, avoiding the top of the psychiatrist's trousers, where his fly was unzipped. 'I cannot believe,' the detective said, 'that this woman was allowed to go out unattended.'

The elderly woman from the dock had been traced. Upon leaving the gift shop, Kinderman had taken her photo around to every Charge Desk, beginning at the hospital's first floor. On the fourth, in Psychiatry, she was recognized as a patient in the Open Ward. Her name was Martina Otsi Lazlo. She was a transfer from the District Hospital where she had been for forty-one years. Her ailment had been classified at first as a mildly catatonic form of dementia praecox, a type of senility that began in adolescence. The diagnosis continued, although the terminology had changed, until Lazlo's transfer to Georgetown General when it opened in 1970.

'Yeah, I looked at her history,' said Temple, 'and I knew it was cockeyed right away. Something else was going on.' He lit a cigarillo and tossed the match carelessly toward an ashtray on his desk. It missed and landed with a *pat* on an open case history of a schizophrenic. Temple eyed the miss glumly. 'Hell, nobody knows what they're doing anymore. She'd been at District so long that nobody knew the first thing about her. They'd lost her early records. Then I took one look at her making these dingbat movements all the time. With her hands. She'd move them like this,' said Temple, beginning to illustrate for Kinderman, but the detective interrupted him. 'Yes, I've seen them,' said Kinderman quietly.

'Oh, you have?'

'She is now in our Holding Ward.'

'Good for her.'

Kinderman immediately took a dislike to him. 'What is the meaning of the movements?' he asked.

A light rapping at the door interrupted the answer. 'Come in,' called Temple. An attractive young nurse in her twenties walked in. 'Do I pick 'em?' asked Temple with a leer at the detective.

'Yes, doctor?'

Temple looked at the nurse. 'Miss Allerton, you signed out Lazlo Saturday?'

'Beg pardon?'

'Lazlo. You signed her out Saturday, correct?'

The nurse looked puzzled. 'Lazlo? No, I didn't.'

'What's this then?' asked Temple. He picked up an Order Form from his desk and began to read its contents aloud to the nurse. 'Subject: Lazlo, Martina Otsi. Action: Permission to visit with brother in Fairfax, Virginia, until March 22.' Temple then handed the Order to the nurse. 'It's dated Saturday and signed by you,' he said.

The nurse's frown deepened as she examined the Order.

'That was your shift,' said Temple. 'Two PM until ten.'

The nurse looked up at him. 'Sir, I didn't write this,' she said.

The psychiatrist's face began to redden. 'Are you kidding me, tootsie?'

The nurse grew agitated and flustered under his gaze. 'No, I didn't. I swear it. She wasn't even gone. I made bed check at nine and I saw her in bed.'

'Isn't that your handwriting?' Temple demanded.

'No. I mean, yes. Oh, I don't know,' exclaimed Allerton. She was looking at the Order Form again. 'Yes, this looks like my writing, but it isn't. Something's different.'

'What's different?' asked Temple.

'I don't know. But I know I didn't write it.'

'Let me see it.' Temple snatched the Order Form from her hand and began to examine it. 'Oh, I see,' he said. 'These little circles, you mean? These little circles over the "i"s in place of dots?'

'May I see that?' asked Kinderman. He was holding out his hand for the form. Temple turned it over to him. 'Sure.'

'Thank you.'

Kinderman examined the document.

'I didn't write that,' the nurse was insisting.

'Yeah, I think you may be right,' murmured Temple.

The detective glanced up at the psychiatrist. 'What was that you just said?' he asked.

'Oh, nothing.' Temple looked up at the nurse. 'It's okay, babe. Come around on your break and I'll buy you some coffee.'

Nurse Allerton nodded, then quickly turned and left the room.

Kinderman handed the Order Form back to Temple. 'This is strange, don't you think? Someone forges a permission to leave for Miss Lazlo?'

'It's a nuthouse.' The psychiatrist threw up his hands.

'Why would someone want to do that?' asked Kinderman.

'I just told you. All the nuts around this place aren't inmates.'

'You mean staff?'

'It's contagious.'

'And who on your staff in particular, please?'

'Ah, well, hell. Never mind.'

'Never mind?'

'I was kidding.'

'You're not terribly concerned about this?'

'No, I'm not.' Temple tossed the Order Form onto his desk and it landed on the ashtray. 'Shit.' He removed it. 'It's probably some half-assed intern's joke, or maybe some jerk who's got something against me.'

'But if that were the case,' the detective pointed out, 'the writing would have doubtless resembled yours.'

'You've got a point.'

'This is known as paranoia, is it not?

'Sharp cookie.' Temple's eyes shuttered down to slits. Blue-grey ash from the cigarillo fell onto the shoulder of his jacket. He brushed it and it darkened into a stain. 'She might have written it herself, I suppose.'

'Miss Lazlo?'

Temple shrugged. 'It could happen.'

'Really?'

'No, it's doubtful.'

'Did anyone see Miss Lazlo leaving? Was anyone with her?'

'I don't know. I'll find out.'

'Would there have been another check of the beds after nine?'

'Yeah, the night nurse makes one at two,' answered Temple.

'Would you ask her if she saw Miss Lazlo in her bed?'

'Yeah, I will. I'll leave a note. Listen, what's so important about this? Is it something to do with the murders?'

'What murders?'

'Well, you know. That kid and the priest.'

'Yes, it is,' said Kinderman.

'I thought so.'

'Why did you think so?'

'Well, I'm not exactly stupid.'

'No, you're not,' said Kinderman. 'You're an extremely intelligent man.'

'So what has Lazlo got to do with these murders?'

'I don't know. She's involved, but not directly.'

'I'm lost.'

'The human condition.'

'Isn't *that* the truth?' said Temple. 'So it's safe to bring her back here?' he asked.

'I would say so. In the meantime, you're convinced that the Order Form was forged?'

'There's not a doubt of it.'

'Who forged it?'

'I don't know. You keep repeating your questions.'

'Is there someone on your staff who makes circles over "i"s?'

Temple stared directly into Kinderman's eyes, and then after a pause he looked away and said, 'No.' He said it emphatically. *Too* emphatically, Kinderman thought. The detective watched him for a moment. Then he asked, 'Now what's the meaning of Miss Lazlo's odd movements?'

Temple turned back to him with a grin of self-satisfaction. 'You know, my work is a lot like yours in many ways. I'm a sleuth.' He leaned forward towards the detective. 'Now here's what I did. You'll appreciate this, I know it. Lazlo's movements have a pattern to them, isn't that right? It's the same thing every time.' Temple mimicked her gestures. 'So one day I'm in a shoemaker's shop, I'm there waiting for my soles to be mended. And I look and see this carpenter stitching up the soles. You know, they do it by machine. So I went over there and asked him, "Tell me, how did you do that before you had machines?" He was old and had an accent, sort of Serbo-Croatian. I was working on a hunch that just came to me sitting there. "We did it by hand," he says, laughing. He thinks I'm dumb. So I said to him, "Show me." He says to me he's busy, but I offered him some money, five bucks I think it was. And he sits down and puts my shoe between his knees and starts to work with these imaginary long leather strips they used to use to attach the soles to the shoe. And don't you know it looked exactly like what Lazlo always does? There it was! The same movements! So as soon as I could I got hold of her brother in Virginia and I asked him some questions. Guess what turned out? Just before she went crazy, Lazlo got jilted by her sweetheart, the guy that she thought was going to marry her. Can you guess his occupation?'

'He was a shoemaker?'

'Right on the money. She couldn't bear losing him, so she became him. When he left her, she was only seventeen years old, but for all of her life she's completely identified with the man. Over fifty-two years now.'

Kinderman felt sad.

'How about that for sleuthing, though?' the psychiatrist said expansively. 'You've either got it or you don't. It's an instinct. It comes early. When I was a resident, I worked up a paper on a patient, a depressive. One of his symptoms was a clicking in the ear that he heard all the time. So when I finished with interviewing the guy, I had a sudden thought. "Which ear is the clicking in?" I asked him. He said to me, "I hear it all the time in the left one." "Not ever in the right one?" I asked him. He said, "No, I hear it only in the left one." "Would you mind if I listened?" I asked him. He said, "No." So I put my ear against his and listened. And Christ, don't you know I could hear the clicking? As loud as could be! The hammer in his tympanum was constantly slipping and making the noise. We cured it with surgery and released him. You know he'd been in there for almost six years? Because of the clicking, he thought he was crazy, and because of that he got depressed. As soon as he knew that the clicking was real he got over his depression overnight.'

'That's really something,' said Kinderman. 'Really.'

'I tend to use hypnosis a lot,' said Temple. 'A lot of doctors don't like it. They think it's too dangerous. But are these people better off the way they are? Christ, you have to be a sleuth and an inventor to be good. Above all, though, you've got to be creative. Always.' He giggled. 'I was just thinking,' he said. 'When I was a resident in Gynaecology, there was this patient, a woman in her forties, who was in for some mysterious pains in her pussy. Hanging around her, I got convinced that she definitely belonged in Psychiatric. I was certain she was loco, but really bananas. So I talked to the psychiatric resident about her, and he went and talked to her for a while, and then later he told me that he didn't agree with me. Well, days went by, and I got more and more certain she was a fruitcake. But the psychiatric resident wouldn't listen. So one day I went to this woman's room. I had a little short stepladder with me and a sheet made out of rubber. I locked her door, put the sheet on top of her up to her neck, and then got up on the ladder, pulled out my dork and pissed on the bed. She couldn't believe what she was seeing. I got down from the ladder, folded up the sheet, and left the room with the sheet and the ladder. Then I bided my time. Maybe one day later, I run into the psychiatric resident at lunch. He looks me in the eye and says "Freeman, you were right about that woman. You'll never believe what she told all the nurses."'' Temple leaned back in his chair with satisfaction. 'Yeah, it takes a lot of doing,' he said. 'It sure does.'

'This has been an education for me, Doctor,' said Kinderman. 'Really. It's opened my eyes in so many ways. You know some doctors, other branches, they keep knocking psychiatry.'

'They're assholes,' snorted Temple.

'Incidentally, I had lunch with your colleague today. You know, Doctor Amfortas? The neurologist?'

The psychiatrist's eyes closed a fraction. 'Yeah, Vince would be knocking psychiatry, all right.'

'Oh, no, no,' protested Kinderman. 'He didn't. No, not him. I just mentioned him because I had this lunch. He was jolly.'

'He was *what*?'

'A nice man. Incidentally, maybe someone could show me around?' He stood up. 'Miss Lazlo's surroundings. I should see them.'

Temple got up and stubbed out the cigarillo in the ashtray. 'I'll do it myself,' he offered.

'Oh, no, no, you're a very busy man. No, I couldn't impose. I really couldn't.' Kinderman's hands were upraised in protestation.

'No sweat,' said Temple.

'You're sure?'

'This place is my baby. I'm proud of it. Come on and I'll show you around.' He opened the door.

'You're positive?'

'Positive,' said Temple.

Kinderman walked through the door. Temple followed. 'It's this way,' said Temple, pointing to the right. He bounded off. Kinderman trailed him, struggling to catch up with the springing steps. 'I feel so guilty,' said the detective.

'Well, you're with the right man.'

Kinderman toured the Open Ward. It was a maze of hallways, most of them lined with the patients' rooms, although in some there were conference rooms and offices for the staff. There was also a snack bar, as well as a physical therapy set-up. But the centre of activity was a large recreation room with a nurse's station, a ping pong table and a television set. When Temple and Kinderman arrived there, the psychiatrist pointed to a large group of patients who were watching something that sounded like a game show. Most of them were elderly and stared dully at the television screen. They were dressed in pyjamas, robes and slippers. 'That's where the action is,' said Temple. 'They bicker all day over what show to watch. The duty nurse spends all her time refereeing.'

'They seem happy with it now,' said Kinderman.

'Just wait. Now there's a typical patient,' said Temple. He was pointing to a man in the group watching television. He was wearing a baseball cap. 'He's a castrophrenic,' Temple explained. 'He thinks enemies are sucking all the thoughts from his mind. I dunno. He could be right. And then there's Lang. He's the guy standing up in the back. He was a pretty good chemist, then he started in to listening to voices on a tape recorder. Dead people. Answering his questions. He'd read some kind of book on the subject. That's what started him.'

Why does that strike me as familiar? wondered Kinderman. He felt a strangeness in his soul.

'Pretty soon he was hearing all these voices in his shower,' said Temple. 'Then in any kind of running water. A faucet. The ocean. Then in branches in the wind or rustling leaves. Pretty soon, he was hearing them in his sleep. Now he can't get away from them. He says the television drowns them out.'

'And these voices made him mentally ill?' asked Kinderman.

'No. The mental illness made him hear all these voices.'

'Like the clicking in the ear?'

'No, the guy is really whacked. Take my word. He really is. See that woman in the crazy hat? Another beauty. But one of my successes. You see her?' He was pointing to an obese middle-aged woman who was sitting with the television crowd.

'Yes, I see her,' said Kinderman.

'Oh-oh,' said Temple. 'Now she sees me. Here she comes.'

The woman was rapidly shuffling toward them. Her slippers slid gratingly against the floor. Soon she was standing directly in front of them. Her hat, made of rounded, blue felt, was covered with candy bars that were held to it with pins. 'No towels,' the woman told Temple.

'No towels,' the psychiatrist echoed.

The woman turned around and listed back toward her group.

'She used to hoard towels,' said Temple. 'She'd steal them from the other patients. But I cured that. For a week, we gave her seven extra towels every day. Then the next week twenty and the next week forty. Pretty soon she had so many in her room she couldn't move, and when we brought her her ration one day, she started screaming and throwing them out. She couldn't stand them any more.' The psychiatrist was quiet for one or two moments, watching as the woman settled into her place. 'I guess the candy comes next,' said Temple tonelessly.

'They're so quiet,' observed the detective. He looked around at some patients in chairs. They were slumping and listless, staring into space. 'Yeah, most of them are vegetables,' said Temple. He tapped a finger against his head. 'Nobody's home. Of course, the drugs don't help.'

'The drugs?'

'Their medication,' said Temple. 'Thorazine. They get it every day. It tends to make them even spacier.'

'The drug cart comes in here?'

'Sure.'

'It has drugs beside Thorazine on it?'

Temple turned his head to look at Kinderman. 'Why?'

'Just a question.'

The psychiatrist shrugged. 'Could be. If the cart is on its way to the Disturbed Ward.'

'And that is where electroshock therapy is done?'

'Well, not so much anymore.'

'Not so much?'

'Well, from time to time,' said Temple. 'When it's needed.'

'Have you patients in this ward who have medical knowledge?'

'Funny question,' said Temple.

'It's my albatross,' said Kinderman. 'My bear. I cannot help it. When I think of a thing, right away I have to say it out loud.'

Temple looked disoriented at this answer, but then turned and made a gesture toward one of the patients, a middle-aged slender man in a chair. He was sitting by a window, staring out. Late afternoon sunlight slanted across him, dividing his body into light and dark. His face was expressionless. 'He was a medic in Korea in the fifties,' said Temple. 'Lost his genitals. He hasn't said a word in thirty years.'

Kinderman nodded. He turned and glanced around at the nursing station. The nurse was busy writing a report. A well-built attendant, a black, stood near her, resting his arm on the station counter while keeping his eye on the patients in the room.

'You have only one nurse here,' Kinderman observed.

'That's all it takes,' said Temple easily. He put his hands on his hips and stared ahead. 'You know, when the television set's turned off, all you hear in this room is the shuffling of slippers. It's a creepy sound,' he said. He continued to stare for a time, then he turned his head to look at the detective. Kinderman was watching the man by the window. 'You look depressed,' said Temple.

Kinderman turned to him and said, 'Me?'

'Do you tend to brood a lot? You've been broody since you came to my office. Are you broody all the time?'

Kinderman recognized with surprise that what Temple was saying was the truth. Since entering his office Kinderman hadn't felt like himself. The psychiatrist had dominated his spirit. How had he done that? He looked at his eyes. There was a whirling within them. 'It's my work,' said Kinderman.

'Then change it. Somebody asked me once, "What can I do about these headaches that I always get from eating pork?" You know what I told him? "Stop eating pork".'

'May I see Miss Lazlo's room now, please?'

'Would you please brighten up?'

'I am trying.'

'Good. Come on, then, I'll take you to her room. It's close by.'

Temple led Kinderman through a hallway, and then into another, and soon they were standing in the room.

'There's very little in it,' said Temple.

'Yes, I see.'

In fact, it was bare. Kinderman looked in a closet. Another blue bathrobe was there. He searched the drawers. They were empty. There were towels and soap in the bathroom; that was all. Kinderman looked around the little room. Suddenly he felt a cold draught against his face. It seemed to flow through him, and then it ebbed. He looked at the window. It was closed. He had an odd feeling. He looked at his watch. It was 3:55.

'Well, I must be going,' said Kinderman. 'Thank you very much.'

'Any time.'

The psychiatrist led Kinderman out of the ward and into a hall of the Neurology Wing. They parted by the doors to the Open Ward. 'Well, I've got to get back inside,' said Temple. 'You know the way out from here?'

'Yes, I do.'

'Have I made your day, Lieutenant?'

'And my evening as well, perhaps.'

'Good. If you're ever depressed again, just call or come in here and see me. I can help you.'

'What school of psychiatry do you follow?'

'I'm a diehard Behaviourist,' said Temple. 'Give me all the facts and I'll tell you ahead of time what a person is going to do.'

Kinderman looked down and shook his head.

'What's the shaking of the head for?' asked Temple.

'Oh, it's nothing.'

'No, it's something,' said Temple. 'What's the problem?'

Kinderman looked up into eyes that were belligerent. 'Well, I've always felt sorry for Behaviourists, Doctor. They can never say, "Thank you for passing the mustard".'

The psychiatrist's mouth tightened up. He said, 'When are we getting back Lazlo?'

'Tonight. I will arrange it.'

'Good. That's swell.' Temple pushed in on a door. He said,

'See you 'round the campus, Lieutenant' and disappeared into the Open Ward. Kinderman stood there a moment, listening. He could hear the rubber soles quickly springing away. When the sound was gone he released a sigh for he felt an immediate sense of relief. He had the feeling he'd forgotten something. What? He felt at a bulge in a pocket of his coat. Dyer's books. He turned right and walked swiftly away.

When Kinderman entered Dyer's room the priest looked up from reading his Office. He was still in his bed. 'Well, it took you long enough,' he complained. 'I've had seven transfusions since you left.'

Kinderman stopped at the side of the bed and dumped the books on Dyer's stomach. 'As you ordered,' he said. '*The Life of Monet* and *Conversations with Wolfgang Pauli*. Do you know why Christ was crucified, Father? He preferred it to carrying these books in public.'

'Don't be snobbish, Lieutenant.'

'There are Jesuit Missions in India, Father. Couldn't you find one to work in? The flies are not as bad as they say. They're very pretty, they're all different colours. Also *Scruples* is translated now into Hindi, you'll still have your comforts and usual *chotchkelehs* by your side. Also several million copies of the *Kama Sutra*.'

'I've read it.'

'No doubt.' Kinderman had moved to the foot of the bed where he picked up Dyer's medical chart, gave it a glance and put it back. 'You'll forgive me if I leave now this mystical discussion? Too much of aesthetics always gives me a headache. I have also two more patients to visit, both priests: Joe DiMaggio and Jimmy the Greek. I am leaving you.'

'Leave then.'

'What's the hurry?'

'I want to get back to *Scruples*.'

Kinderman turned on his heel and walked out.

'Is it something I've said?' asked Dyer.

'Mother India is calling you, Father.'

Kinderman went out into the hall and out of sight. Dyer

stared at the empty, open doorway. 'Bye, Bill,' he murmured with a fond, warm smile. After a moment he returned to his Office.

Back at the precinct, Kinderman waddled through the noisy squad room, entered his office and closed the door. Atkins was waiting for him. He was leaning against a wall. He wore bluejeans and a thick, black turtleneck sweater underneath a shiny black leather jacket. 'We're going too far down, Captain Nemo,' said Kinderman, eyeing him bleakly from the door. 'The hull cannot take all this pressure.' He strode towards his desk. 'And neither can I. Atkins, what are you thinking of? Stop it. *Twelfth Night* is at the Folger, already, not here. What's this?' The detective leaned over his desk and picked up two composite sketches. He eyed them numbly, then darted a querulous look at Atkins. 'These are the suspects?' he said.

'No one got a clear look,' said Atkins.

'I can see that. The old man looks like a senile avocado trying to pass for Harpo Marx. The other one, meanwhile, boggles my mind. The man in the windbreaker had a moustache? No one mentioned a moustache in the church, not a word.'

'That was Miss Volpe's contribution.'

'Miss Volpe.' Kinderman dropped the sketches and rubbed a hand across his face. '*Meshugge*. Miss Volpe, meet Julie Febré.'

'I have something to tell you, Lieutenant.'

'Not now. Can't you see a man trying to die? It takes absolute, total concentration.' Kinderman wearily sat at his desk and stared at the sketches. 'Sherlock Holmes had it easy,' he gloomily complained, 'He had no sketches of the Hound of the Baskervilles to cope with. Also, Miss Volpe is doubtless worth ten of his Moriarty.'

'The Gemini file came in, sir.'

'I know that. I see it on the desk. Are we surfacing, Nemo? My vision is no longer blurred.'

'I have some news for you, Lieutenant.'

'Hold your thought. I've had a fascinating day at Georgetown General. Are you going to ask me about it?'

'What happened?'

'I'm not ready to discuss it at this time. However, I want your opinion on something. This is all academic. Understand? Just assume these hypothetical facts. A learned psychiatrist, someone like the Chief of Psychiatry at the hospital, makes a clumsy effort to make me think that he is covering up for a colleague; let's say a neurologist who is working on the problem of pain. This happens, in this hypothetical case, when I ask this imaginary psychiatrist if anyone on his staff has a certain eccentricity about his handwriting. This make-believe psychiatrist looks me in the eye for two or three hours, then he looks away and says "no" very loud. Also, like a fox, I find there's friction between them. Maybe not. But I think so. What do you deduce from this nonsense, Atkins?'

'The psychiatrist wants to finger the neurologist, but he doesn't want to do it openly.'

'Why not?' the detective asked. 'Remember, this man is obstructing justice.'

'He's guilty of something. He's involved. But if he's seemingly covering for someone else, you would never suspect him.'

'He should live so long. But I agree with your opinion. In the meantime, I have something more important to tell you. In Beltsville, Maryland, years ago they had this hospital for patients who were dying of cancer. So they gave them big doses of LSD. Couldn't hurt. Am I right? And it helps the pain. Then something funny happens to all of them. They all have the same experience, no matter what their background or their religion. They imagine they are going straight down through the earth and through every kind of sewage and filth and trash. While they're doing it, they *are* these things; they're the same. Then they start to go up and up and up, and suddenly everything is beautiful and they are standing in front of God, who then says to them, "Come up here with me, this isn't Newark." Every one of them had this experience, Atkins. Well, okay, maybe ninety percent. That's enough. But the main thing is one other thing that they said. They said they felt the whole universe was them. They were all one thing, they said; one person. Isn't it amazing that all of them would say that? Also, consider Bell's Theorem, Atkins: in any two-particle system, say the physicists, changing the spin of one of the particles simultaneously changes the spin of the other, *no matter what the distance is between them, no matter if it's galaxies or light years!*'

'Lieutenant?'

'Please be silent when you're speaking to me! I have something else to tell you.' The detective leaned forward with glittering eyes. 'Think about the autonomic system. It does all of these seemingly intelligent things to keep your body functioning and alive. But it hasn't got intelligence of its own. Your conscious mind is not directing it. "So what directs it?" you ask me. Your unconscious. Now think of the universe as your body, and of evolution and the Hunting Wasps as the autonomic system. What is directing it, Atkins? Think about that. And remember the collective unconscious. In the meantime, I cannot sit and chit-chat forever. Did you see the old lady or not? It doesn't matter. She belongs to Georgetown General Hospital. Give a call and have her sent right over. She's a psychiatric patient there. She's a lifer.'

'The old lady is dead,' said Atkins.

'What?'

'She died this afternoon.'

'What killed her?'

'Heart failure.'

Kinderman stared; then at last he lowered his head and nodded. 'Yes, that would be the only way for her.' He felt a deep and poignant sadness. 'Martina Otsi Lazlo,' he said fondly. He looked up at Atkins. 'This old lady was a giant,' he told him softly. 'In a world where love doesn't last, she was a giant.' He opened a drawer and took out the barrette they had found at the dock. He held it in his hand for a moment, staring. 'I hope she is with him now,' he murmured. He put the barrette in the drawer, which he closed. 'She has a brother in Virginia,' he said wearily to Atkins. 'Her last name is Lazlo. Call the hospital and make the arrangements. The contact is Temple, Doctor Temple. He's the Chief of Psychiatry there, a *goniff*. Don't allow him to hypnotize you. He can do it on the telephone, I'm thinking.'

The detective stood up and walked toward the door, only to stop and come back to his desk. 'Walking is good for the heart,' he said. He picked up the binder containing the Gemini file and threw a look at Atkins. 'Impudence is not,' he warned. 'Do not speak.' He walked to the door, pulled it open, then turned. 'Run a computer check for succinylcholine prescriptions written in the District this month and the last. The names are Vincent Amfortas and Freeman Temple. Are you going to Mass every Sunday?'

'No.'

'Why not? As they say among the blackrobes, Nemo, you're a "three sprinkle job"? Baptism, wedding, and death?'

Atkins shrugged. 'I don't think of it,' he said.

'Most illuminating. In the meantime, one final little question, Atkins, then I throw you to the torturers forthwith. If Christ hadn't let himself be crucified, would we have heard of the resurrection? Don't answer. It's obvious, Atkins. I thank you for your effort and your time. Enjoy your voyage to the bottom of the sea, in the meantime. I assure you you will find there only fish looking stupid, except for their leader, a giant carp weighing thirteen tons and with the brain of a porpoise. He's very unusual, Atkins. Avoid him. If he thinks we're connected, he might do something crazy.' The detective turned and walked away. Atkins saw him pause in the middle of the squad room, where he cast his gaze upward while his fingertips touched at the brim of his battered hat. A policeman with a suspect in tow bumped into him, and Kinderman said something to them. Atkins couldn't hear it. Finally, Kinderman turned and was gone.

Atkins walked over to the desk and sat down. He opened the drawer and looked at the barrette and wondered what Kinderman had meant about love. He heard footsteps and looked up. Kinderman was standing at the door. 'If I find so much as one Almond Roca missing,' he said, 'then it's no more Batman and Robin. In the meantime, what time did the old lady die?'

'Around 3:55,' answered Atkins.

'I see,' said Kinderman. He stared into space for a while, then abruptly he turned and left without a word. Atkins pondered the meaning of his question.

Kinderman went home. In the hall he removed his hat and coat, then went into the kitchen. Julie was sitting at the maple table, reading a fashion magazine while Mary and her mother pottered at the stove. Mary looked up from a pot she was stirring. 'Hi, sweetheart,' she smiled. 'Glad you made it for dinner.'

'Hi, Dad,' said Julie, still engrossed in her reading. Mary's mother turned her back on the detective and wiped the kitchen counter with a rag. 'Hello, dumpling,' said Kinderman. He gave Mary a kiss on the cheek. 'Without you, life is little glass beads and stale pizza,' he said. 'What's cooking?' he added. 'I smell brisket.'

'It has no smell,' grunted Shirley. 'Fix your nose.'

'I am leaving this to Julie,' said Kinderman darkly. He sat opposite his daughter at the table. The Gemini file was on his lap. Julie's arms were folded and propped on the table, and her long black hair touched the pages of *Glamour*. She absently pulled back a tress and turned a page. 'So what's this about Febré?' the detective asked her.

'Daddy, please don't get excited,' said Julie laconically. She turned to another page.

'Who's excited?'

'I'm just thinking about it.'

'Me too.'

'Bill, don't bug her,' said Mary.

'Who's bugging? Only, Julie, this will make for us a very big problem. So one person in a family changes names. This is easy. But when three all at once make a change, and all different, I don't know; this could finally lead to mass hysteria, not to mention a miniscule confusion. Could we maybe coordinate all this?'

Julie lifted her beautiful blue eyes to her father's. 'I don't understand you, Dad.'

'Your mother and I, we are changing our name to Darlington.'

A wooden ladle slammed into the sink, and Kinderman saw Shirley walking quickly from the room. Mary turned to the refrigerator, silently giggling.

'*Darlington*?' said Julie.

'Yes,' said Kinderman. 'Also we are converting.'

Julie covered a gasp with her hand. 'You're becoming Catholics?' she asked in amazement.

'Don't be foolish,' said Kinderman blandly. 'This is as bad as being a Jew. We are thinking now Lutheran, maybe. We're all finished with those swastikas on the temple.' Kinderman heard Mary racing out of the kitchen. 'Your mother is upset a little bit,' he said. 'Change is always hard in the beginning. She'll get over it. We don't have to do this all at once. We'll make it gradual. First we change the name, after that we convert, and *then* we are subscribing to *The National Review*.'

'I don't believe this,' said Julie.

'Believe it. We are entering the blender of the times. We are becoming purée, if not Febré. Never mind. It was inevitable. The only question now is how do we coordinate this business. We are open to suggestions, Julie. What do you think?'

'I think you shouldn't change your name,' Julie told him emphatically.

'Why not?'

'Well, it's your *name*!' she said. She saw her mother returning. 'Are you *serious* about this, Momma?'

'It doesn't have to be "Darlington", Julie,' said Kinderman. 'We'll pick another name that we all can agree on. What about "Bunting"?'

Mary nodded sagely. 'I like it.'

'Oh, God, this is gross,' said Julie. She got up and flounced out of the kitchen as Mary's mother was coming back in. 'You're all through talking all your craziness?' asked Shirley. 'In this house I can't tell who is a person and who's not. It's all maybe some dummies talking *shtuss* to torment me and make me hear voices and then put me in a home.'

'Yes, you're right,' said Kinderman sincerely. 'I apologize.'

'You see what I mean?' squealed Shirley. 'Mary, tell him to stop it!'

'Bill, stop it,' said Mary.

'I am done.'

Dinner was ready at 7:15. Afterwards Kinderman soaked in the bathtub, trying to make his mind a blank. As usual he found himself unable to do it. *Ryan does it so easily*, he reflected. *I must ask him his secret. I will wait until he's done something right and feels expansive.* His mind went from the concept of a secret to Amfortas. *The man is so mysterious, so dark.* There was something he was hiding, he knew. What was it? Kinderman reached for a plastic bottle and poured some more bubble fluid into the tub. He could barely keep from dozing off.

The bath over, Kinderman put on a robe and carried the Gemini file to his den. Its walls were covered with movie posters, black-and-white classics from the thirties and forties. The dark wooden desk was strewn with books. Kinderman winced. He was barefoot and had stepped on a sharp-edged copy of Teilhard de Chardin's *The Phenomenon of Man*. He bent down and picked it up and then placed it on the desk. He turned on the desk lamp. The light caught tinfoil candy wrappers lurking in the rubble like gleaming felons. Kinderman cleared away a space for the file, scratched his nose, sat down and tried to focus. He searched among the books and found a pair of reading glasses. He cleaned them with the sleeve of his robe and then put them on. He still couldn't see. He shut one eye and then the other, then he took off the glasses and did it again. He decided he saw better without the left lens. He wrapped his sleeve around the lens and banged it sharply on a corner of the desk. The lens fell out in two pieces. *Occam's Razor*, Kinderman thought. He put the glasses back on and tried again.

It was no use. The problem was fatigue. He took off the glasses, left the den and went straight to bed.

Kinderman dreamed. He was sitting in a theatre watching a film with the inmates of the Open Ward. He thought he was watching *Lost Horizon*, although what he saw on the screen was *Casablanca*. He felt no discrepancy about this. In Rick's Café the piano player was Amfortas. He was singing 'As Time Goes By' when the Ingrid Bergman character entered. In Kinderman's dream she was Martina Lazlo and her husband was played by Doctor Temple. Lazlo and Temple approached the piano and Amfortas said, 'Leave him alone, Miss Ilse.' Then Temple said, 'Shoot him' and Lazlo took a scalpel from her purse and stabbed Amfortas in the heart. Suddenly Kinderman was in the movie. He was sitting at a table with Humphrey Bogart. 'The letters of transit are forged,' said Bogart. 'Yes, I know,' said Kinderman. He asked Bogart whether Max, his brother, was involved, and Bogart shrugged his shoulders and said, 'This is Rick's.' 'Yes, everyone comes here,' said Kinderman, nodding; 'I've seen this picture twenty times.' 'Couldn't hurt,' said Bogart. Then Kinderman experienced a feeling of panic because he had forgotten the rest of his lines, and he began a discussion of the problem of evil and gave Bogart a summary of his theory. In the dream it took a fraction of a second. 'Yes, Ugarte,' said Bogart, 'I do have more respect for you now.' Then Bogart began a discussion of Christ. 'You left him out of your theory,' he said; 'the German couriers will find out about that.' 'No, no, I include him,' said Kinderman quickly. Abruptly Bogart became Father Dyer, and Amfortas and Miss Lazlo were sitting at the table, although now she was young and extremely beautiful. Dyer was hearing the neurologist's confession, and when he gave the absolution Lazlo gave Amfortas a single white rose. 'And I said I'd never leave you,' she told him. 'Go and live no more,' said Dyer.

Instantaneously, Kinderman was back in the audience and he knew that he was dreaming. The screen had grown larger, filling his vision, and in place of *Casablanca* he saw two lights against a pale green wash of endless void. The light at the left was large and coruscating, flashing with a bluish radiance. Far to its right was a small white sphere that glowed with the brilliance and power of suns, yet it did not blind or flare; it was serene. Kinderman experienced a sense of transcendence. In his mind he heard the light on the left begin to speak. 'I cannot help loving you,' it said. The other light made no answer. There was a pause. 'That is what I am,' the first light continued. 'Pure love. I want to give you love freely,' it said. Again there was no answer from the brilliant sphere. Then at last the first light spoke again. 'I want to create myself,' it said.

The sphere then spoke. 'There will be pain,' it said.

'I know.'

'You do not understand what it is.'

'I choose it,' said the bluish light. Then it waited, quietly flickering. Many more moments passed before the white light spoke again. 'I will send Someone to you,' it said.

'No, you mustn't. You must not interfere.'

'He will be a part of you,' said the sphere.

The bluish light drew inward upon itself. Its flarings were muted and minute. Then at last it expanded again. 'So be it.'

Now the silence was longer, much stiller than before. There was a heaviness about it.

At last the white light spoke quietly. 'Let time begin,' it said.

The bluish light flared up and danced in colours, and then slowly it steadied to its state of before. For a time there was silence. Then the bluish light spoke softly and sadly. 'Goodbye. I will return to you.'

'Hasten the day.'

The bluish light began to coruscate wildly now. It grew larger and more radiant and beautiful than ever. Then it slowly compacted, until it was almost the size of the sphere. There it seemed to linger for a moment. 'I love you,' it said. The next instant it exploded into far-flinging brilliance, hurtling outward from itself with unthinkable force in a trillion shards of staggering energies of light and shattering sound.

Kinderman bolted awake. He sat upright in bed and felt at his forehead. It was bathed in perspiration. He could still feel the light of the explosion on his retinas. He sat there and thought for a while. Was it real? The dream had seemed so. Not even the dream about Max had this texture. He didn't think about the portion of the dream in the cinema. The other segment blotted it out.

He got out of bed and went down to the kitchen where he put on the light and squinted at the pendulum clock on the wall. *Ten after four? This is craziness*, he thought. *Frank Sinatra is just now going to sleep.* Yet he felt awake and extremely refreshed. He put the tea kettle on and stood by the stove. He had to watch it and catch it before it whistled. Shirley might come down. While he waited, he thought about his dream of the lights. It had affected him deeply. What was this emotion he was feeling? he wondered. It was something like poignance and unbearable loss. He had felt it at the ending of *Brief Encounter*. He reflected on the book about Satan that he'd read, the book written by the Desert Fathers, French Carmelites. Satan's beauty and perfection were described as breathtaking. 'Bearer of light.' 'The Morning Star'. God must have loved him very much. Then how could he have damned him for all of eternity?

He felt at the kettle. Just warm. A few more minutes. He thought about Lucifer again, that being of unthinkable radiance. The Catholics said his nature was changeless. *And so?* Could he really have brought sickness and death to the world? Be the author of nightmarish evil and cruelty? It didn't make sense. Even old Rockefeller had handed out dimes now and then. He thought of the gospels, all those people possessed. By what? Not fallen angels, he thought. *Only goyim mix up devils with dybbuks. It's a joke. These were dead people trying to make a comeback. Cassius Clay can do it endlessly but not a poor dead tailor?* Satan didn't run around invading bodies; not even the gospels said that, reflected Kinderman. *Oh, yes, Jesus made a joke about it once*, he conceded. The apostles had just come to him, breathless and full of themselves with their successes in casting out demons. Jesus nodded and kept a straight face as he told them, 'Yes, I saw Satan falling like lightning from heaven.' It was a wryness, a gentle little pulling of the leg. But why 'lightning'? wondered Kinderman. Why 'Prince of this world'?

A few minutes later, he made a cup of tea and took it up to his den. He closed the door softly, felt his way to the desk, and then turned on the light and sat down. He read the file.

The Gemini killings were confined to San Francisco and had spanned a range of seven years from 1964 to 1971, when the Gemini was killed by a rain of bullets while climbing a girder of the Golden Gate Bridge, where the police had entrapped him after countless failed attempts. While he lived, he was charged with twenty-six murders, each one savage and involving mutilations. The victims were of random sex and age, and were sometimes children, and the city lived in terror, even though Gemini's identity was known. The Gemini had offered it himself in a letter to the *San Francisco Chronicle* immediately after the first of his murders. He was James Michael Vennamun, the thirty-year-old son of a noted evangelist whose meetings had been televised nationally every Sunday night at ten o'clock. But the Gemini, in spite of this, could not be found, even with the help of the evangelist, who retired from public view in 1967. When finally killed, the Gemini's body fell into the river, and though days of dredging had failed to turn it up there was little doubt about his death. A fusillade of hundreds of bullets hit his body. And the murders then ceased.

Kinderman quietly turned the page. This section concerned the mutilations. Abruptly he stopped and stared at a paragraph. The hairs on his neck prickled up. *Could this be?* he thought. *My God, it couldn't!* And yet there it was. He looked up and breathed and thought for a while. Then he went on.

He came to the psychiatric profile, based largely on the Gemini's rambling letters, as well as a diary he'd kept in his youth. The Gemini's brother, Thomas, was a twin. He was mentally retarded and lived in a trembling terror of darkness. He slept with a light on. The father, divorced, took little care of the boys, and it was James who parented and cared for Thomas.

Kinderman was soon absorbed in the story.

With vacant, meek eyes Thomas sat at a table while James made more pancakes for him. Karl Vennamun lurched into the kitchen clad only in pyjama bottoms. He was drunk. He was carrying a shot glass and a bottle of whisky and that was almost drained. He looked at James blearily. 'What are you doing?' he demanded harshly.

'Fixing Tommy more pancakes,' said James. He was walking past his father with a plateful when Vennamun savagely struck his face with the back of his hand and knocked him to the floor. 'I can see that, you snotty little bastard,' snarled Vennamum. 'I said no food for him today! He dirtied his pants!'

'He can't help it!' James protested. Vennamun kicked him in the stomach, then advanced on Thomas, who was shaking with fear. 'And you! You were told not to eat! Didn't you hear me?' There were dishes of food on the table, and Vennamun swept them to the floor with his hand. 'You little ape, you'll learn obedience and cleanliness, damn you!' The evangelist pulled the boy uprig'.t with his hands and began to drag him towards a door that led outside. Along the way, he cuffed him. 'You're like your mother! You're filth. You're a filthy Catholic bastard.'

Vennamun dragged the boy outside and to the doors of the cellar. The day was bright on the hills of the wooded Reyes Peninsula. Vennamun pulled open a cellar door. 'You're going down in the cellar with the rats, goddamn you!'

Thomas started trembling and his large, doe-eyes were shining with fright. He cried, 'No! No, don't put me in the dark! Papa, please! Please, –'

Vennamun slapped his face and then hurled him down the stairs. Thomas cried out, 'Jim! Jim!'

The cellar door was closed and bolted. 'Yeah, the rats'll keep him busy,' snarled Vennamun drunkenly.

The terrified screaming began.

Later, Vennamun tied his son James to a chair, and then sat and watched television and drank. At last he fell asleep. But James heard the shrieking throughout the night.

By daybreak, there was silence. Vennamun awakened, untied James, and then went outside and opened the cellar. 'You can come out now,' he shouted down the darkness. He got no reply. Vennamun watched as James ran down the stairs. Then he heard someone *weeping. Not Thomas. James. He knew that his brother's mind was gone.*

Thomas was permanently institutionalized in the San Francisco State Mental Hospital. James saw him whenever he could, and at the age of sixteen ran away from home and went to work as a packing boy in San Francisco. Each evening he went to visit Thomas. He would hold his hand and read children's storybooks to him. He would stay with him until he was asleep. This went on until one evening in 1964. It was a Saturday. James had been with Thomas all day.

It was nine p.m. Thomas was in bed. James was in a chair at his bedside, close to him, while a doctor checked Thomas's heart. He removed the stethoscope from his ears and smiled at James. 'Your brother's doing just fine.'

A nurse put her head in the door and spoke to James. 'Sir, I'm sorry, but visiting hours are over.'

The doctor motioned James to remain in his chair, and then walked to the door. 'Let me speak to you a moment, Miss Keach. No, out here in the hall.' They stepped outside. 'It's your first day here, Miss Keach?'

'Yes, it is.'

'Well, I hope you're going to like it here,' said the doctor.

'I'm sure I will.'

'The young man with Tom Vennamun is his brother. I'm sure you couldn't miss it.'

'Yes, I noticed,' said Keach.

'For years he's come faithfully every night. We allow him to stay until his brother falls asleep. Sometimes he stays the whole night. It's all right. It's a special case,' said the doctor.

'Oh, I see.'

'And, look, the lamp in his room. The boy is terrified of darkness. Pathologically. Never turn it off. I'm afraid of his heart. It's terribly weak.'

'I'll remember,' said the nurse. She smiled.

The doctor smiled back. 'Well, I'll see you tomorrow, then. Goodnight.'

'Goodnight, Doctor.' Nurse Keach watched him walk down the

hall, and her smile immediately turned down to a scowl. She shook her head and muttered, 'Dumb.'

In the room, James gripped his brother's hand. He had the storybook in front of him, but knew all the words; he had said them a thousand times before: '"Goodnight little house and goodnight mouse. Goodnight comb and goodnight brush. Goodnight nobody. Goodnight mush. And goodnight to the old lady whispering 'hush'. Goodnight stars. Goodnight air. Goodnight noises everywhere."' Weary, James closed his eyes for a moment. Then he looked to see if Thomas was asleep. He wasn't. He was staring up at the ceiling. James saw a tear rolling down from his eye. Thomas stammered. 'I l-l-l-love you, J-j-j-james.'

'I love you, Tom,' his brother said softly. Thomas closed his eyes and was soon asleep.

After James left the hospital, Nurse Keach walked past the room. She stopped and came back. She looked in. She saw Thomas alone and asleep. She came into the room, turned off the lamp, and then closed the door behind her when she left. 'A special case,' she muttered. She returned to her office and her charts.

In the middle of the night, a shriek of terror sounded in the hospital. Thomas had awakened. The shrieks continued for several minutes. Then the silence was abrupt. Thomas Vennamun was dead.

And the Gemini Killer was born.

Kinderman looked up at a window. It was dawn. He felt strangely moved by what he had read. Could he have pity for such a monster? He thought again of the mutilations. Vennamun's logo had been God's finger touching Adam's; thus always the severing of the index finger. And there was always the 'K' at the start of one of the victims' names. Vennamun, Karl.

He finished reading the report: 'Subsequent killings of initial 'K' victims indicate proxy murders of the father, whose eventual dropout from public life suggests the Gemini's secondary motive, specifically destruction of the father's career and reputation by way of connection with the Gemini's crimes.'

Kinderman stared at the file's last page. He removed his

glasses and looked again. He blinked. He didn't know what to make of it.

He jumped just as the telephone rang. 'Yes, Kinderman here,' he said softly. He looked at the time and felt afraid. He heard Atkins' voice. Then he didn't. Only buzzings. He felt cold and numb and sick to his soul.

Father Dyer had been murdered.

PART TWO

The greatest event in the history of the Earth, now taking place, may indeed be the gradual discovery, by those with eyes to see, not merely of Some Thing *but of* Some One *at the peak created by the convergence of the evolving Universe upon itself.*

There is only one Evil: Disunity.

Pierre Teilhard de Chardin

WEDNESDAY, MARCH 18

Chapter Nine

———

Wednesday, March 18

Dear Father Dyer,

Soon you may be asking yourself, 'Why me? Why does a stranger place this burden in *my* hands rather than in those of his colleagues who are scientists and surely better suited to the task?' Well, they aren't better suited. Science leans to these matters like a child to his medicine. I would guess that you'll be sceptical about it yourself. 'Another nut with a weeping statue of Jesus that cries real tears,' you'll probably say. 'Just because I'm a priest, he must think I'll swallow any old miraculous cow, and in this case a purple one at that.' Well, I really don't think that at all. I'm putting this on you because I can trust you. Not your priesthood, Father – *you*. If you were planning to betray me, you already would have done it. But you haven't. You've kept your word. That's really something. When we spoke, it wasn't under the seal of the confessional. Any other priest – any other person – would probably have blown the whistle on me. But before I laid my burden upon you, I gauged you. I'm so sorry your reward is yet another obligation. But I know you'll follow through. That's the thing of it. You'll do it. Aren't you glad that you met me, Father?

I don't quite know how to do this. It's awkward as hell. I

want so much for you to trust in my judgement, to believe me. I'm afraid that won't be easy. What I'm going to be saying will make you cringe. So let's go about it this way, please: it might be best. Just suspend your curiosity for a while and read no further until after you have followed these few instructions, which I'm now about to give you. First, get your hands on a reel-to-reel tape recorder, one with controls that allow for rapid replay. Better yet, use mine. I'll Scotch-tape a key to my house to this letter. Now look in the cardboard box that I've sent you. It contains a few reel-to-reel recordings that I've made. Find the one marked 'January 9, 1982'. Thread it onto the recorder. The footage counter has to be resting at zero when the end of the leader hits the capstan at the left. When this is done, fast-forward to 383, then plug in the earphones, set the volume controls to maximum (not the Output, only Microphone and Line), and set the speed at Low. Then push 'Play' and listen. You're going to hear amplifier hiss and static at uncomfortable levels. Please bear with it. Then shortly you will hear the sound of somebody speaking. It ends at 388 on the counter. Keep playing and replaying the section with the voice until you're sure that you know what's being said. It's fairly loud, but the static tends to blur intelligibility. When you know what's being said, set the speed at High – which is double – and repeat the procedure. That's right. I want you to repeat the procedure. Forget what you heard the first time. Listen again. Please follow these instructions and do not read further until you have done so.

Though I trust you, this continues on a separate page. We all need the help of grace now and then.

Now you've listened. What you heard at the slower speed, I'm sure, is a clear male voice saying, 'Lacey'. And at the faster speed, the same information on the tape becomes the equally distinct words, 'Hope it'. Now here you must take the leap of faith and of common sense that I have nothing to gain by misrepresenting. And now I will tell you how I made that tape. I put a blank reel of tape – unused – on the recorder, plugged in a diode (it screens out all sound from the room or the environment, yet acts like a microphone of sorts); I set the speed to Low, said out loud 'Does God exist?', set the Microphone and Line to the highest settings, and then pushed the buttons for recording. For the next three minutes, I did nothing at all but breathe and wait. Then I stopped recording. When I played back the tape, the voice was there.

I sent the tape to a friend at Columbia University. He ran it through a spectrograph for me. He sent me a letter and some copies of the spectrographic readings. You'll find them in the box. The letter says the spectrographic analysis concludes that the voice cannot possibly be human; that to get that effect you would have to construct an artificial larynx and then have it programmed to say those words. My friend says the spectrograph can't be wrong. Furthermore, he couldn't understand how a word like 'Lacey' transmuted into 'Hope it' at twice the speed. Note also – and this is my comment, not his – that the answer to my question is unresponsive, if not totally meaningless, unless it is played at twice the speed of the original recording. That rules out any freak sort of radio reception – which tape recorders cannot do anyway, Father – that might be invoked as an explanation, along with coincidence. You will doubtless want to satisfy yourself on these matters; in fact, I urge you very strongly to do so. My friend at Columbia is Professor Cyril Harris. Call him. Better yet, get a second opinion, another spectrographic analysis, preferably done by someone else. I am certain you will find that the result is the same.

I started making these recordings a few months after the death of Ann. There is a patient in the psychiatric ward of the hospital, a schizophrenic named Anton Lang. Please don't talk to him about this; he has very real problems which will only tend to lessen the phenomenon's credibility, along with mine, I would have to suppose. Lang had complained of a chronic headache, which caused me to come into contact with him. I, of course, read his history, and found that for years he'd been making tape recordings of what he characterized simply as 'the voices'. I asked him about them, and he told me some things that were intriguing and suggested that I read a book on the subject. The title was *Breakthrough*. It was written by a Latvian, Konstantin Raudieve, and is available in English through a British publisher. I ordered a copy and read it. Are you with me so far?

Most of the book consisted of Raudieve's transcriptions of voice recordings, I fear. They were trifling and inane. If these were the voices of the dead, as this Latvian professor was convinced that they were, was this really all that they had to tell us? 'Kosti is tired today.' 'Kosti works.' 'Here there are customs at the border.' 'We sleep.' It put me in mind of the ancient *Tibetan Book of the Dead*. Do you know it, Father? It's a curious work, a manual of instructions preparing the dying for what they would face on the other side. The first experience, they believed, was a decisive and immediate confrontation with transcendence, which they called 'The Clear Light'. The newly dead spirit could opt to join with it; but few did, because most were not ready, for their earthly lives had not properly prepared them; and so far after this initial confrontation, the dead went through stages of deterioration as they dwindled towards eventual rebirth into the world. Such a state, it struck me, might produce the inanities and banalities recorded not only in Raudieve's book, but also in most of the spiritualist literature. It's pretty sickening, discouraging stuff. And so, to say the least, I wasn't exactly thrilled by *Breakthrough*. But it had a preface by another author named Colin Smythe, and this I found to be quite understated and credible. So were various testimonials written by physicists, engineers and even a Catholic archbishop from Germany, who had all made recordings of their own and who seemed not so anxious to proselytize the reader as they were to speculate on the causes of the voices, considering, among other things, the possibility that the voices were imprinted on the tape in some way by the experimenter's unconscious.

I decided to try it. Let's face it, I was crazy with grief over Ann. I own a little Sony portable recorder. It's small enough to stuff in the pocket of a coat, but you can rapidly reverse and replay with this model, something I was soon to discover was important. One evening – it was summer and still quite light out – I sat down in my living room with the Sony, and invited any voices who could hear me to communicate and manifest themselves on the tape. Then I pushed 'Record' and let the blank cassette run from start to end. Then I replayed it. I heard nothing except for some noise in the street, and some loud static and amplifier sounds. I then forgot the whole thing.

A day or two later I decided to listen to the tape again. Somewhere in the middle I heard something anomalous, a little *click* and then a faint, odd sound that was barely audible; it seemed embedded in the hissing and the static, if not at some level underneath those sounds. But it struck me as something that was – well – a little curious. So I went back to that spot and kept playing it over and over. With each repetition, the sound grew louder and more distinct until finally I heard – or thought I heard – a clear male voice shouting my name. 'Amfortas.' Just that. It was loud and distinct and not a voice that I recognized. I think my heart began to race a little bit. I went through the rest of the tape and heard nothing, then returned to the spot where I'd heard the voice. But now I couldn't hear it. My hopes fell away like a poor man's wallet falling over a cliff. I began to replay the section repeatedly again, and then again heard the faint odd sound. About three repetitions after that, I could hear the voice clearly again.

Was my mind playing tricks? Was I superimposing intelligibility onto scraps of random noise? I played more of the tape and now, where I hadn't heard a thing before, another voice popped out at me. It was a woman. No, not Ann. Just a woman. She was speaking a rather long sentence, the first part of which, even after many repetitions, I was simply unable to understand. The whole thing had a very odd pitch and rhythm, and the accents on the words were not where they belonged. The words also had a very lilting effect; they valleyed, then continuously ascended. The latter was the portion I could understand: 'Continue to hear us,' the woman was saying; but because of the lilt, it sounded like a question. I was simply astonished. There wasn't any doubt that I was hearing it. But why hadn't I heard it before? I decided that my brain had probably accommodated to the faintness of the voice and its oddities, and had learned how to knife through the veil of static and hiss to the voice just beneath it.

Now doubts set in again. Had my tape recorder simply picked up voices from the street, or perhaps from next door? There were times when I could hear my neighbours talking. One of them might have mentioned my name. I went into the kitchen which is a little more removed from the street, and I made a new recording with a fresh cassette. I asked aloud that anyone 'communicating' with me repeat the word 'Kirios', which had been my mother's maiden name. But on playback I heard nothing, just the usual odd sound here and there. One of them resembled the sudden braking of automobile tyres. No doubt from the street, I thought. I was tired. Listening had taken intense concentration. I did no more recording that night.

The following morning, while waiting for the water to boil for coffee, I listened again to both the tapes. 'Continue to hear us' and 'Amfortas' I heard quite clearly. On the second tape, I focused on the braking sound, replaying it again and again, and suddenly my brain made a strange accommodation, for instead of the noise I heard the words 'Anna Kirios' spoken in the high-pitched voice of a woman with a rapid-fire speed. I let the water for the coffee boil over. I was stunned.

When I went to the hospital that day I brought along the tapes and the tape recorder, and over the lunch break I played the key selections for one of the nurses, Emily Allerton. She didn't hear anything, she told me. Later I tried it on Amy Keating, one of the Charge Desk nurses in Neurology. I keyed to a selection from tape number one and she held the speaker pressed close against her ear. After just one playing, she handed me the tape recorder and nodded. 'Yes, I hear your name,' she said, and then returned to whatever she'd been doing. I decided to rest the matter at that; at least with the nurses.

Over the following weeks, I was obsessed. I bought a reel-to-reel tape recorder, a pre-amplifier and earphones, and I began to spend hours each night making tapes. And now it seemed that I never failed to get a result. In fact, the tapes were virtually filled with voices in an almost continuous, even overlapping stream. Some were too faint to even bother deciphering, while others had varying degrees of clarity. Some were at normal speed, while others were intelligible only when I slowed them down to half speed. Some were not even apparent until I'd done this. I kept asking for Ann, but I never heard her. Now and then I'd hear a woman's voice saying, 'I'm here,' or 'I'm Ann'. But it wasn't. It wasn't her voice.

One night in October I was listening to a playback of a tape that I'd made the week before. It had an interesting fragment on it, a voice saying, 'Earth control'. After several repetitions I went a little past it, and then suddenly I caught my breath. I heard a voice saying, 'Vincent, this is Ann'. I felt a tingling from the base of my spine up to my neck. It wasn't just my mind saying this was her voice; it was my body and my blood; my memories; my being; my unconscious mind. I played and replayed it, and each time I felt that same tingling, like a thrilling. I even tried to suppress it, but I couldn't. It was Ann.

The next morning my hopes and my doubts were inseparable. Wasn't this voice a projection of my wish?

Intelligibility superimposed over random noises indigenous to tape? I decided now to settle this matter decisively.

I consulted Eddie Flanders, an instructor at the Georgetown Institute of Languages, and a friend who had once been my patient. God knows what I told him, but I got him to listen to the voice of Ann. When he took off the earphones, I asked what he'd heard. He said, 'Somebody's talking. But it's really so faint.' I said, 'What are they saying? Can you make it out?' He said, 'It sounds like my name.'

I took the earphones away from Ed and ascertained he was listening to the proper section. Then I had him listen to it again. The result was the same. I was utterly baffled. 'But it is a voice,' I asked him, 'not just noise?' 'No, it's clearly a voice,' he said. 'Isn't it yours?' 'You hear the voice of a man?' I asked. He said, 'Yes. It sounds like you.' That more or less ended my research that day. But the week after that I came back. The Institute maintained its own recording studio for the making of instructional tapes. They had powerful amplifiers and professional Ampex recorders. They also had a microphone that was installed in a soundproof booth. I prevailed upon Eddie to help me make a recording. I went into the booth, turned away from Eddie's view while I made my little speech inviting the voices to manifest on tape. I also asked two direct questions, requesting as replies the words 'affirmative' or 'negative', as these would be easier to detect on playback than merely a simple 'yes' or 'no'. Then I left the booth and closed the booth door behind me and signalled Eddie to turn on the tape and begin to record. He said, 'What are we recording?' I said, 'Molecules of air. It has to do with some studies of the brain that I'm doing.' Eddie seemed satisfied and we recorded at maximum gain and at a speed of $7\frac{1}{2}$ i.p.s. After three minutes or so we stopped and listened to the playback at maximum gain. Something rather odd was on the tape. It wasn't quite a voice. It was more of a gurgling sound and approximately ten times louder than any of the voices I thought I was hearing on my home recordings. Its approximate duration was seven seconds. We could hear nothing else on the rest of the tape. 'Is that a normal sort of noise you get at times when you're taping?' I asked. I was thinking of sound propagation by something within the equipment itself. Ed said, no, that couldn't be. He seemed genuinely puzzled and he told me that the sound should not be there. I suggested a defect in the tape. He thought possibly this was so. After minutes of replaying the sound, we thought it seemed to have something of the quality of a voice. We couldn't come close to making out its sense. We called it a day.

I went on with my experiments at home and continued to hear the soft, fleet voices either answering my questions or taking my cue for topics of discussion, though I never again heard a voice like Ann's. From all this, I formed the following impressions. I seemed to be in touch with personalities in some place or condition of transition. They were not clairvoyant. They did not know the future, for example; but their knowledge extended past the scope of my own. They could tell me, for example, the name of the duty nurse at any moment on some ward with which I had no contact or familiarity. They often had opinions that were contradictory to one another's. Sometimes when I asked a factual question, such as the date of my mother's birth, they gave several answers, none of them correct, and gave me the impression, perhaps, of not wanting to lose my interest. A few of their statements were flatout lies of a trouble-making nature, or designed to upset me, I would think. I came to recognize these voices and ignored them, as I did with the occasional speaker of obscenities. Some voices asked for help, but when I asked – and many times – what it was that I could do to help them, the answer was usually something like, 'Happy. We're fine.' Some asked me to pray for them, and still others said they prayed for me. I couldn't help thinking of the Communion of Saints.

A sense of humour was in evidence. Early on in the experiments I wore an old bathrobe one night as I was taping. It had gaudy-coloured stripes and a very large tear around the upper right shoulder. I heard a voice saying, 'Horse-blanket'. Among the numerous occasions when I asked, 'Who created the material universe?', once a voice answered clearly, 'Me'. And one night I'd invited an intern over to join me in an experiment. He'd expressed an interest in psychic phenomena and I felt comfortable discussing this with him. Through the evening, he told me that he couldn't hear a thing, although, as usual, I did. I heard 'What's the use?', 'Why bother?' and 'Go play Pac-Man', among other things. I learned weeks later that the intern was terribly hard of hearing, but didn't want it known.

The voices helped me at times by suggesting other modes of recording. One was the use of a diode, and the other was to find a band of 'white noise' – the space between stations – on a radio receiver and connect this to the tape recorder. The latter I never tried as here one would expect to receive and record actual radio voices from ordinary sources. The microphone was best when in a soundproof or extremely quiet room; but I finally opted for the use of the diode, for this ruled out misinterpretation of ordinary sounds from the surrounding environment.

Sometimes the voices criticized my technical abilities. I would have a wrong button pushed in now and then and I was apt to get a voice saying, 'You don't know what you're doing.' (That particular one sounded exasperated. I was tired and had been making miscues throughout the session.) Such responses were a part of what gave me the impression that I was dealing with personalities that were highly individual and quite ordinary. Just like people. They often said 'Goodnight' toward the end of the tape, and then I'd find that I was tired and headed for bed. On occasion there were many 'Thanks' and 'Thank you's' from different voices. One curious thing. Once I asked if it was important that I try to promulgate this phenomenon, and the answer was a very clear, 'Negative'. That surprised me.

In mid-1982 I decided to write to Colin Smythe, the man who had written the preface for *Breakthrough*. He's the one who seemed so credible. I asked him a number of questions and he answered me immediately, referring me to a book of his own that he had written on the subject. (It's called *Carry on Talking*.) In his letter he seemed reticent about the subject, as inevitably, especially in the London press, it had become overblown and somewhat lurid. People were claiming to have talked to John F. Kennedy and Freud and that sort of thing. But he told me something fascinating. A group of neurologists from Edinburgh, while in London for a medical conference, had looked him up and played for him tape recordings of their own. They had made them in the presence of people in coma, or with incapacitating injuries which prevented them from speaking; and on the tapes were the voices of these patients.

Not long after that, I took my portable Sony recorder to the hospital. It was two or three AM and I went to the Disturbed Ward where I made a recording of a patient who was severely catatonic, an amnesiac who'd been in Psychiatric for years. None of us had ever known his actual identity. The police had picked him up wandering 'M' Street in a daze around 1970 or so, and he hadn't said a single word since that time. Although maybe he has. In his room, I turned on the tape recorder having asked him who he was and whether he could hear me. I let the tape run its entire length. Once back home, I played it back. The result was very odd. First of all, in that entire half hour of tape there were only two fragments of speech that I could hear. Ordinarily, the tape would be literally jammed with them, even though most might be just barely audible. This time – except for the two that I mentioned – the silence was exceptional and very strange. The other odd thing – well, I'd say 'eerie' is probably more like it – were the voices on the tape. They were both the same person, a man, and I felt virtually certain that I was hearing the voice of the catatonic patient. I thought I heard it saying, 'I'm beginning to remember.' That was the first thing. Then I heard what I presumed was the patient's name in answer to the question that I'd asked about that; something close to 'James Vennerman', as I recall. I didn't like the sound of it for some reason and I never attempted this experiment again.

Toward the end of the last year a decisive event occurred. Up until then I was still in doubt about what I was hearing. That rapidly changed. I traded in my tape recorder for a Revox with a built-in variable pitch control. I also got a band pass filter, which excluded all frequencies of sound that were not within the range of the human voice. On a Saturday a rather young man from the stereo shop delivered the new equipment and wired it up. When he had finished, I had a thought. The young have almost vastly better hearing than we, and this youngster's business, after all, was sound. So I brought out the tape with the rather loud rumbling sound and I asked him to listen through the earphones. When he had finished, I asked him what he'd heard. He said immediately, 'Somebody talking.' This took me by surprise. 'Is the voice a man's or a woman's?' I asked him. He answered, 'A man's.' 'Can you tell what he's saying?' He said, 'No, it's too slow.' Another surprise. I was accustomed to the voices being too fast. 'No, you mean too fast,' I said. 'No, slow. At least I *think* it's too slow.' He put the earphones back on, rewound the tape to the spot, and then manually speeded up the tape with his hands as he listened to the playback. Then he took off the earphones and nodded. 'Yeah, too slow.' He handed me the earphones. 'Here, you listen,' he said, 'and I'll show you.' I put on the earphones and listened as he once again speeded up the tape. And I heard the distinct, loud voice of a man say the words, 'Affirmative. Can you hear me?'

This experience seemed to open a door, for not long after that I began to get some clear, loud voices on my tapes, perhaps one in every three or four sessions of taping. 'Lacey/Hope it' was the first of these. Even that intern could probably hear them.

Three of them I sent to my friend at Columbia, with the results of which I've already told you. Listen to them. Then make tapes of your own. You may fail at first and get only the fainter, more emphemeral voices. If so, and if you haven't learned the trick of how to listen, of knifing through the veil of hiss and static, then take my louder tapes and build a case from them. They must first be cleaned up. There is equipment available that will remove all the static and the hiss. After that, run them through another spectrographic analysis. There is also a way of determining the original speed at which they were recorded. This, as I stressed, will absolutely rule out freak radio reception as an explanation.

The voices are real. I believe they are the voices of the dead. This can never be proved; but that they emanate from intellects without bodies – at least as we know them – can be forcefully and scientifically demonstrated. The Catholic Church has the means – and God knows, should have the interest – in developing a scientific body of proof that these voices exist, have no earthly source, defy a materialistic explanation, and can be replicated time and again in a laboratory by hard-headed men and machines.

There was that voice that said it wasn't important to do this. But not important for whom? I have to wonder. The men of the earth cry out against death and the terror of a final extinction and oblivion; they weep through the nights with each loss of a loved one. Must faith be enough to rid us ever of this anguish? Can it be enough?

These tapes are my prayer for those who mourn. They may prove no more than a hand in Christ's side, not enough to overcome that final doubt, just as the raising of Lazarus failed to convince even some who were there and had seen it with their eyes. But what is it that Jesus asks us to do? If our cup for the thirsty isn't full to the brim are we then to withold it? If God cannot intervene, men can. It is surely His intention that we should. This is our world.

Thank you for not telling me that my decision is the sin of despair. I know that it is not. I do nothing. I only wait. Maybe in your heart you really thought it was wrong. But you didn't say so. I can have a good parting.

In the days to come, you may hear some very strange things about me. I dread that possibility, but should it ever come to pass, please know that I have never meant harm to anyone. Think the best of me, Father, won't you?

How long have I known you? Two days? Well, I shall miss you. Yet I know that I will see you again someday. When you read this, I will be with my Ann. Please be glad.

With respect and affection,
    Vincent Amfortas

Amfortas looked over the letter. He made a few small corrections, then he checked the time and decided he had best have a steroid injection. He had learned not to wait for the headaches to come. Now every six hours he would take six milligrams automatically. Soon it would alter his mind. He'd had to write the letter now.

He went up to the bedroom in the early morning light, took the shot, and then came back to the typewriter where it was resting on the breakfast nook table. He consulted some notes and then decided he should add a postscript to the letter:

'P.S.,' he typed. 'In the many, many months that I've been making these recordings, I have time and again asked the question, "Describe your condition, state of being or location as concisely as you can." A few times I've been able to elicit an answer, at least an answer I was able to hear, and since substantive questions like this are so often evaded by the voices, I thought you might like to know what answers I've gotten.

They are as follows:

We come here first.
Here one waits.
Limbo.
Dead.
It's like a ship.
It's like a hospital.
Doctor angels.

I also asked, "What should we the living be doing?" and one answer that I heard rather clearly was "Good works". It sounded like a woman.'

   Amfortas drew the letter out of the typewriter, and slipped in an envelope in its place. On the front of it he typed:

Rev. Joseph Dyer, S. J.
Georgetown University
To be delivered in the event of my death.

Chapter Ten

Kinderman approached the hospital entrance, his pace growing slower with every step. When he reached the doors he turned around and looked up at the drizzling sky for a moment, searching for a dawn that he'd somehow misplaced; but there were only the flashing red lights of the squad cars turning implacably and in silence, splashing the dark, wet slick of the streets.

Kinderman felt that he was walking in a dream. He couldn't feel his body. The world was an edge. When he noticed the television news team arriving, he quickly turned around and walked into the hospital. He rode the elevator up to Neurology and stepped off into quiet chaos. Newsmen. Cameras. Uniformed policemen. By the Charge Desk there were curious interns and residents, most of them assigned to some other ward. In the hallways there were patients, robed and frightened: some of the nurses were reassuring them, easing and cajoling them back to their rooms.

Kinderman looked around. Opposite the Charge Desk, a uniformed policeman stood guarding the door to Dyer's room. Atkins was there. He was listening as newspeople pummeled him with questions, their stridencies blending together into noise. Atkins kept shaking his head, saying nothing. Kinderman approached him. Atkins saw him coming and met his gaze. The sergeant looked stricken. Kinderman leaned in close to his ear. 'Atkins, get these reporters down to the lobby,' he said; then he squeezed the sergeant's arm and for a fraction of an instant looked into his eyes in a momentary sharing of his pain. He allowed himself no more. He went into Dyer's room and closed the door.

The sergeant beckoned to a group of policemen. 'Get these

people downstairs!' he called out to them sharply. An outcry of protest arose from the reporters. 'You're disturbing the patients,' said Atkins. There were groans. The policemen started herding the reporters away. Atkins sauntered to the Charge Desk and leaned his back against it. He folded his arms. His haunted eyes were fixed on the door to Dyer's room. Beyond it lay a horror that was unimaginable. His mind could not fully grasp it.

Stedman and Ryan emerged from the room. They looked drawn and pale. Ryan's gaze was on the floor and he never looked up as he hastened away and down the hall. He turned a corner by the Charge Desk and soon was out of sight. Stedman had been watching him. Now he turned his gaze to Atkins. 'Kinderman wants to be alone,' he said. His voice had a hollow sound.

Atkins nodded.

'Do you smoke?' Stedman asked him.

'No.'

'I don't either. But I'd like a cigarette,' said Stedman. He averted his head for a moment, thinking. When he lifted a hand to his eyes and examined it, he saw that it was trembling. 'Jesus Christ,' he said softly. The trembling grew stronger. Suddenly the hand stabbed into a pocket and Stedman was swiftly walking away. He was following the direction that Ryan had taken. Atkins could still hear him murmuring, 'Jesus! Jesus! Jesus Christ!' Somewhere a buzzer sounded. A patient was summoning a nurse.

'Sergeant?'

Atkins shifted his gaze. The policeman at the door was staring at him oddly, 'Yes, what is it?' Atkins answered.

'What the hell is going on here, Sergeant?'

'I don't know.'

Atkins heard some arguing coming from his right. He looked and saw a television news team confronting two policemen close to the elevators. Atkins recognized an anchorman from the local six o'clock news. His hair was pomaded and his manner was belligerent and obstreperous. The policemen were gradually pushing them back toward the bank of elevators. At one point the anchorman tripped and fell backwards a little, almost losing his balance, then he cursed and gave up and left with the others, pounding a section of rolled up newspaper in his palm.

'Can you tell me who's in charge here, please? I had a notion at one time that it was me.'

Atkins looked to his left and saw a short, slender man in a blue flannel suit. Behind rimmed glasses were small, alert eyes. 'Are you in charge?' asked the man.

'I'm Sergeant Atkins, sir. Can I help you?'

'I'm Doctor Tench. I'm the Chief of Staff of this hospital, I think,' he said with heat. 'We have a number of patients here in serious to critical condition. All this upset isn't helping them, you know.'

'I understand, sir.'

'I don't want to sound callous,' said Tench, 'but the sooner the deceased is removed, the sooner it will stop. Will that be soon, do you think?'

'Yes, I think so, sir.'

'You understand my position.'

'Yes, I do.'

'Thank you.' Tench walked away with a brisk, officious step.

Atkins noticed it was quieter now. He glanced around and saw the television crew. They were almost gone. The anchorman still slapped at his palm with the paper and was boarding an elevator from which Stedman and Ryan were emerging. They walked towards Atkins with their heads down. Neither said a word. The television anchorman was watching them. 'Hey, what happened in there?' he called out. The elevators doors slid shut.

Atkins heard the door to Dyer's room coming open. He looked and saw Kinderman emerging. The detective's eyes were red and rubbed. He stopped and faced Stedman and Ryan for a moment. 'All right, you can finish,' he said. His voice was cracked and low.

'Lieutenant, I'm sorry,' said Ryan gently. His face and his voice were filled with compassion.

Kinderman nodded, staring down at the floor. He murmured, 'Thank you, Ryan. Yes, thank you.' Then without looking up he hurried away from them. He was headed for the elevators. Atkins caught up with him quickly.

'I'm just going for a walk now, Atkins.'

'Yes, sir.' The sergeant kept walking beside him. As they reached the elevators, one opened. It was going down. Atkins and Kinderman stepped in and turned around.

'Guess we picked the right elevator, Chick,' said a voice.

Atkins heard machinery running. His head spun around. The television anchorman was grinning while a camera churned in another man's hands. 'Was the priest decapitated?' asked the anchorman, 'or was he –?'

Atkins' fist smashed into his jaw and the anchorman's head cracked into a wall and rebounded from the fury of the blow. Blood spurted from his lips and he crumpled to the floor, where he lay unconscious. Atkins glared at the cameraman, who quietly lowered the camera. Then the sergeant looked at Kinderman. The detective seemed oblivious. He was staring down into space, his hands plunged deep in the pockets of his coat. Atkins pushed a button and the elevator stopped at the second floor. He took the detective by the arm and led him out. 'Atkins, what are you doing?' asked Kinderman dazedly. He seemed a helpless, confused old man. 'I want to go walking,' he said.

'Yes, we're going, Lieutenant. This way.'

Atkins led him to another wing of the hospital and took an elevator down from there. He wanted to avoid the reporters in the lobby. They walked through more hallways and soon they were standing outside the hospital on the side facing out to the campus of the University. A narrow portico above them sheltered their bodies from the rain; it was coming down harder now and they watched the downpour in silence. In the distance students in raincoats and brightly coloured slickers were walking to breakfast. Two coeds ran laughing out of a dormitory, both holding newspapers over their heads. 'The man was a poem,' said Kinderman softly. Atkins said nothing. He stared at the rain.

'I want to be alone, please, Atkins. Thank you.'

Atkins turned his head to examine the detective. He was staring straight ahead. 'All right, sir,' said the sergeant. He turned and went back inside the hospital, returning at last to the Neurology wing where he started to question possible witnesses. All the staff on the night to morning shift had been asked to remain for that purpose, including the nurses, doctors and attendants from Psychiatric. Some of these were clustered by the desk. While Atkins was talking to the Charge Nurse on duty in Neurology at the time of Dyer's death, a doctor approached him and interrupted with, 'Would you forgive me, please? I'm sorry.' Atkins looked him over. The man seemed shaken. 'I'm Doctor Amfortas,' he said. 'I was treating Father Dyer. Is it true?'

Atkins nodded gravely.

Amfortas stood staring at him for a while, his complexion growing paler, his eyes more withdrawn. Then at last he said, 'Thank you,' and walked away. His steps were unsteady. Atkins watched him, and then turned to the nurse. 'What time does he come on duty?' he asked her.

'He doesn't,' she told him. 'He doesn't do ward work any more.' She was fighting back the tears.

Atkins jotted down a few words in his notebook. He was turning to the nurse again when he looked and saw Kinderman approaching. His hat and coat were soaking wet. He must have been walking in the rain, thought Atkins. Soon he was standing in front of the sergeant. His manner had changed completely. His gaze was firm and clear and determined. 'All right, Atkins, stop loitering around with pretty nurses. This is business, not *Young Detectives In Love*.'

'Nurse Keating was the last one to see him alive,' said Atkins.

'When was that?' the detective asked Keating.

'About half-past four,' she said.

'Nurse Keating, may I speak to you alone?' asked Kinderman. 'I'm sorry, but this has to be done.'

She nodded, and dabbed at her nose with a handkerchief. Kinderman pointed to a glass-enclosed office behind the Charge Desk. 'Perhaps in there?'

Again she nodded. Kinderman followed her into the office. It contained a writing shelf, two chairs and shelves filled with files of various papers. The detective motioned the nurse to be seated, and then closed the door. Through the glass, he saw Atkins quietly watching. 'So you saw Father Dyer at half-past fourish,' he said.

She said, 'Yes.'

'And where did you see him?'

'In his room.'

'And what were you doing there, please?'

'Well, I'd gone back there to tell him that I couldn't find the wine.'

'You said "the wine"?'

'Yes, he'd buzzed me a little bit before and said he needed some bread and wine and did we have some?'

'He wanted to say Mass?'

'Yes, that's right,' said the Nurse. She coloured a little, and then shrugged. 'One or two on the staff – well, they keep some liquor around sometimes.'

'I understand.'

'I looked around in the usual places,' she said. 'Then I went back and told him, "I'm sorry," that I just couldn't find it. But I gave him some bread.'

'And what did he say?'

'I don't remember.'

'Would you tell me your hours, Miss Keating?'

'Ten to six.'

'Every day?'

'When I'm working.'

'And what are your working days, please?'

'I'm on Tuesday through Saturday,' she answered.

'Had Father Dyer said Mass here before?'

'I don't know.'

'But he never before wanted bread and wine.'

'That's correct.'

'Did he tell you why he wanted to say Mass today?'

'No.'

'When you told him that you couldn't find the wine, did he say something?'

'Yes.'

'And what did he say, Miss Keating?'

She needed the handkerchief again, then she paused and appeared to be composing herself. '"You drank it all?", he said.' Her voice cracked, and now her face puckered up into grief. 'He was always making jokes,' she said. She turned away her head and started weeping. Kinderman noticed a box of tissues on one of the shelves, and he pulled out a handful and gave them to her; her handkerchief by now was a crumpled, wet ball. She said, 'Thank you,' and took them. Kinderman waited. 'I'm sorry,' said Keating.

'Never mind. Did Father Dyer tell you anything else at the time?'

The nurse shook her head.

'And when did you see him next?'

'When I found him.'

'When was that?'

'Around ten before six.'

'Between half-past four and ten to six, did you see someone entering Father Dyer's room?'

'No, I didn't.'

'Did you see someone leaving it?'

'No.'

'And at those times, you were opposite the room at this Charge Desk.'

'That's right. I was writing up reports.'

'But you were here the whole time.'

'Well, except for some times when I gave out medication.'

'How long did it take you to give the medication?'

'Oh, a couple of minutes for each, I would guess.'

'What rooms?'

'418, 420 and 411.'

'You left your desk three times?'

'No, twice. Two medications were together.'

'And what times did you give them at, please?'

'Mister Bolger and Miss Ryan had a codeine at a quarter to five, and Miss Freitz in four-eleven had a heparin and dextran about an hour later.'

'These rooms, they are on the same hallway as Father Dyer's?'

'No, they're just around the corner.'

'So if someone else had entered Father Dyer's room around a quarter to five you wouldn't have seen it; and the same if someone left the room an hour later?'

'Yes, that's right.'

'These medications are given every day at those times?'

'No, the heparin and dextran for Miss Freitz are new. I never saw it on the log until today.'

'And who prescribed it, please? Can you remember?'

'Yes, Doctor Amfortas.'

'You're certain? Would you like to check the records?'

'No, I'm positive.'

'Why are you positive?'

'Well, it's unusual. The resident usually does that. But I think he's got a sort of special interest in her case.'

The detective looked puzzled. 'You said Doctor Amfortas doesn't work on the ward now.'

'That's right. That was as of last night,' said the nurse.

'But he was in this girl's room?'

'That's not unusual. He visits her a lot.'

'At such hours?'

Keating nodded. 'The girl's got insomnia. So has he, I would think.'

'Why is that? I mean why do you think that?'

'Oh, for months now he suddenly pops up on my shift and just stands there and chats with me, or just sort of roams around. Up here we call him "The Phantom".'

'When was the last time that he spoke to Miss Freitz at such an hour? Or was there such a time?'

'Yes, there was. That was yesterday.'

'What time, please?'

'Maybe four or five a.m. Then he went into Father Dyer's room and talked for a while.'

'He went into Father Dyer's room?'

'Yes.'

'Were you able to hear any part of their discussion?'

'No, the door was closed.'

'I see.' Kinderman thought for a while. He was staring through the window at Atkins. The sergeant was leaning on the desk, staring back. Kinderman returned his attention to the nurse. 'Who else did you see around the ward at this time?'

'You mean staff?'

'I mean anyone. Anyone walking around in the hall.'

'Well, there was only Mrs Clelia.'

'Who is she?'

'She's a patient in Psychiatric.'

'She was walking in the hall?'

'Well, no. I found her sprawled in the hall.'

'You found her sprawled?'

'She was sort of in a stupor.'

'Where exactly in the hallway?'

'It was just around the corner from here near the entrance to Psychiatric.'

'And what time was this, please?'

'It was just before I found Father Dyer. I called over to the Open Ward in Psychiatric and they came here and got her.'

'Mrs Clelia is senile?'

'I really couldn't tell you. I would guess so. I don't know. She looked a little catatonic, I would say.'

'Catatonic?'

'I'm just guessing,' said Keating

'I see.' Kinderman thought for a moment, then stood up. He said, 'Thank you, Miss Keating.'

'Sure.'

Kinderman handed her another tissue and then left the light office and spoke to Atkins. 'Get the telephone number for

Doctor Amfortas and bring him in for questioning, Atkins. In the meantime, I am going to Psychiatric.'

Soon Kinderman was standing in the Open Ward. The events of the morning had not touched it. The usual throng of silent starers was already gathered around the television; all the dreamers were in their chairs. An old man in his seventies approached the detective. 'I want cereal this morning and figs,' he said. 'Don't forget the damned figs. I want figs.' An attendant was slowly coming towards them. Kinderman looked for the nurse at the Charge Desk. She was back in her office, talking on the telephone. Her face looked drawn and strained. Kinderman started to move toward the desk. The old man remained behind and continued to address the empty air where the detective had been standing. 'I don't want any goddamned figs,' he was saying. Suddenly Temple appeared. He came springing through the door and looked around. He looked dishevelled and half-awake; his eyes were still caked with sleep. He saw Kinderman and met him at the desk. 'Jesus Christ,' he exclaimed. 'I can't believe this. Is it true the way he died?'

'Yes, it's true.'

'They called and woke me up. Jesus Christ. I can't believe it.'

Temple flicked a glance at the nurse and looked sour. She saw him and quickly got off the phone. The attendant was leading the old man to a chair. 'I would like to see one of your patients,' said Kinderman. 'Mrs Clelia. Where would she be?'

Temple eyed him. 'I can see you've been getting acquainted,' he said. 'What do you want with Mrs Clelia?'

'I'd like to ask her some questions. One or two. It couldn't hurt.'

'Mrs *Clelia*?'

'Yes.

'You'd be talking to a wall,' said Temple.

'I am used to this,' Kinderman assured him.

'What did you mean by that?'

'I'm just talking.' Kinderman's shoulders raised and he offered up the palms of his hands. 'My mouth opens, it comes out before I know what I'm saying. It's just *shtuss*. For the

177

meaning, we would need the *I Ching*.'

Temple appraised him with a calculating look, and then turned to the nurse. She was standing at the Charge Desk, gathering papers and looking busy. 'Where's Mrs Clelia, snooks?' Temple asked her.

The nurse did not look up. 'In her room.'

'You'll indulge an old man and let me see her?' asked Kinderman.

'Sure, why not?' said Temple. 'Come on.'

Kinderman followed him and they were soon in a narrow room. 'There's your girl,' said Temple. He'd gestured towards an elderly, white-haired woman who was sitting in an easy chair by a window. She was staring at her slippers and grasping at the ends of a red woollen shawl, pulling it tighter around her shoulders. She didn't look up. The detective took his hat off and held it by the brim. 'Mrs Clelia?'

The woman looked up with empty eyes. 'Are you my son?' she said to Kinderman.

'I would be proud to believe so,' he said gently.

For a moment Mrs Clelia held his gaze, but then looked away. 'You're not my son,' she murmured. 'You're wax.'

'Can you remember what you did this morning, Mrs Clelia?'

The old woman started crooning softly. The air was tuneless and unpleasantly discordant.

'Mrs Clelia?' prodded the detective.

She seemed not to hear.

'I told you,' said Temple. 'Of course, I could try to put her under for you.'

'Put her under?'

'Hypnosis. Shall I try it?' said Temple.

'Absolutely.'

Temple closed the door and pulled up a chair so that he faced the old woman.

'You don't make the room dark first?' Kinderman wondered.

'No, that's nonsense,' said Temple. 'Oogah-boogah.' From an upper pocket of his medical jacket he extracted a small medallion. It hung from a short length of chain and was triangular. 'Mrs Clelia,' said Temple. She immediately turned her gaze to the psychiatrist. He lifted the medallion and let it swing gently before her eyes. Then he spoke the words, 'Dream time'. Instantly, the old woman closed her eyes and seemed to slump in her chair. Her hands fell gently to her lap. Temple turned a self-satisfied look to the detective. 'What should I ask her?' he said. 'Same thing?'

Kinderman nodded.

Temple turned back to the woman. 'Mrs Clelia,' he said, 'can you remember what you did this morning?'

They waited but she made no answer. The woman sat motionless. Temple began to look puzzled. 'What did you do this morning?' he repeated. Kinderman shifted his weight a little. There was still no reply. 'Is she sleeping?' the detective asked softly. Temple shook his head. 'Did you see a priest today, Mrs Clelia?' the psychiatrist asked her.

Suddenly the woman broke her silence. 'Noooooo,' she answered in a tone that was low and drawn out, like a groan. It had an eeriness about it.

'Did you go for a walk this morning?'

'Noooooo.'

'Did somebody take you somewhere?'

'Noooooo.'

'Shit,' whispered Temple. He turned his head and looked at Kinderman. The detective said, 'All right. That's enough.'

Temple turned back to Mrs Clelia. He touched her forehead and said, 'Wake up.'

Slowly, the old woman began to sit up. She opened her eyes and looked at Temple. Then she stared at the detective. Her eyes were innocent and blank. 'Did you fix my radio?' she asked him.

'I will fix it tomorrow, ma'am,' said Kinderman.

'That's what they all say,' replied Mrs Clelia. She stared at her shoes and hummed.

Kinderman and Temple stepped into the hall. 'Did you like that question about the priest?' asked Temple. 'I mean, why cock around? Get right to it. And how about the one about

179

somebody *taking* her over to Neurology? I thought that was a good one.'

'Why couldn't she answer you?' asked Kinderman.

'I dunno. To tell you the truth it kind of beats me.'

'You've hynotized this lady many times before?'

'Once or twice.'

'She went under so quickly,' said Kinderman.

'Well, I'm good,' said Temple. 'I told you. Jesus Christ, I can't get over what was done to that priest. I mean, how is that possible, Lieutenant?'

'We will see.'

'And he was mutilated?' asked Temple.

Kinderman stared at him intently. 'His left index finger was severed,' he said, 'and on his right hand palm the killer had carved a zodiacal sign. The Twins. The Gemini,' Kinderman told him. His gaze probed unwaveringly into Temple's. 'What do you make of that?' he asked.

'I dunno,' said Temple. His face was a blank.

'No, you wouldn't,' said Kinderman. 'Why should you? Incidentally, you have somewhere a Pathology section?'

'Sure.'

'Where they are making autopsies and so on?'

Temple nodded. 'Down below on Level "B". You take the elevator down from Neurology and turn left. Are you going there?'

'Yes.'

'You can't miss it.'

Kinderman turned and walked away. 'What do you want in Pathology anyway?' Temple called out to his back. Kinderman shrugged and kept on walking. Temple cursed underneath his breath.

Atkins was leaning against the Charge Desk when he saw Kinderman coming down the hall. He pushed off from the desk and walked forward to meet him. 'You reached Amfortas?' the detective asked him.

'No.'

'Keep trying.'

'Stedman and Ryan are finished.'

'I am not.'

'There were prints on the jars,' said Atkins. 'All over them, in fact, and very clear.'

'Yes, the killer is bold. He is mocking us, Atkins.'

'Father Healy's downstairs. He says he wants to see the body.'

'No, don't let him. Go down there and talk to him, Atkins. Be vague. And tell Ryan to hurry up with the prints. I want comparisons immediately with the prints that he took from the confessional. In the meantime, I am going to Pathology.'

Atkins nodded and both men walked to the elevators and caught one going down. When Atkins got off at the Lobby floor, the detective caught a glimpse of Father Healy. He was sitting in a corner with his head in his hands. The detective looked away and was glad when the elevator doors had closed.

Kinderman found his way to Pathology and at last to a quiet room where medical students were dissecting cadavers. He tried not to see them. A doctor in an office faced with glass looked up from the desk where he was working and saw the detective prowling around. He got up and came out and confronted Kinderman. 'Can I help you?' he asked.

'Could be.' Kinderman flashed his identification. 'Have you any sort of instrument used in dissection that resembles a shears, perhaps? I was curious.'

'Sure,' said the doctor. He led the detective over to a wall where various instruments were sheathed. He plucked one down and gave it to Kinderman. 'Be careful with that,' he warned.

'I will,' said Kinderman. He was holding a gleaming cutting instrument made of stainless steel. It resembled a shears. The blades curved sharply into a crescent, and when Kinderman turned them they flashed with reflected light from above. 'This is something,' the detective murmured. The instrument gave him a feeling of dread. 'What do you call this?' he asked.

'Shears.'

'Yes, of course. In the land of the dead there is no jargon.'

'What was that?'

'Nothing.' Kinderman carefully pulled at the handles in an effort to separate the blades. He had to strain. 'I'm so weak,' he complained.

'No, they're stiff,' said the doctor. 'They're new.'

Kinderman looked up with his eyebrows raised. 'You said "new"?'

'This just came in.' The doctor reached out and peeled a sticker from a handle. 'It's still got the shipping tag on it,' he said. He crumpled it up and let it drop in a pocket of his jacket.

'You replace these very often?' the detective asked him.

'You must be kidding. These things are expensive. Anyway, there's no way to damage them. I don't know why we'd be getting in a new one,' said the doctor. He looked up and scanned the rows of hooks and sheaths on the wall. 'Well, the old one's not around,' he said at last. 'Maybe one of the medical students copped it.'

Kinderman gingerly handed him the shears. He said, 'Thank you very much, Doctor – What was your name?'

'Arnie Derwin. Is that all you wanted?'

'It's enough.'

When Kinderman arrived at the Neurology desk, a group of nurses were gathered around as Atkins and the Chief of Staff, Doctor Tench, stood head to head in a confrontation. Kinderman reached them in time to hear Tench saying, 'This is a hospital, sir, not a zoo and the patients come first! Do you understand?'

'What's all this *tsimmis*?' asked Kinderman.

'This is Doctor Tench,' said Atkins.

Tench turned around and jutted his chin up toward the detective. 'I'm the Chief of Staff. Who are you?' he demanded.

'A poor lieutenant of police chasing phantoms. You will kindly step aside? We have business,' said Kinderman.

'Jesus Christ, you've got a nerve!'

The detective had already turned to Atkins. 'The killer is

someone in this hospital,' he told him. 'Call the precinct. We are going to need many more men.'

'Now listen *here*!' exploded Tench.

The detective ignored him. 'Post two men on every floor. Lock all exits to the street and put a man on each. No one enters or leaves without proper credentials.'

'You can't *do* that!' said Tench.

'Whoever leaves must be searched. We are looking for a surgical shears. We must also search the hospital for them.'

Tench had purpled. 'Would you *listen* to me, please, god-damnit!'

The detective now whirled on him grimly. 'No, you listen to *me*,' he said sharply. His voice was low and even and commanding. 'I want you to know what we are facing,' he said. 'Have you heard of the Gemini Killer?'

'What?' Tench's manner continued to be querulous.

'I said the Gemini Killer,' said Kinderman.

'Yes, I've heard of him. So what? He's dead.'

'Do you remember any published accounts of his *modus operandi*?' pressed Kinderman.

'Look, what are you driving at?'

'Do you remember them?'

'Mutilations?'

'Yes,' said Kinderman intently. He leaned his head forward, close to the doctor's. 'The middle finger of the victim's left hand was always severed. And on the victim's back he would carve out a sign of the zodiac – the Gemini, the Twins. And the name of each victim began with "K". Is it all coming back to you, Doctor Tench? Well, forget it. Put it instantly out of your mind. The truth is that the missing finger was *this* one!' The detective extended his right index finger. 'Not the middle but the *index* finger! Not the left hand at all, but the *right*! And the sign of the Gemini was not on the back, it was carved on the left hand palm! Only San Francisco Homicide knew this, no one else. But they gave the press the false information on purpose so they wouldn't be bothered every day with some looney coming in and confessing that he was the Gemini and then wasting all their time with the investigations; so they could know the real thing when they found him.' Kinderman moved his face in closer. 'But in *this* case, Doctor, this and another two besides, we have the true M.O!'

Tench looked shocked. 'I can't believe it,' he said.

'Believe it. Also, when the Gemini wrote letters to the press, he always doubled his final "L"s on every word even when it was wrong. Does this tell you something, Doctor?'

'My God.'

'Do you now understand? Is it clear?'

'But what about Father Dyer's name? It doesn't start with a "K",' said Tench in puzzlement.

'His middle name was *Kevin*. And now will you kindly let us go about our business and try to protect you?'

Ashen-faced, Tench mutely nodded. 'I'm sorry,' he said. He walked away.

Kinderman sighed and looked wearily at Atkins; then he glanced at the Charge Desk. One of the nurses from another ward was standing with her arms folded, staring intently at the detective. As he met her gaze she looked strangely anxious. Kinderman returned his attention to Atkins. He took him by the arm and drew him a few steps away from the desk. 'All right, do as I told you,' he said. 'And Amfortas. Have you reached him?'

'No.'

'Keep trying. Go on. Go ahead.' He turned him gently away, and then watched him as he moved toward the inner office phone. And now a great weight came down upon his being and he walked to the door of Dyer's room. He avoided the gaze of the policeman on guard, put his hand on the doorknob, opened the door and stepped inside.

He felt as though he'd entered another dimension. He leaned back against the door and looked at Stedman. The pathologist was sitting in a chair numbly staring. Behind him the rain spattered down against a window. Half the room was in shadow and the greyness from outside washed the rest in a pale spectral light. 'There isn't a stain or a drop of blood anyplace in the room,' said Stedman softly. His voice was toneless. 'Not even on the mouths of the jars,' he added.

Kinderman nodded. He took a deep breath and looked at the body where it lay on the bed underneath a white drape. Beside it, on a tray cart, were twenty-two specimen jars arranged neatly in symmetrical rows. They contained Father Dyer's entire blood supply. The detective shifted his gaze to the wall behind the bed, where the killer had written something in Father Dyer's blood:

It's A Wonderfull Life

Towards sundown the mystery deepened past reason. Sitting in the squad room, Ryan told Kinderman the results of the fingerprint comparison. The detective looked at him, stunned. 'Are you telling me two different people did these murders?'

The prints from the confessional panels did not match the prints from the jars.

THURSDAY, MARCH 19

Chapter Eleven

The eye passed on to the brain a hundredth part of the data it received. The odds that what it relayed was due to chance was a billionth of a billionth of a billionth of one percent. One sense datum felt like any other. What decided what ought to be relayed to the brain?

A man decided to move his hand. His motor responses were triggered by neurons, which were triggered by others that led to the brain. But what neuron decided to make that decision? Assuming that the chain in the firing of neurons could be lengthened by the billions of neurons in the brain, when you came to the end of them, what remained that had triggered a man's free act of will? Could a neuron decide? Prime Neuron Untriggered? First Decider Undecided? Or perhaps the entire brain decided. Would that give to its whole what none of its single parts possessed? Could zero times billions yield more than a zero? And what made the decision for the brain as a whole to make a decision?

'"May the angels lead you into paradise",' Father Healy read softly from the book. '"May the choirs of angels be there to welcome you. And with Lazarus, once a beggar, may you have eternal rest."'

Kinderman watched as Healy sprinkled holy water onto the casket. The Mass in Dahlgren Chapel had ended, and now they were standing in a grassy hollow of the Georgetown campus at beginning of day. A new grave had been dug in the Jesuit Cemetery. Parish priests from Holy Trinity were there, and the campus Jesuits, who were few; most of the faculty were laymen these days. No family was present. There hadn't been time. Jesuit burials were swift in their coming. Kinderman studied the shivering men in black cassocks and coats huddled close by the graveside. Their faces were stoic and unreadable. Were they thinking of their own mortality?

'"A dawning light from on high will visit us to shine upon those who are in darkness and entering the shadowland of death".'

Kinderman thought of his dream of Max.

'"I am the resurrection and the life",' Healy prayed. Kinderman looked up at the old red classroom buildings towering above and around them, making them small in this quiet valley. Like the world, they continued their implacable existence. How could Dyer be gone? Every man who ever lived craved perfect happiness, the detective poignantly reflected. *But how can we have it when we know we're going to die?* Each joy was clouded by the knowledge it would end. And so nature had implanted in us a desire for something unattainable? *No. It couldn't be. It makes no sense.* Every other striving implanted by nature had a corresponding object that wasn't a phantom. Why this exception? the detective reasoned. It was nature making hunger when there wasn't any food. *We continue. We go on.* Thus death proved life.

The priests began drifting away in silence. Only Father Healy remained. He stood motionless, staring at the grave; then, softly, he began to recite from John Donne: '"Death be not proud, though some have called thee mighty and dreadful, for thou art not so",' he intoned with tenderness. His eyes began filling with tears. '"For those whom thou think'st thou dost overthrow die not, poor Death, nor canst thou kill me. From rest and sleep, which but thy pictures be, much pleasure – then, from thee much more must flow; and soonest our best men with thee do go, rest of their bones and soul's delivery. Thou'rt slave to fate, chance, kings and desperate men, and dost with poison, war, and sickness swell; and poppy or charms can make us sleep as well, and better than thy stroke. Why swell'st thou then? One short sleep passed, we wake eternally, and death shall be no more. Death, thou shalt die."'

The priest waited, and then wiped away his tears on a sleeve. Kinderman walked over to him. 'I'm so sorry, Father Healy,' he said.

The priest nodded, staring down at the grave. Then at last he looked up and met Kinderman's gaze, his eyes full of anguish and pain and loss. 'Find him,' he said grimly. 'Find the bastard who did it and cut off his balls.' He turned and walked away through the hollow. Kinderman watched him.

Men also craved justice.

When the Jesuit was finally out of sight, the detective wandered over to a tombstone and read the inscription:

DAMIEN KARRAS, S. J.
1928–1971

Kinderman stared. The inscription was telling him something. What? Was it the date? He couldn't piece it together. Nothing made sense any more, he brooded. Logic had fled with the fingerprint comparison. Chaos ruled this corner of the earth. What to do? He didn't know. He looked up at the campus Administration Building.

Kinderman went to Healy's office. He removed his hat. Healy's secretary tilted her head. 'May I help you?' she asked him.

'Father Healy. Is he in? May I see him?'

'Well, I doubt that he's seeing people now,' she sighed. 'I know he hasn't been taking any calls. But your name, please?'

Kinderman told her.

'Oh, yes,' she said. She picked up a telephone and buzzed the inner office. When she finished talking to Healy, she put down the phone and told Kinderman, 'He'll see you. Please go in.' She gestured towards the door.

'Thank you, Miss.'

Kinderman entered a spacious office. The furnishings were

mostly of dark rubbed wood and on the walls there were lithographs and paintings of Jesuits prominent in Georgetown's past. Saint Ignatius Loyola, the founder of the Jesuits, stared down mildly from a massive gold-framed oil. 'What's on your mind, Lieutenant? Want a drink?'

'No, thank you, Father.'

'Please sit down.' Healy gestured at a chair in front of his desk.

'Thank you, Father.' Kinderman settled down. He felt a sense of security in this room. Tradition. Order. He needed these now.

Healy downed a shot glass filled with Scotch. It made a muffled little sound as he set it back down on the polished leather hide that covered his desk. 'God is great and mysterious, Lieutenant. What's up?'

'Two priests and a crucified boy,' said Kinderman. 'There is clearly some religious connection. But what is it? I don't know what I'm looking for, Father; I am groping. But besides being priests, what might Bermingham and Dyer have had in common? What connective little link might be between them? Do you know?'

'Sure, I know,' said Healy. 'Don't you?'

'No, I don't. What is it?'

'You. And that goes for the Kintry kid as well. You knew them all. Hadn't you thought of that?'

'Yes, I had,' the detective admitted. 'But it's surely a coincidence,' he said. 'Thomas Kintry's crucifixion – that's a statement with no relevance to me whatsoever.' He opened up his hands in a rhetorical gesture.

'Yeah, you're right,' said Healy. He'd turned himself sideways and was looking out a window. Class had just broken and students were milling toward their next assignment. 'It could be that exorcism,' he murmured.

'What exorcism, Father? I don't understand.'

Healy turned his head to him. 'Come on, you know *something* about it, Lieutenant.'

'Well, a little.'

'I'll bet.'

'Father Karras was involved in some way.'

'If you want to call dying an involvement,' said Healy. He looked out the window again. 'Damien was one of the exorcists. Joe Dyer knew the victim's family. And Ken Bermingham gave Damien permission to investigate, and then helped to select the other exorcist. I don't know what it could possibly mean, but that's certainly a connection of sorts, don't you think?'

'Yes, of course,' said Kinderman. 'It's very strange. But then it leaves us with Kintry.'

Healy turned to him. 'Does it? His mother teaches languages at the Institute of Linguistics. Damien had brought them a tape recording that he wanted them to analyze. He wanted to know if the sounds on the tape were a language or just a lot of gibberish. He wanted evidence the victim was speaking in some kind of language she'd never learned.'

'And was she?'

'No. It was English in reverse. But the person who discovered it was Kintry's mother.'

Kinderman lost his feeling of security. This connective thread led to darkness. 'This case of possession, Father – you believe that it was real?'

'I can't be bothered with goblins,' said Healy. '"The poor are always with us". That's enough for me to think about, most days.' He picked up the shot glass and toyed with it absently, turning it around and around with his fingers. 'How did they do it, Lieutenant?' he asked quietly.

Kinderman hesitated before answering. Then at last he said softly, 'With a catheter.'

Healy kept turning the shot glass around. 'Maybe you *should* be looking for a demon,' he murmured.

'A doctor will do,' answered Kinderman.

The detective left the office and was soon breathing shallowly and quickly as he wearily hurried out the campus main gate. He walked down 36th Street. The rain had just stopped and the red brick sidewalks glistened with wetness. At the corner he turned right and went directly to Amfortas's narrow row house. He noticed all the window drapes had been drawn. He went up the steps and rang the doorbell. A minute went by. He rang again but still no one came. Kinderman gave up. He turned away from the door and hurried towards the hospital, lost in a maze but moving swiftly as if hoping that action would generate thought.

At the hospital, Kinderman couldn't find Atkins. None of the policemen knew where he was. Kinderman approached the Neurology Charge Desk. The nurse on duty was Allerton. Kinderman asked her about Amfortas. 'Do you know where I can reach him, please?' he said.

'No, he doesn't make rounds any more,' explained Allerton.

'Yes, I know, but he sometimes still comes. Have you seen him?'

'No, I haven't. Let me check in his lab,' said the nurse. She picked up a phone and dialled an extension. No one answered. She hung up the phone and said, 'I'm sorry.'

'Has he maybe gone away on a trip?' asked Kinderman.

'I really couldn't say. We've got messages for him. Let me check them.' Allerton moved to a rack of pigeonholes and from one of them she plucked a sheaf of message slips. She went through them and then handed them to Kinderman. 'You can look at these yourself, if you like.'

'Thank you.' Kinderman examined the messages. One was from a medical equipment supply house regarding an order for a laser probe. All the others were calls from the same individual, a Doctor Edward Coffey. Kinderman held up a slip to the nurse. 'It's the same as some others,' he said. 'May I keep it?'

She told him, 'Yes.'

Kinderman pocketed the message slip and gave the rest of them back to the nurse. 'I'm obliged,' he told her. 'Meantime, should you happen to see Doctor Amfortas, or possibly hear from him, you will ask him to call me, please?' He handed her a business card. 'At this number.' He pointed it out.

'Of course, sir.'

'Thank you.'

Kinderman turned and walked to the elevators. He pressed the button marked 'Down'. An elevator came and, after a nurse stepped out, he entered it. Then the nurse stepped back inside. Kinderman remembered her. She was the one who had stared at him so oddly the morning before. 'Lieutenant?' she said. She was frowning and her manner was hesitant. She folded her arms across her chest and over the white leather purse that she carried.

Kinderman removed his hat. 'May I help you?'

The nurse looked away. She seemed uncertain. 'I don't know. It's sort of crazy,' she said. 'I don't know.'

They'd arrived at the lobby. 'Come, let's find someplace and talk,' said Kinderman.

'I feel silly. It's just something . . .' She shrugged. 'Well, I don't know.'

The elevator door slid open. They stepped out and the detective guided the nurse to a corner of the lobby, where they sat down on blue naugahyde chairs. 'This is really awfully stupid,' said the nurse.

'Nothing's stupid,' the detective reassured her. 'If someone now said to me, "The world is an orange", I would ask him what kind, and after that who knows what. No, really. Who knows what is what anymore?' He glanced at her nametag: Christine Charles, 'So what is it, Miss Charles?'

She blew out a breath between her lips.

'It's all right,' the detective said. 'Now what is it?'

She lifted her head and met his gaze. 'I work in Psychiatric,' she said. 'The Disturbed Ward. There's this patient.' She shrugged. 'I wasn't there when he came in. It was years ago,' she said. 'Ten or twelve. I looked it up in his file.' She was fumbling through her purse and now extracted a package of cigarettes. She shook one out and then lit it with a match. It took her several tries to make the match strike fire. She averted her head and blew out smoke in a thick grey column. 'I'm sorry,' she said.

'Go ahead, please.'

'Well, this man. The police had picked him up down on

"M" Street. He was wandering around in a kind of a daze. He couldn't talk, I guess, and he had no I.D. Well, at any rate, he finally wound up here with us.' She took a nervous, quick puff of the cigarette. 'He was diagnosed as a catatonic, although who the heck really knows? I'm being frank. Anyway, the man never talked for all these years, and we kept him in the Open Ward. Until recently. I'll come to all that in a second. This man had no name, so we made one up. We all called him Tommy Sunlight. In the rec room he'd move around all day from chair to chair just following the sunlight. He'd never sit in shadow if he could help it.' Again she shrugged. 'There was something sort of gentle about him. But then everything changed, like I said. Around the first of this year, he started – well – coming out of his withdrawal, I guess. And then little by little he began to make sounds like he wanted to talk. It was clear in his head, I think, but he hadn't used his vocal equipment in so long that it all came out grunts and moans for a while.' She leaned over to an ashtray and stubbed out the cigarette with quick, hard pokes. 'God, I'm making such an awfully long story out of nothing.' She looked back at the detective. 'In a nutshell, he finally turned violent and we put him into isolation. Straitjacket. Padded cell. The whole drill. He's been in there since February, Lieutenant, so there's no way on earth he could be involved. But he says he's the Gemini Killer.'

'Excuse me?'

'He insists he's the Gemini Killer, Lieutenant.'

'But you say he's locked up?'

'Yes, that's right. I mean, that's why I hesitated telling you this. He could as easily have said that he's Jack the Ripper. You know? So what? But it's just . . .' Her voice trailed away and her eyes grew troubled and vaguely distant. 'Well, I guess it's what I heard him say last week,' she said. 'One day when I gave him his Thorazine.'

'And what did he say, please?'

'"The priest".'

Admittance to the Disturbed Ward was controlled by a nurse who was stationed in a circular booth made of glass. It was set in the centre of a widened-out square space forming the confluence of three halls. The nurse pressed a button now and a metal door slid back. Temple and Kinderman stepped into the ward and the door slid quietly shut behind them. 'There's just no *way* to get out of here,' said Temple. His manner was irritated and brusque. 'She either sees you through the window of her door and buzzes you out or you have to press a four-digit combination that's changed every week. Do you *still* want to see him?' he demanded.

'Couldn't hurt.'

Temple stared in disbelief. 'The man's cell is locked. He's in a straitjacket. Leg restraints.'

The detective shrugged. 'I'll just look.'

'It's your nickel, Lieutenant,' the psychiatrist said gruffly. He started to walk and Kinderman followed him to a hallway that was dimly lit. 'They keep changing these goddamned bulbs,' grumbled Temple, 'and they keep going out.'

'All across the world.'

Temple fished in a pocket and extracted a ring that was heavy with keys. 'He's in there,' he said. 'Cell 12.' Kinderman peered through a one-way window at a padded room that was starkly equipped with a straightbacked chair, a wash basin, a toilet and a drinking fountain. On a cot against the wall at the end of the room sat a man in a straitjacket. Kinderman could not see his face. The man's head was bent down low to his chest, and long black hair fell down in oily, matted strands.

Temple unlocked and opened the door. He gestured inside. 'Be my guest,' he said. 'When you're finished, push the buzzer by the door. It brings the nurse. I'll be in my office,' he said. 'I'm going to leave the door unlocked.' He gave the detective a look of disgust and then bounded down the hall.

Kinderman entered the cell and pulled the door shut softly behind him. A naked light bulb hung from a wire in the centre of the ceiling. Its filaments were weak and it cast a saffron glow on the room. Kinderman glanced at the white wash basin. A faucet was dripping slow drops, one at a time; in the silence their sound was heavy and distinct. Kinderman walked toward the cot and then stopped.

'It's taken you a long time to get here,' said a voice. It was low and had whispers at its edge. It was sardonic.

Kinderman looked puzzled. The voice seemed familiar. Where had he heard it before? he wondered. 'Mister Sunlight?' he said.

The man raised his head and when Kinderman looked at the dark, rugged features, he staggered backward a step in shock. 'My God!' he gasped. His heart began to race.

The patient's mouth was cracked in a grin. 'It's a wonderful life,' he leered, 'don't you think?'

Kinderman blindly backed to the door, stumbled, turned around, pressed the buzzer for the nurse and then bolted from the room with a face drained of colour. He rushed to Freeman Temple's office.

'Hey, pal, what's wrong?' asked Temple, frowning, when Kinderman burst into his office. Seated at his desk, he put aside a late issue of a psychiatric journal and appraised the perspiring, panting detective. 'Hey, sit down. You don't look too good. What's the matter?'

Kinderman sank down into a chair. He could not speak or even focus his thoughts. The psychiatrist stood up and leaned over him, examining his face and eyes. 'You all right?'

He shut his eyes and nodded. 'Could you give me some water, please?' he asked. He put a hand to his chest and felt his heart. It was still beating quickly.

Temple poured ice water out of a carafe into a plastic cup on his desk. He picked it up and gave it to Kinderman. 'Here, drink this.'

'Thank you. Yes.' Kinderman took the cup from his hand. He sipped at the water once, then again, and then quietly waited for his heart to slow down. 'Yes, that's better,' he sighed at last. 'Much better.' Soon Kinderman's breathing slowed to normal and he shifted his gaze to the anxious Temple. 'Sunlight,' he said. 'I want to look at his file.'

'What for?'

'*I want to see it!*' the detective shouted.

Startled, the psychiatrist jerked backward. 'Yeah, okay, pal. Take it easy, I'll go get it.' Temple bounded from the office in a step, jostling Atkins as he came to the door.

'Lieutenant?' said Atkins.

Kinderman looked at him blankly. 'Where were you?' he asked him.

'Picking out a wedding ring, Lieutenant.'

'This is good. This is normal. Good, Atkins. Stay near.' Kinderman turned his gaze to a wall. Atkins didn't know what to make of this, or of what the detective had said. He frowned and walked over to the Charge Desk where he leaned and watched and waited. He had never seen Kinderman look like this.

Temple returned and placed the file in Kinderman's hands. The detective started reading it while Temple sat down and watched him. The psychiatrist lit a cigarillo and carefully studied Kinderman's face. He looked down at the hands that were turning the pages of the file so rapidly. They had a tremor.

Kinderman looked up from the file. 'Were you here when this man was brought in?' he asked sharply.

'Yes.'

'Stretch your memory, please, Doctor Temple. What was he wearing?'

'Jesus Christ, that was such a long time ago.'

'Can you remember?'

'No.'

'Were there signs of any injuries? Bruises? Lacerations?'

'That would be in the file,' said Temple.

'It is *not* in the file! It is *not!*' The detective slapped the file on the desk with each 'not'.

'Hey, take it easy.'

Kinderman stood up. 'Have you or any nurse told the man in

Cell 12 about Father Dyer's murder?'

'*I* haven't. Why the hell would we tell him that?'

'Ask the nurses,' Kinderman told him grimly. 'Ask them. I want to know the answer by morning.'

Kinderman turned and strode from the room. He walked up to Atkins. 'I want you to check with Georgetown University,' he said. 'There was a priest there, Father Damien Karras. See if they still have his medical records, and his dental records as well. Also, call Father Healy. I want him to come over here right now.'

Atkins stared quizzically into Kinderman's haunted eyes. The detective answered his unspoken question. 'Father Karras was a friend of mine,' said Kinderman. 'Twelve years ago he died. He fell down the Hitchcock Steps to the bottom. I attended his funeral,' he said. 'I just saw him. He is here in this ward in a straitjacket.'

Chapter Twelve

In the Midnight Mission in downtown Washington DC, Karl Vennamun ladled out soup to the derelicts seated at the long communal table. When they thanked him, he said 'Bless you' in a warm, low voice. The founder of the Mission, Mrs Tremley, followed him, passing out bread in thick slabs.

While the derelicts ate with trembling hands, the old Vennamun stood behind a small wooden podium and read passages aloud from the Scriptures. Afterwards, while coffee and cake were consumed, he delivered a homily, his eyes aglow with fervour. His voice was rich and his stops and cadences were hypnotic. The room was in his grip. Mrs Tremley looked around at the faces of the derelicts. One or two of them were dozing, overcome by the food and the warmth of the room; but the others were rapt and their faces glowed. One man wept.

After dinner, Mrs Tremley sat alone with Vennamun at the end of the empty table. She blew at hot coffee in her mug. Wisps of steam were curling up. She took a sip. Vennamun's hands were clasped on the table and he stared at them thoughtfully in silence. 'Karl, you preach wonderfully,' said Mrs Tremley. 'You have such a great gift.'

Vennamun said nothing.

Mrs Tremley set her mug down on the table. 'You must think again of sharing it with the world,' she said. 'They've forgotten all about it now; all that terrible tragedy; it's over. You should start your public ministry again.'

For a time the old Vennamun did not move. When at last he looked up and met Mrs Tremley's gaze he said softly, 'I've been thinking of doing just that.'

FRIDAY, MARCH 20

Chapter Thirteen

It was said that every man had a double, thought Kinderman; an identical physical counterpart who existed somewhere in the world. Could that be the answer to the mystery? he wondered. He looked down at the gravediggers excavating grimly, digging up the coffin of Damien Karras. The Jesuit psychiatrist had no brothers, no member of a family who might account for the startling resemblance between the priest and the man in the hospital Disturbed Ward. No medical or dental records were available; they'd been discarded after Karras's death. There was nothing to be done now, thought Kinderman, but this, and he stood at the gravesite with Atkins and Stedman, praying that the body in the coffin was Karras. The alternative was horror that was almost unthinkable, a shifting of the mind from its axis. *No. It couldn't be*, thought Kinderman. *Impossible*. Yet even Father Healy thought Sunlight was Karras.

'You mention light,' the detective pondered. Atkins hadn't mentioned it, but he listened, buttoning the collar of his leather jacket. It was noon, yet the wind had grown knifing and bitter. Stedman remained intent on the digging. 'What we see is only part of the spectrum,' brooded Kinderman; 'a tiny slot between the gamma rays and radio waves, a little fraction of the light that there is.' He squinted at the silvery disc of the sun, its edges hard and bright behind a cloud. 'So when God said, "Let there be light",' he pondered, 'it could be that He was really saying, "Let there be reality".'

Atkins didn't know what to say.

'They're finished,' said Stedman. Hé looked over at Kinderman. 'Shall we open it up?'

'Yes, open it.'

Stedman gave an instruction to the diggers, and they carefully pried back the lid of the coffin. Kinderman, Stedman and Atkins stared. The wind was keening and their coat bottoms flapped.

'Find out who that is,' said Kinderman quietly.

It wasn't Father Karras.

Kinderman and Atkins went into the Disturbed Ward. 'I want to see the man in Cell 12,' said Kinderman. He felt like a man in a dream and wasn't sure who or where he was. He doubted so simple a fact as his breathing.

Nurse Spencer, the Charge Nurse, checked his I.D. When she met his gaze, her eyes held anxiety and a shadow of something like fear. Kinderman had seen it throughout the staff. A general silence had descended on the hospital. Figures dressed in white moved like phantoms on a ghost ship. 'All right,' she said reluctantly. She picked up keys from the desk and started to walk. Kinderman followed her and she was soon unlocking Cell 12. Kinderman looked up at the corridor ceiling. As he watched, another light bulb flickered out.

'Go on in.'

Kinderman looked at the nurse.

'Shall I lock it behind you?' she asked him.

'No.'

She held his gaze for a moment, then left. She was wearing new shoes and her thick crêpe soles squished loud against the tiles in the silent corridor. For a moment the detective watched her, then he stepped inside the room and closed the door. He looked at the cot. Sunlight was watching him, his face devoid of expression. The dripping in the basin came at regular intervals; each *plop* was heartbeats apart. Looking into those eyes, the detective felt a dread fluttering up in his chest. He walked to the straightbacked chair against the wall and was acutely aware of the sound of his footsteps. Sunlight followed him with his eyes. His look was ingenuous and blank. Kinderman sat down and met his gaze. For an instant his glance flicked up to the scar above the patient's right eye, then dropped back to that disquieting, motionless stare. Kinderman still could not believe what he was seeing. 'Who are you?' he asked. In the small, padded room the sound of his words had a strange distinctness. He almost wondered who had spoken them.

Tommy Sunlight did not answer. He continued to stare.

Plop. Silence. Then another *plop*.

A sense of panic crept up on the detective. 'Who are you?' he repeated.

'I am someone.'

Kinderman stared. He was taken aback. Sunlight's mouth curved into a smile and in the eyes there was a mocking, malevolent glint.

'Yes, of course, you are someone,' Kinderman responded, struggling for a grip on his self-control. 'But who? Are you Damien Karras?'

'No.'

'Then who are you? What is your name?'

'Call me "Legion", for we are many.'

An unreasoning chill passed through Kinderman's body. He wanted to be out of this room. He couldn't move. Abruptly Sunlight put his head back and crowed like a rooster; then he neighed like a horse. The sounds were authentic, not at all like imitations, and inwardly Kinderman gasped at the performance.

Sunlight's chuckle was a thick and bitter syrup cascading. 'Yes, I do my imitations rather well, don't you think? After all, I've had the time to perfect them. Practice, practice! Ah, yes, that's the key. It's the secret to the slickness of my butchery, Lieutenant.'

'Why do you call me "Lieutenant"?' asked Kinderman.

'Don't be devious.' The words were a snarl.

'Do you know my name?' asked Kinderman.

'Yes.'

'What is it?'

'Do not rush me,' Sunlight hissed. 'I will show you my powers by and by.'

'Your powers?'

'You bore me.'

'Who are you?'

'You know who I am.'

'No, I don't.'

'You do.'

'Then tell me.'

'The Gemini.'

Kinderman paused for a moment. He listened to the dripping of the faucet. At last he said, 'Prove it.'

Sunlight put his head back and brayed like a donkey. The detective felt the hair prickling up on his hands. Sunlight looked down and said matter-of-factly, 'It's often good to change the subject now and then, don't you think?' He sighed and averted his gaze to the floor. 'Yes, I've had such good times in my life. So much fun.' He shut his eyes and a blissful expression came over his face, as if he were inhaling a delicious fragrance. 'Ah, Karen,' he crooned. 'Pretty Karen. Little ribbons, yellow ribbons in her hair. It smelled of Houbigant Chantilly. I can almost smell it now.'

Kinderman's eyebrows rose involuntarily and the blood started draining from his face. Sunlight looked up at him. His eyes read Kinderman's expression. 'Yes, I killed her,' said Sunlight. 'After all, it was inevitable, wasn't it? Of course. A divinity shapes our ends and all that. I picked her up in Sausalito and then later dropped her off at the city dump. At least some of her. Some of her I kept. I'm a rank sentimentalist. It's a fault, but who is perfect, Lieutenant? In my defence, I kept her breast in my freezer for a time. I'm a saver. Pretty dress she was wearing. A little peasant blouse with pink and white ruffles. I still hear from her occasionally. Screaming. I think the dead should shut up unless there's something to say.' He looked cross, then put his head back and lowed like a steer. The sound was shatteringly real. He abruptly broke it off and looked back at Kinderman. 'Needs work,' he said with a frown. For a time he was silent, studying Kinderman with a motionless, unblinking stare. 'Be calm,' he said in a flat, dead voice. 'I hear the sound of your terror ticking like a clock.'

Kinderman swallowed and listened to the dripping, unable to wrench away his gaze.

'Yes, I also killed the black boy by the river,' said Sunlight. 'That was fun. They're all fun. Except for the priests. The priests were different. Not my style. I kill at random. That's the thrill of it. No motive. That's the fun. But the priests were different. Oh, of course, they had a "K" at the start of their names. Yes, that much I was able to insist upon, finally. We must keep on killing Daddy, must we not? Still in all, the priests were different. Not my style. Not random. I was obliged – well, obliged to settle a score on behalf of – a friend.' He fell silent and continued to stare. Waiting.

'What friend?' asked Kinderman at last.

'You know, a friend over here. The other side.'

'You are on the other side?'

An odd change came over Sunlight. The air of distant mockery disappeared and was replaced by a manner of uneasiness and fear. 'Don't be envious, Lieutenant. There is suffering over here. It isn't easy. No, not easy. They can sometimes be cruel. Very cruel.'

'Who are "they"?'

'Never mind. I cannot tell you. It's forbidden.'

Kinderman thought for a time. He leaned forward. 'Do you know my name?' he said.

'Your name is Max.'

'No, it isn't,' said Kinderman.

'If you say so.'

'Why did you think it was Max?'

'I don't know. You remind me of my brother, I suppose.'

'You have a brother named Max?'

'Someone does.'

Kinderman probed the expressionless eyes. Was there something sardonic in them? Something taunting? Abruptly Sunlight lowed like a steer again. When he'd finished, he looked satisfied. 'It's getting better,' he rumbled. Then he belched.

'What is your brother's name?' asked Kinderman.

'Keep my brother out of this,' Sunlight growled. The next instant, his manner became expansive. 'Do you know that you're talking to an artist?' he asked. 'I do special things with my victims sometimes. Things that are creative. But of course, they take knowledge and a pride in your work. Did you know, for example, that decapitated heads can continue to see for about – oh, possibly twenty seconds. So when I have one that's gawking, I hold it up so it can see its body. That's an extra I throw in for no added charge. I must admit it makes me chuckle every time. But why should I have all the fun? I like to share. But of course, I got no credit for that in the media. They just wanted to print all the bad things about me. Is that fair?'

Kinderman suddenly said sharply, '*Damien*!'

'Please don't shout,' said Sunlight. 'There are sick people here. Observe the rules or I shall have you ejected. Incidentally, who's this Damien you insist that I am?'

'Don't you know?'

'I sometimes wonder.'

'Wonder what?'

'The prices of cheese and how Daddy's getting on. Are they calling these Gemini killings in the papers? It's important, Lieutenant. You must get them to do that. Dear Daddy's got to know. That's the point. That's my motive. I'm so glad we could have this little chat to convince you.'

'The Gemini is dead,' said Kinderman.

Sunlight froze him with a look of menace. 'I'm alive,' he hissed. 'I go on. See to it that it's known, or I will punish you, fat man.'

'How will you punish me?'

Sunlight's manner abruptly turned amiable. 'Dancing is fun,' he said. 'Do you dance?'

'If you're the Gemini, prove it,' said Kinderman.

'Again? Christ, I've given you every fucking proof you could need,' Sunlight rasped. His eyes shone with anger and icy venom.

'You couldn't have killed the priests and the boy.'

'I did.'

'The boy's name was what?'

'It was Kintry, the little black bastard.'

'How could you get out of here to have done that?'

'They let me out,' said Sunlight.

'What?'

'They let me out. They take off my straitjacket, open the door, and then send me out to prowl the world. All the doctors and the nurses. They're all in it with me. Sometimes I bring them back pizza or a copy of the Sunday *Washington Post*. Other times, they just ask me to sing. I sing well.' He put back his head and began to sing with flawless pitch and in a high falsetto, 'Drink To Me Only With Thine Eyes.' He sang it all. Kinderman again felt a fear in his soul.

Sunlight finished and grinned at the detective. 'Did you like that? I think I'm pretty good. Don't you think? I'm multifaceted, as they say. Life is fun. It's a *wonderful* life, in fact. For some. Too bad about poor Father Dyer.'

Kinderman stared.

'You know I killed him,' Sunlight said quietly. 'An interesting problem. But it worked. First a bit of the old succinylcholine to permit me to work without annoying distractions; then a three-foot catheter threaded directly into the inferior *vena cava* – or in fact, the superior *vena cava*. It's a matter of taste, don't you think? Then the tube moves through the vein from the crease of the arm, and then into the vein that leads into the heart. Then you hold up the legs and squeeze blood manually from the arms and from the legs. It isn't perfect; there's a little blood left in the body, I'm afraid, but regardless, the total effect is astonishing, and isn't that what really counts in the end?'

Kinderman looked stunned.

Sunlight chuckled. 'Yes, of course. Good showbiz, Lieutenant. The effect. All done without spilling a drop of blood. I call that showmanship, Lieutenant. But of course, no one noticed. Pearls before –'

Sunlight did not finish. Kinderman had risen, rushed over to the couch, and struck Sunlight's face with a savage, smashing backhand slap. Now he loomed over Sunlight, his body trembling. Blood began to trickle from Sunlight's mouth and from his nose. He leered up at Kinderman. 'A few boos from the gallery, I see. That's fine. Yes, that's all right. I understand. I've been dull. Well, I shall liven things up for you a bit.'

Kinderman looked puzzled. Sunlight's words were growing slurry, his eyelids heavy with a sudden drowsiness. His head was beginning to sag. He was whispering something. Kinderman leaned over to catch the words. 'Goodnight moon. Goodnight cow – jumping over – the moon. Goodnight – Amy. Sweet little –'

Something extraordinary happened. Though Sunlight's lips were barely moving, another voice emerged from his mouth. It was the younger, lighter voice of a man, and he seemed to be shouting from a distance. 'S-s-s-stop him!' the voice cried in a stutter. 'D-d-d-don't let him –!'

'Amy,' whispered Sunlight's voice.

'N-n-n-no!' cried the other far away. 'J-j-j-ames! No-n-n-no! D-d-d –!'

The voice stopped. Sunlight's head drooped over and he seemed to fall unconscious. Kinderman stared down at him, awed, uncomprehending. 'Sunlight,' he said. There was no answer.

Kinderman turned and walked to the door. He buzzed for the nurse and then stepped outside. He waited for the nurse to come rushing up to him. 'He passed out,' he said.

'Again?'

Kinderman watched her rush into the cell, his eyebrows knitting into a question. When the nurse reached Sunlight Kinderman turned and began to walk rapidly down the hall. He felt shame and regret as he heard the nurse cry out, 'His goddam nose is broken!'

Kinderman hurried to the Charge Desk where Atkins was

waiting with some papers. He handed them over to the detective. 'Stedman said you'd want this right away,' said the sergeant.

'What is it?' asked Kinderman.

'The pathology report on the man in the coffin,' said Atkins.

Kinderman stuffed the papers in a pocket. 'I want a policeman stationed in the hall outside Cell 12,' he told Atkins urgently. 'Tell him not to leave here tonight until I speak to him. Point two, find the Gemini's father. His name is Karl Vennamun. Try to get access to the National Computer. I need him here quickly. Get to it, please Atkins. It's important.'

Atkins said, 'Yes, sir,' and hurried away. Kinderman leaned against the Charge Desk and took the papers from his pocket. He skimmed them hurriedly, but then went back and reread one section. It gave him a start. He heard shoes squeaking towards him. He looked up. Nurse Spencer stood before him accusingly. 'Did you hit him?' she asked.

'May I speak to you in private?'

'What's wrong with your hand?' she said. She was staring at it. 'It's swollen.'

'Never mind, it's all right,' the detective told her. 'Could we talk in your office, please?'

'Go on in,' she said. 'I need to get something.' She walked away and around a corner. Kinderman entered her little office and sat at the desk. While he waited, he studied the report again. Already shaken, he fell deeper into doubt and confusion.

'Okay, let me have that hand.' The nurse was back with a few supplies. Kinderman held out his hand and she started to pad it with gauze and then bandage it. 'That's very kind of you,' he said.

'Don't mention it.'

'When I told you Mister Sunlight passed out, you said "again",' said Kinderman.

'Did I?'

'Yes.'

'Well, it's happened before.'

The detective winced from a pressure on his hand.

'You want to hit people, that's what happens,' said the nurse.

'How often has he fallen unconscious before?'

'Well, actually, just this week. I think the first time was Sunday.'

'Sunday?'

'Yes, I think so,' said Spencer. 'Then again the next day. If you want exact times, I can check the chart.'

'No, no, no, not just yet. Any others?' he asked.

'Well –' Nurse Spencer looked uncomfortable. 'About four o'clock Wednesday morning. I mean, just before we found –' She paused and looked flustered.

'That's all right,' said Kinderman. 'You're very sensitive. Thank you for that. In the meantime, when this happens is it normal sleep?'

'Not at all,' responded Spencer, snipping the bandage roll with a scissors. She taped the loose end. 'His autonomic system slows to almost nothing: heartbeat, temperature, respiration. It's like hibernation. But his brainwave activity's just the opposite. It speeds up like crazy.'

Kinderman stared at her in silence.

'Does that mean something?' Spencer asked him.

'Has anyone mentioned to Sunlight what happened to Father Dyer?'

'I don't know. *I* haven't.'

'Doctor Temple?'

'I don't know.'

'Does he spend a lot of time treating Sunlight?'

'You mean Temple?'

'Yes, Temple.'

'Yes, I think so. Guess he thinks it's a challenge.'

'Does he use hypnosis on him?'

'Yes.'

'Very often?'

'I don't know. I'm not sure. I can't be sure.'

'And when was the last time you saw Temple doing this, please?'

'Wednesday morning.'

'At what time?'

'Around three. I was working the shift for a girl on vacation. Move your fingers a little.'

Kinderman wiggled his swollen hand.

'Feel all right?' she asked. 'Not too tight?'

'No, it's fine, Miss. Thank you. And thank you for talking to me.' He stood up. 'One little thing,' he said. 'Could you keep our discussion confidential?'

'Sure. And the broken nose as well.'

'He's all right now, Sunlight?'

She nodded. 'They're giving him an EEG right now.'

'You'll let me know if the results are as usual?'

'Yes. Lieutenant?'

'Yes?'

'This is all very strange,' she said.

Kinderman met her gaze in silence. Then he told her, 'Thank you,' and left the office. He walked hurriedly through the halls and found Temple's office. The door was closed. He lifted his bandaged hand to knock, then remembered his injury and knocked with the other hand. He heard Temple say, 'Come in.' Kinderman entered.

'Oh, it's you,' said Temple. He was sitting at his desk, his white medical jacket stained with ashes. His tongue wet the end of a fresh cigarillo and he pointed to a chair. 'Have a seat. What's the problem? Hey, what's wrong with your hand?'

'A little scratch,' the detective told him. He eased himself down in the chair.

'Big scratch,' said Temple. 'So what can I do you for, Lieutenant?'

'You have the right to remain silent,' Kinderman told him, speaking in a deadly, flat tone of voice. 'If you give up the right to remain silent, anything you say can and will be used against you in a court of law. You have the right to speak with an attorney and to have the attorney present during questioning. If you so desire, and cannot afford one, an attorney will be appointed for you without charge prior to questioning. Do you understand each of these rights that I've explained to you?'

Temple looked staggered. 'What the hell are you talking about?'

'I have asked you a question,' snapped Kinderman. 'Answer it.'

'Yes.'

'You understand your rights?'

The psychiatrist looked cowed. 'Yes, I do,' he said softly.

'Mister Sunlight in the Disturbed Ward, Doctor – have you treated him?'

'Yes.'

'You've done so personally?'

'Yes.'

'You've used hypnosis?'

'Yes.'

'How often?'

'Maybe once or twice a week.'

'For how long?'

'A few years.'

'And to what end?'

'Just to get him to talk, at first; and then later to find out who he is.'

'And did you?'

'No.'

'You didn't?'

'No.'

Kinderman stared in steely silence. The psychiatrist shifted a little in his chair. 'Well, he said he's the Gemini Killer,' he blurted. 'That's crazy.'

'Why?'

'Well, the Gemini's dead.'

'Doctor, isn't it a fact that by the use of hypnosis you implanted Mister Sunlight's conviction he's the Gemini?'

The psychiatrist's face began to crimson. He shook his head vigorously, once, and said, 'No.'

'You did not?'

'No, I didn't.'

'Did you tell Mister Sunlight the manner in which Father Dyer was murdered?'

'No.'

'Did you tell him my name and rank?'

'No.'

'Did you forge a so-called Order Form involving Martina Lazlo?'

Temple stared silently, flushing, then said, 'No.'

'You are positive?'

'Yes.'

'Doctor Temple, it's a fact, is it not, that you worked with the Gemini Squad in San Francisco as their chief psychiatric consultant on the case?'

Temple looked stricken.

'Is that a fact or is it not?' said Kinderman harshly.

The psychiatrist said, 'Yes,' in a weak, cracked voice.

'Mister Sunlight has specific information known generally only to the Gemini Squad about the murder of a woman named Karen Jacobs killed by the Gemini in 1968. Did you give Mister Sunlight this information?'

'No.'

'You did not?'

'No, I didn't. I swear it.'

'Isn't it a fact that through hypnosis you've implanted the conviction in the man in Cell 12 that he is the Gemini Killer?'

'I said, *no!*'

'Do you now wish to change any part of your testimony?'

'Yes.'

'What part?'

'About the Order Form,' Temple said weakly.

The detective cupped a hand to his ear.

'The Order Form,' said Temple, raising his voice.

'You forged it?'

'Yes.'

'To make trouble for Doctor Amfortas?'

'Yes.'

'To make him a suspect?'

'No. It wasn't that.'

'Then why?'

'I don't like him.'

'Why not?'

Temple seemed to hesitate. At last he said, 'His manner.'

'His manner?'

'So superior,' said Temple.

'And for this you forge an Order Form, Doctor?'

Temple stared.

'When I spoke to you on Wednesday about Father Dyer, I described the authentic Gemini M.O. Yet you made no comment. Why was that? Why did you conceal your background, Doctor?'

'I didn't conceal it.'

'Why didn't you offer it?'

'I was scared.'

'You were what?'

'Afraid. I was sure you'd suspect me.'

'You achieved a notoriety during the Gemini case and have since become obscure. Isn't it a fact that you have an interest in resurrecting the Gemini murders?'

'No.'

Kinderman drilled his eyes with a deadly, grim, unblinking stare. He did not move at all or speak. Finally, Temple's face turned ashen and he quavered, 'You're not going to arrest me, are you?'

'Intense dislike,' the detective said firmly, 'is not probable cause for making an arrest. You are a terrible, indecent man, Doctor Temple, but for the moment the only restriction upon you is that you disengage from Mister Sunlight. You will not treat him or enter his cell until you are given further notice. And stay out of my sight,' said Kinderman harshly. He stood up and walked out of Temple's office, pulling the door shut loudly behind him.

For much of the remainder of the afternoon, Kinderman wandered around the Disturbed Ward waiting for the man in

Cell 12 to grow conscious. He waited in vain. At approximately half-past five he left the hospital. The cobbled streets were slick with rain as he rounded 'O' Street onto 36th and walked south to Amfortas's tight frame house. There he rang the doorbell and knocked repeatedly. No one answered and at last he left. He walked up 'O' Street and entered the gates of the University. He went up to Father Healy's office. The little reception room was empty; the secretary wasn't at her desk. Kinderman started to glance at his watch when he heard Father Healy calling to him gently from the inner office, 'I'm here, friend. Come in.'

The Jesuit was sitting behind his desk, his hands clasped together at the back of his head. He looked tired and depressed. 'Sit down and relax,' he told the detective.

Kinderman nodded and sat in a chair to the side of the desk. 'You've been well, Father?'

'Yes, thank God. And you?'

Kinderman cast his eyes down and nodded; then he remembered to remove his hat. 'I'm sorry,' he murmured.

'What can I do for you, Lieutenant?'

'Father Karras,' the detective said. 'From the time he was taken away in the ambulance, what happened, Father? Would you know? I mean precisely, Father – the schedule of events from the time he died until he was buried.'

Healy told him what he knew and when he'd finished both men fell silent for a time. Outside on the campus the wind rattled windowpanes in the darkness of the winter night. Then the lid of a Scotch bottle rasped metallically as the Jesuit slowly unscrewed it. He poured two fingers into a glass and then sipped and grimaced. 'I don't know,' he breathed softly. He stared through a window at the lights of the city. 'I just don't know anything any more.'

Kinderman nodded in mute agreement. He bent over in his chair, hands clasped together, and he groped for some thread that he could follow toward reason. 'He was buried the next morning,' he said, recapping what Healy had told him. 'Closed coffin. The usual thing with your burials. But what person was the last one to see him, Father Healy? Would you know? Do

213

you remember? I mean, who was the last one to see him in the coffin?'

Healy swirled the Scotch around in his glass with a gentle movement of his wrist, staring down at the amber fluid reflectively. Then, 'Fain,' he murmured. 'Brother Fain.' He paused as though checking his memory, then looked up with a nod of his head. 'Yes, that's right. He was left to dress the body and seal up the coffin. Then no one ever saw him again.'

'What was that?'

'I said, no one ever saw him again.' Healy shrugged and shook his head. 'Sad case,' he sighed. 'He'd always griped about the Order not treating him well. He had a family in Kentucky and kept asking for assignment someplace near them. Towards the end he –'

'Towards the end?' interjected Kinderman.

'He was elderly; eighty – eighty-one. He always said when he died he'd make sure he died at home. We always figured he just split because he sensed it was coming. He'd already had a couple of pretty bad coronaries.'

'Two coronaries precisely?'

'Yes,' said Healy.

Kinderman's flesh began to tingle. 'The man in Damien's coffin,' he said numbly. 'You remember he was dressed like a priest?'

Healy nodded.

'The autopsy,' said Kinderman, pausing for a moment. 'The man was elderly and showed the scarring of three major heart attacks: two before plus the one that killed him.'

The two men stared at one another in silence. Father Healy waited for what came next. Kinderman held his eyes and told him, 'We have every indication that he died of fright.'

The man in Cell 12 did not regain consciousness until approximately six the next morning, a few minutes before Nurse Amy Keating was discovered in an empty room in Neurology. Her torso had been slit open, her organs removed, and her body – before being sewn back up – had been stuffed with light switches.

Chapter Fourteen

He sat in a space between fear and longing, a portable tape recorder clutched in one hand as he listened to cassettes of the music they had shared. Was it day or night outside? He didn't know. The world was veiled beyond his living room, and the light from the lamps seemed dim. He couldn't remember how long he'd been sitting there. Was it hours or only minutes? Reality danced in and out of his focus in a silent, baffling Harlequinade. He'd doubled the steroid dosage, he remembered; the pain had eased to an ominous throbbing, a price that his brain had exacted for its ruin, for the drug ate away at its vital connections. He stared at a sofa and watched as it shrank to half its size. When he saw it smile he closed his eyes and gave himself totally to the music, a haunting song from a show they had seen:

> '*Touch me*
> *It's so easy to leave me*
> *All alone with my memories*
> *Of my days in the sun.*'

The song swept through his soul and filled it. He wanted it louder and he fumbled for the volume control on the recorder when he heard a cassette fall softly to the floor. When he groped to pick it up two more of the cassettes slipped off his lap. He opened his eyes and saw the man. He was staring at his double.

The figure sat crouched in mid-air as though seated, mimicking Amfortas' posture precisely. Dressed in the same denim jeans and blue sweater, it was staring back with an equal astonishment.

Amfortas leaned back; it leaned back. Amfortas put a hand to his face; it did the same. Amfortas said, 'Hello'; it said, 'Hello'.

Amfortas felt his heart begin to beat faster. The 'double' was an often-reported hallucination in serious disorders of the temporal lobe, but looking into those eyes and at that face was eerily disquieting, almost frightening. Amfortas shut his eyes and began to breathe deeply, and slowly his heart rate began to slow down. Would the double be there when he opened his eyes again? he wondered. He looked. It was there. Now Amfortas grew fascinated. No neurologist had ever seen 'the double'. The reports of its behaviour were vague and contradictory. A clinical interest overcame him. He picked up his feet and held them out. The double did the same. He put his feet down. The double followed. Then Amfortas started crossing and uncrossing his feet with a timing that he tried to make random and unplanned, but the double imitated, matching the movements simultaneously without flaw or variation.

Amfortas paused and thought for a moment. Then he held up the tape recorder in his hand. As the double imitated the action, its hand was empty, curled around the air. Amfortas wondered why the delusion stopped short of including the tape recorder. The double wore clothing, after all. He could not think of an explanation.

Amfortas looked down at the double's shoes. Like his own, they were blue-and-white striped Nikes. He looked at his feet and pigeoned them inward, making sure he could not see if the double was matching him. Would it mimick if he were not observing its action as it happened? He shifted his gaze to the double's feet. They were already pigeoned in. Amfortas was wondering what to try next when he noticed that a tip on the double's left shoelace had something like an ink mark on it or a scuff. When he checked his own shoe he saw that his shoelace tip was the same. He thought that was odd. He didn't think he had known of such a marking until now. How had he seen it on the double? Perhaps his unconscious had known, he decided.

Amfortas lifted his gaze to the double's. It was haggard and burning. Amfortas leaned closer; he thought he saw lamplight reflected in the eyes. How could this be? the neurologist wondered. Again he experienced a sense of disquiet. The double was staring at him intently. Amfortas heard voices coming from the street, students shouting back and forth; then they faded to silence and he thought he could hear the beating of his heart when suddenly the double grasped at its temple and gasped in pain, and Amfortas was unable to distinguish the action of the double from his own as the searing pincers clutched at his brain. He rose unsteadily to his feet and cassettes and the tape recorder tumbled to the floor. Amfortas lurched blindly towards the stairs, knocking over an end table and a lamp. Moaning, he stumbled up to his bedroom, opened the medical bag on the bed and groped for the hypodermic and the drug. The pain was unbearable. He flopped on the edge of the bed and with shaking hands filled up the syringe. He could barely see. He stabbed the syringe through the fabric of his trousers and pressed twelve milligrams of steroid into his thigh. He'd done it so rapidly that the drug hit his muscle like a hammer; but soon he felt an easing of the pain in his head, and a calm and a clarity of thought. He exhaled a long and fluttering breath and allowed the disposable syringe to slip from his fingers to the floor. It rolled on the wood and then stopped at a wall.

When Amfortas looked up, he was staring at the double. It was sitting in mid-air calmly meeting his gaze. Amfortas saw a smile on its lips, his own. 'I'd lost track of you,' they said in perfect unison. Now Amfortas began to feel giddy. 'Can you sing?' they said; then together they hummed a piece of the *Adagio* from Rachmaninoff's Symphony in C. When they broke it off, they chuckled in amusement. 'What very good company you are,' they said. Amfortas shifted his glance to the night-stand and the green and white ceramic of the duck. He picked it up and held it with tenderness while his eyes brushed over it, remembering. 'I bought this for Ann while we were still dating,' they said. 'At Mama Leone's in New York. The food was awful but the duck was a hit. Ann cherished this crazy little thing.' He looked up at the double. They smiled fondly. 'She said it was romantic,' said Amfortas and the double. 'Like those flowers in Bora Bora. She said she had a painting of that in her heart.'

Amfortas frowned and the double frowned back. The doubling of his voice had abruptly begun to annoy the neurologist. He felt an odd sensation of floating, of becoming disconnected with his surroundings. Something smelled horrible. 'Go away,' he said to the double. It persisted, simultaneously mimicking his words. Amfortas stood up and walked unsteadily to the stairs. He could see the double at his side, a mirror image of his movements.

The next instant, Amfortas found himself sitting in the living room chair. He didn't know how he'd gotten there. He was holding the duck in his lap. His mind seemed clear again and tranquil, though he felt himself suffering in some way at a distant remove from his perceptions. He could hear a dull pounding in his head but could not feel it. He looked at the double with distaste. It was facing him, sitting in the air and scowling. Amfortas closed his eyes to escape from the vision.

'Do you mind if I smoke?'

For a moment the voice didn't register; then Amfortas opened his eyes and stared. The double was sitting on the sofa, one leg comfortably stretched on its cushions. It lit a cigarette and exhaled smoke. 'God knows, I've been trying to give it up,' it said. 'Oh well, I've at least cut down.'

Amfortas was stunned.

'Have I upset you?' asked the double. It frowned as if in sympathy. 'Awfully sorry.' It shrugged its shoulders. 'Strictly speaking I shouldn't be relaxing like this, but for heaven's sakes, I'm tired. That's all. I need a break. And in this case, what's the harm? Do you know what I mean?' It was staring at Amfortas with an air of expectancy, but the neurologist was still speechless. 'I understand,' it said at last. 'It takes a bit of getting used to, I suppose. I've never learned how to make a subtle entrance. I suppose I could have tried it an inch at a time.' It gave a shrug of surrender, and then said, 'Hindsight. Anyway, I'm here, and I do apologize. All these years I've been aware of you, of course, but you've never known about me. Too bad. There are times when I've wanted to shake you, so to speak; to set you straight. Well, I suppose I can't do that, even now.

Stupid rules. But at least we can have a chat.' It looked suddenly solicitous. 'Feeling better? No. I see the cat still has your tongue. Never mind, I'll keep talking until you're used to me.' A cigarette ash fell on its sweater. It looked down and brushed it away, and murmured, 'Careless.'

Amfortas started giggling.

'It's alive,' said the double. 'How nice.' It stared as Amfortas continued to laugh. 'Only nice to a point,' said the double sternly. 'Do you want me to mimick you again?'

Amfortas shook his head, still chuckling. Then he noticed that the table and lamp he'd knocked over were back in place. He stared, looking puzzled.

'Yes, I picked them up,' said the double. 'I'm real.'

Amfortas returned his gaze to the double. 'You're in my mind,' he said.

'Four words. Well done. We're progressing. I'm referring to the form,' said the double, 'not content.'

'You're an hallucination.'

'And the lamp and the table as well?'

'I went into a fugue coming down the steps. I picked them up myself and then forgot it.'

The double breathed out smoke with a sigh. 'Earth souls,' it murmured, shaking its head. 'Would it help to convince you if I were to touch you? If you could feel me?'

'Perhaps,' said Amfortas.

'Well, it can't be done,' said the double. 'That's out.'

'That's because I'm hallucinating.'

'If you say that again I will vomit. Listen, who do you think that it is you're talking to?'

'Myself.'

'Well, that's partially correct. Congratulations. Yes. I'm your other soul,' said the double. 'Say "Pleased to meet you", or something, would you? Manners. Oh, that puts me in mind of a story. About introductions and what-not. It's lovely.' The double sat up for a moment, smiling. 'This was told to me by Noël Coward's double, and Coward himself says it's true, that it happened. It seems he was standing in a Royal reception line.

He was right beside the Queen and to the other side of him stood Nicol Williamson. Well, along came a man named Chuck Connors. An American actor. You know? Of course. Well, he thrust out his hand to shake Noël's and said, "Mister Coward, I'm Chuck Connors"! And Noël said immediately in a soothing, reassuring tone, "Why, my dear boy, of *course* you are." Isn't that lovely?' The double leaned back against the sofa. "What a wit, that Coward. Too bad he's moved on past the border. Good for him, of course. Bad for us." The double looked meaningfully at Amfortas. 'Good conversationalists are so rare,' it said. 'Do you get my drift or do you not?' It flicked the cigarette stub to the floor. 'Don't worry. It's not going to burn,' it said.

Amfortas felt a mixture of doubt and excitement. There was something of reality about the double, a flavour of life that was not his own. 'Why don't you prove that I'm not hallucinating,' he said.

The double looked puzzled. 'Prove it?'

'Yes.'

'How?'

'Tell me something I don't know.'

'I can't stay here forever,' said the double.

'Some fact I don't know that I can check.'

'Did you know that little story about Noël Coward?'

'I made it up. It isn't a fact.'

'You are utterly insatiable,' said the double. 'Do you think you had the wit to make that up?'

'My unconscious does,' said Amfortas.

'Once again, you are close to the truth,' said the double. 'Your unconscious is your other soul. But not exactly in the way you suppose.'

'Please explain that.'

'Prevenient,' said the double.

'What?'

'That's a fact you don't know. It just came to me. "Prevenient". That's a word. I heard it from Noël. There. Are you satisfied?'

'I know the Latin roots of the word.'

'This is absolutely maddening if not insufferable,' said the double. 'I give up. You're hallucinating. And I suppose now you're going to tell me that you didn't commit those murders. Speaking of facts you don't know, old boy.'

Amfortas froze. The double peered over at him slyly. 'Not denying it, I see.'

The neurologist's tongue was thick in his mouth. 'What murders?' he asked.

'You know. The priests. That boy.'

'No.' Amfortas shook his head.

'Oh, don't be stubborn. Yes, I know, you weren't consciously aware of it. Still in all.' The double shrugged. 'You knew. You knew.'

'I had nothing to do with those murders.'

The double looked angry and suspicious. It sat up. 'Oh, I suppose now you're going to blame *me*. Well, I haven't got a body, so that let's me out. Besides that, we don't meddle. Do you understand? It was you and *your* anger that committed those murders. Yes, your anger, over God taking Ann from you. Face it. That's the reason you're allowing yourself to die. It's your guilt. Incidentally, that's a stupid idea. It's the coward's way out. It's premature.'

Amfortas looked down at the ceramic. He was squeezing it, shaking his head. 'I want to be with Ann,' he said.

'She isn't there.'

Amfortas looked up.

'I see I have your attention,' said the double. He leaned back against the sofa. 'Yes, you're dying, you think, because you want to join Ann. Well, I'm not going to argue that now. You're too stubborn. But it's pointless. Ann's moved on to another wing. With all that blood on your soul, I rather doubt that you'll ever catch up. Awfully sorry to be telling you this, but I'm not here to feed you lies. I can't afford it. I've got trouble enough as it is.'

'Where is Ann?' The neurologist's heart was beating faster, the pain growing closer to his field of awareness.

'Ann is being treated,' said the double. 'Like the rest of us.' He abruptly looked sly. 'Do you know where I come from now?'

Amfortas turned his head and stared numbly at the tape recorder in the corner, and then back at the double.

'Amazing. A landmark in the history of learning. Yes, you've heard my voice before on your tapes. I'm from there. Would you like to know all about it?'

Amfortas was mesmerized. He nodded.

'I'm afraid I can't tell you,' said the double. 'Sorry. There are rules and regulations. Let's just say that it's a place of transition. As for Ann, as I told you before, she's gone on. That's just as well. You were bound to find out about her and Temple.'

The neurologist held his breath and stared. The pounding in his head was growing louder, the pain more present and insistent. 'What do you mean?' he said, his voice breaking.

The double shrugged and looked away. 'Would you like to hear a nice definition of jealousy? It's the feeling that you get when someone you absolutely detest is having a wonderful time without you. There could be some truth in that. Think it over.'

'You aren't real,' said Amfortas huskily. His vision was blurring. The double's body was undulating on the sofa.

'Christ, I'm out of cigarettes.'

'You're not real.' The light was growing dim.

The double was a voice amid shimmering movement. 'Oh, I'm not? Well, by God, I'm going to break another rule. No, really. My patience has come to its limit. There's a nurse who joined your staff today. Her name is Cecily Woods. You couldn't possibly know that. She's on duty this minute. Go ahead, pick up the telephone and see whether or not I'm right. You want a fact you didn't know? That's it. Go ahead. Call Neurology and ask for Nurse Woods.'

'You're not real.'

'Call her now.'

'You're not *real*!' Amfortas was shouting. He stood up from the chair, the ceramic in his hand, his body trembling, the pain pushing upward, tearing and crushing and making him cry out, 'God! Oh, my God!' He moved blindly towards the sofa, stumbling, sobbing, and as the room began to whirl he tripped and fell forward, smashing his head against the corner of the coffee table with a force that opened up a red wound. He thudded to the floor and the green and white ceramic gripped in his hand smashed to pieces with a splintering sound of loss. In moments the blood seeping out from his temple was lapping at the shards and staining the fingers still tightly clutching a piece of the inscription. It said, 'ADORABLE'. The blood soon covered it over. Amfortas whispered, 'Ann.'

SATURDAY, MARCH 21

Chapter Fifteen

The old man's name was Perkins and he was a patient in the Open Ward. He'd been found unconscious in Room 400, where the body of Keating had been discovered by the Charge Nurse coming on duty at six. The room was around the corner from the Charge Desk and out of view of the uniformed policemen posted at the stairwells and the elevator banks. The old man had blood on his hands. 'Will you answer me?' Kinderman said to him. The old man's stare was blank. He was seated on a chair. 'I like dinner,' he said.

'That's all he ever says,' Nurse Lorenzo told Kinderman. She was a nurse from the Open Ward. The Neurology Charge Nurse who'd discovered the body was standing by a window, controlling her horror. She was new on the ward.

'I like dinner,' the old man repeated dully. He smacked his lips over toothless gums.

Kinderman turned to the nurse from Neurology, appraising the tightness of her neck and face. His glance flicked down to her nametag. 'Thank you, Miss Woods,' he said. 'You may go.'

She left hurriedly and closed the door behind her. Kinderman turned to Miss Lorenzo. 'Would you help the old man into the bathroom, please?'

Nurse Lorenzo hesitated a moment, then assisted the elderly man to his feet and guided him toward the bathroom door. The detective was standing inside. The nurse and the old man stopped at the doorway and Kinderman pointed to a mirror on the door of the medicine chest above the sink where a message had been scrawled in blood. 'Did you write this?' the detective demanded. With a hand, he turned the old man's head so that his gaze was on the mirror. 'Did someone make you write this?'

'I like dinner,' drooled the patient.

Kinderman stared without expression, then he lowered his head and told the nurse, 'Take him back.'

Nurse Lorenzo nodded and assisted the senile old man from the room. Kinderman listened to their hesitant footsteps. When he heard the door to the room close softly, he slowly looked up at the writing on the mirror. He licked at dry lips as he read the message:

call me legion, for we are many

Kinderman hastened out of the room and picked up Atkins at the Charge Desk. 'Come with me, Nemo,' the detective ordered, not slackening his pace as he passed the sergeant. Atkins followed in his wake until at last they were standing in the isolation section in front of the door to Cell 12. Kinderman peered through the observation window. The man in the cell was awake. He was sitting on the edge of the cot in his straitjacket, grinning at Kinderman, his eyes mocking. His lips began moving and he seemed to be saying something but Kinderman couldn't hear him. The detective turned away and questioned the policeman standing by the door. 'How long have you been here?' he asked him.

'Since midnight,' answered the policeman.

'Has anyone entered the room since that time?'

'Just the nurse a few times.'

'Not a doctor?'

'No. Just the nurse.'

Kinderman considered this for a moment, then he turned to Atkins. 'Tell Ryan I want fingerprints taken of every member of the hospital staff,' he said. 'Start with Temple, and then everyone working in Neurology and Psychiatric next. After that we'll see. I want no exceptions. None. Get extra help to take the prints and then run the comparisons with the prints from the murder scenes. Get as many men as possible. I want it done quickly. Go ahead, Atkins. Hurry. And tell the nurse to come back here with her keys.'

Kinderman watched him hurrying away. When he'd rounded a corner, the detective kept listening to his footsteps as if they were the dwindling sound of reality. They faded away to silence and again there was darkness in Kinderman's soul. He glanced up at the light bulbs in the ceiling. Three were still out. The hallway was dim. Footsteps. The nurse was approaching. He waited. She reached him and he pointed to the door of Cell 12. The nurse probed his eyes with a shifting glance, then unlocked the door. He walked inside. Sunlight's nose had been taped and bandaged and his eyes were riveted to Kinderman's, unblinking and unwaveringly following him as he walked to the chair and sat down. The silence was thick and claustrophobic. Sunlight was perfectly immobile, a frozen image with eyes staring wide. He was like a figure in a wax museum. Kinderman looked up at the dangling light bulb. It was flickering. Now steady. The detective heard a chuckle.

'Yes, let there be light,' said the voice of Sunlight.

Kinderman looked hard into Sunlight's eyes. They were wide and vacant. 'Did you get my message, Lieutenant?' he asked. 'I left it with Keating. Nice girl. Good heart. Incidentally, I'm delighted that you're summoning Daddy. One thing, though. A favour. Might you call United Press and make sure Daddy's photographed together with Keating? That's why I kill, you know – to disgrace him. Help me. I'll make it worth your while. Death will take a holiday. Just once. For one day. I assure you, you'll be grateful. In the meantime, I could speak to my friends here about you. Put in a good word. They don't like you, you know. Don't ask me why. They keep mentioning your name begins with "K" but I ignore them. Isn't that good of me? And brave. They're so capricious with their angers.' He seemed to be thinking of something and shuddered. 'Never mind. Let's not talk about them now. Let's go on. I pose an

226

interesting problem for you, don't I, Lieutenant? I mean, presuming you're convinced now I really am the Gemini.' His face became a threatening mask. '*Are you convinced?*'

'No,' replied Kinderman.

'You're being very foolish,' rasped Sunlight with menace. 'And issuing a clear invitation to the dance.'

'I don't know what you mean by that,' said Kinderman.

'Neither do I,' said Sunlight blankly. His face was ingenuous. 'I'm a madman.'

Kinderman stared and listened to the dripping. Finally, he spoke. 'If you're the Gemini, how do you get out of here?'

'Do you like opera?' asked Sunlight. He began to sing from *La Bohème* in a deep, rich voice, then abruptly broke it off and looked at Kinderman. 'I like plays much better,' he said. '*Titus Andronicus* is my favourite. It's sweet.' He laughed softly. 'How is your friend Amfortas?' he asked. 'I understand he had a little visitation of late.' Sunlight started quacking like a duck, then fell silent. He looked away. 'Needs work,' he growled. He turned back to Kinderman, staring intently. 'You want to know how I get out?' he said.

'Yes, tell me.'

'Friends. Old friends.'

'What friends?'

'Tell me.'

'No, it's boring. Let's discuss something else.'

Kinderman waited, holding his gaze.

'It was wrong of you to hit me,' said Sunlight evenly. 'I can't help myself. I'm insane.'

Kinderman listened to the dripping of the faucet.

'Miss Keating ate tuna fish,' said Sunlight. 'I could smell it. Damned hospital food. It's disgusting.'

'How do you get out of here?' Kinderman repeated.

Sunlight leaned his head back and chuckled. Then he fixed a shining stare on Kinderman. 'There are so many possibilities. I think of them a lot. I try to figure it out. Do you think this might be true? I think possibly I *am* your friend Father Karras.

Perhaps they pronounced me dead but I wasn't. Later I resuscitated at – well – an embarrassing moment and then wandered the streets not knowing who I was. I still don't, for that matter. And needless to say, of course, I'm quite naturally and hopelessly mad. I have frequent dreams of falling down a long flight of steps. Is that something that really happened? If it did then I surely must have damaged my brain. Did that happen, Lieutenant?'

Kinderman kept silent.

'Other times I dream that I'm someone named Vennamun,' said Sunlight. 'These dreams are very nice. I kill people. Still, I can't sort out the dreams from the truth. I'm insane. You're quite wise to be sceptical, I'd say. Still in all, you're a homicide detective. So it's clear there are people being killed. That makes sense. Do you know what I think? It's Doctor Temple. Mightn't he have hypnotized his patients into – well – certain actions that are socially unacceptable these days? Ah, the times, they keep changing for the worse, don't you think? In the meantime, perhaps I'm telepathic or have psychic abilities that give me all my knowledge of the Gemini crimes. It's a thought, is it not? Yes, I see that you're thinking about it. Good for you. Bye the bye, chew on this. You haven't thought of it yet.' Sunlight's eyes glittered tauntingly and he leaned his body forward a little. 'What if the Gemini had an accomplice?'

'Who killed Father Bermingham?' asked Kinderman.

'Who is he?' Sunlight asked him innocently. His eyebrows were gathered in puzzlement.

'You don't know?' the detective asked.

'I can't be everywhere at once.'

'Who killed Nurse Keating?'

'"Put out the light, and then put out the light."'

'Who killed Nurse Keating?'

'The envious moon.' Sunlight put his head back and lowed like a steer. He looked back at Kinderman. 'I think I've almost got it now,' he said. 'It's fairly close. Tell the press that I'm the Gemini, Lieutenant. Last warning.'

He was staring ominously at Kinderman. The seconds ticked

by in silence. 'Father Dyer was silly,' said Sunlight at last. 'A silly person. How's your hand, by the way? Still swollen?'

'Who killed Nurse Keating?'

'Troublemakers. Persons unknown and no doubt uncouth.'

'If you did it, what happened to her vital organs?' asked the detective. 'You would know that. What happened to them? Tell me.'

'I like dinner,' said Sunlight in a monotone.

Kinderman stared at the expressionless eyes. *'Old Friends.'* The detective's heart skipped a beat.

'Daddy's got to know,' said Sunlight at last. His gaze broke away from Kinderman's and he vacantly stared into space. 'I'm tired,' he said softly. 'My work is never done, it seems. I'm tired.' He looked curiously helpless for a moment. Then he seemed to grow somnolent. His head drooped. 'Tommy doesn't understand,' he murmured. 'I tell him to go on without me but he won't. He's afraid. But he doesn't – understand. Tommy's – angry – with me.'

Kinderman stood up and moved closer. He leaned his ear close to Sunlight's mouth to catch whispered words. 'Little – Jack Horner. Child's – play.' Kinderman waited but nothing else came. Sunlight fell unconscious.

Kinderman hurriedly left the room. He felt an awful foreboding. On the way out he buzzed for the nurse. When she arrived he went back to the neurology wing and looked for Atkins. The sergeant was standing at the Charge Desk, talking on the telephone. When he saw the detective beside him, he hurried through the rest of his conversation.

A child was being checked into Neurology, a boy aged six. A hospital attendant had just pushed him up to the desk in a wheelchair. 'Here's a nice little fellah for you,' the attendant told the Charge Nurse. She smiled at the boy and said, 'Hi.'

Kinderman's attention was fixed on Atkins.

'Last name?' asked the nurse.

The attendant said, 'Korner. Vincent P.'

'Vincent *Paul*,' said the boy.

'Is that with a "C" or a "K"?' the nurse asked the attendant.

He handed her some papers. 'K'.

'Atkins, hurry,' said Kinderman urgently.

Atkins finished in another few seconds and the boy was wheeled away to a room in Neurology. Atkins hung up the phone.

'Put a man at the entrance to the Open Ward in Psychiatric,' Kinderman told him. 'I want someone there around the clock. No patient goes out, no matter what. No matter *what*!'

Atkins reached for the telephone and Kinderman grabbed his wrist. 'Call later. Give me someone right now,' he insisted.

Atkins signalled to a uniformed policeman stationed at the elevators. He came over. 'Come with me,' said Kinderman. 'Atkins, I am leaving you. Goodbye.'

Kinderman and the policeman hurried towards the Open Ward. When they'd reached the entrance Kinderman stopped and instructed the policeman, 'No patient comes out of here. Only staff. Understand?'

'All right, sir.'

'Do not leave for any reason unless relieved. Do not go to the bathroom, even.'

'Yes, sir.'

Kinderman left him and entered the ward and soon he was standing in the recreation room a few feet to the right of the Charge Desk. He looked around slowly, checking each face with a sense of wariness and a quickening feeling of dread. And yet all seemed in order. What was wrong? Then he noticed the quiet. He looked towards the crowd around the television set. He blinked and moved closer but abruptly he stopped a few feet from the group. Rapt and staring, their eyes were riveted to a television screen that was blank. The set was not on.

Kinderman glanced around the room and for the first time noticed there were neither any nurses nor attendants around. He squinted at the office behind the Charge Desk. No one was there. He looked at the silent group around the television set. His heart began to thump. The detective moved rapidly toward the Charge Desk, slipped around it and opened the door to the little office. He flinched in shock: A nurse and an attendant were sprawled on the floor, unconscious, blood seeping out of head wounds. The nurse was nude. No part of her uniform was anywhere in sight.

'*Child's play!*' '*Vincent Korner!*'

The words struck Kinderman's mind like a blow. Quickly he turned and rushed out of the office, only to freeze in his tracks at what he saw. Every patient in the room was moving towards him, approaching in a cordon that was closing in, the shuffling of their slippers the only sound in an awful, terrifying silence. They were leering, their glittering eyes fixed upon him, and from separated points of the room came their voices, lilting and staggered and eerily pleasant:

'Hello.'

'Hello.'

'So nice to see you, dear.'

They began to whisper unintelligibly. Kinderman shouted for help.

The boy had been medicated and was sleeping. The Venetian blinds at the window had been closed and the darkness of the room was dimly illuminated by the flickering of cartoons that were running on the television set without sound. The door opened silently and a woman in nurse's uniform entered. She was carrying a shopping bag. She closed the door quietly behind her, set the shopping bag down and took something out of it. She stared at the boy intently and then slowly and softly she approached him. The boy began to stir. He was on his back and he sleepily opened his eyes in a squint. As she leaned her body over the boy, the woman slowly raised her hands. 'Look what I've got for you, dearie,' she crooned.

Suddenly Kinderman burst into the room. Shouting hoarsely, '*No!*' he seized the woman from behind in a desperate chokehold. She made croaking, strangling noises, weakly flailing her arms behind her while the boy sat up, crying out in terror as Atkins and a uniformed policeman charged into the room behind the detective. 'I've got her!' croaked Kinderman. 'The light! Hit the light! Get the light!'

'Mommy! Mommy!'

The lights came on.

'You're choking me!' gurgled the nurse. A teddy bear dropped from her hands to the floor. Kinderman eyed it, looking stunned and slowly he released his frenzied grip. The nurse whipped around and kneaded her neck. 'Jesus *Christ*!' she exclaimed. 'What the hell is the *matter* with you? Are you *crazy*?'

'I want Mommy!' wailed the boy.

The nurse put her arms around him, pulling him close. 'You nearly broke my neck!' she squalled at Kinderman.

The detective was straining for breath. 'I'm sorry,' he wheezed; 'very sorry.' He pulled out a handkerchief and held it against his cheek where a long, deep scratch continued to bleed. 'My apologies.'

Atkins picked up the shopping bag and looked into it. 'Toys,' he said.

'What toys?' said the boy. He was suddenly calm and pulled away from the nurse.

'Search the hospital!' Kinderman instructed Atkins. 'She's after someone! Find her!'

'What toys?' the boy repeated.

More policemen appeared at the door, but Atkins held them back and gave them new instructions. The policeman in the room went out and joined them. The nurse brought the shopping bag over to the boy. 'I don't believe you,' the nurse said to Kinderman. She dumped out the contents of the bag on the bed. 'Do you treat your own family like this?'

'My family?' Kinderman's mind began to race. Abruptly he saw the nurse's nametag: Julie Fantozzi.

'. . . *an invitation to the dance.*'

'Julie! *My God*!'

He raced from the room.

Mary Kinderman and her mother were in the kitchen preparing dinner. Julie was sitting at the kitchen table reading a novel. The telephone rang. Julie was farthest away but she got it. 'Hello? Oh, hi, Dad. Sure. Here's Mom.' She held out the telephone to her mother. Mary took it while Julie went back to her reading.

'Hi, sweetheart. Are you coming for lunch?' Mary listened for a while. 'Oh, really?' she said. 'Why is that?' She listened some more. At last she said, 'Sure, honey, if you say so. In the meantime, dinner or no?' She listened. 'Okay, dear. I'll keep a plate warm. But hurry. I miss you.' She hung up the phone and went back to the bread that she was baking.

'*Nu?*' said her mother.

'It's nothing,' said Mary. 'Some nurse is coming over with a package.'

Again the telephone rang.

'Now they're cancelling,' muttered Mary's mother.

Julie jumped up to get the phone again, but her mother waved her back. 'No, don't answer,' she said. 'Your father wants the line kept clear. If he calls, he'll give a signal: two rings.'

Kinderman stood at the Neurology Charge Desk, his anxiety mounting with each unanswered dull ring of the telephone as he pressed the receiver to his ear. *Someone answer! Answer!* he thought in a frenzy. He let the phone ring for another minute, slammed down the receiver and raced to a stairway. He didn't even think of waiting for an elevator.

Panting, he arrived in the lobby and breathlessly rushed out into the street. He hurried to a squad car, got in and slammed the door. A helmeted policeman sat behind the wheel. 'Two-oh-seven-eighteen Foxhall Road and hurry!' gasped Kinderman. 'The siren! Break laws! Hurry, hurry!'

They took off with a screech of grasping tyres, the squad car siren wailing shrilly, and soon they were careering down Reservoir Road and then up onto Foxhall toward Kinderman's house. The detective was praying, his eyes shut tightly throughout the ride. When the squad car bumped to a jarring stop, he opened his eyes. He was in his driveway. 'Go around! The back door!' he ordered the policeman, who jumped from the car and began to run, drawing a snub-nosed revolver from its holster.

233

Kinderman squeezed himself out of the car, drew a gun and fished house keys out of a pocket as he rushed toward his door. With a shaky hand he was trying to insert a key in the lock, when the door flew open. Julie glanced at the gun, and then called back inside the house, 'Mother, Daddy's home!' The next second, Mary appeared at the door. She looked at the gun and then at Kinderman severely. 'The carp is dead already. What on earth do you think you're doing?'

Kinderman lowered the gun and moved quickly forward, embracing Julie. 'Thank God!' he whispered.

Mary's mother appeared. 'There's a Storm Trooper out in the back,' she said. 'It's beginning. What should I tell him?'

'Bill, I want an explanation,' said Mary.

The detective kissed Julie's cheek and pocketed the gun. 'I am crazy. That is all. That's the whole explanation.'

'I'll just tell him we're Febré,' Mary's mother grunted. She went back into the house. The telephone rang and Julie ran to the living room to get it. Kinderman stepped inside the house and moved toward the back. 'I will tell the policeman,' he said.

'Tell him what?' demanded Mary. She started to follow him into the kitchen. 'Bill, what is going *on* here? Will you talk to me, please?'

'I am talking.'

Kinderman froze. Against the wall by the doorway to the kitchen he saw a shopping bag. He rushed forward to pick it up when he heard the elderly, lilting voice of a woman in the kitchen saying, 'Hello.' Kinderman instantly drew his gun, stepped into the kitchen, and aimed toward the table where an elderly woman in nurse's uniform was seated, staring at him blankly.

'Bill!' screamed Mary.

'Oh, dear, I'm so tired,' said the woman.

Mary put her hands on Kinderman's arm and pushed it down. 'I don't want any *guns* in this house, do you hear me?'

The policeman charged into the kitchen, his gun drawn and levelled.

'Put that gun down!' screamed Mary.

'Could you please hold it down?' cried out Julie from the living room. 'I'm talking on the phone!'

Mary's mother muttered, '*Goyim*,' and continued to stir a pan of gravy at the stove.

The policeman looked at Kinderman. 'Lieutenant?'

The detective's eyes were glued to the woman. In her face was a look of confusion and weariness. 'Put it down, Frank,' Kinderman said. 'It's all right. Go on back. Go on back to the hospital.'

'Okay, sir.' The policeman sheathed the gun and left.

'How many for dinner?' asked Mary's mother. 'I have to know now.'

'What kind of shenanigan is this, Bill?' demanded Mary. She gestured at the woman. 'What kind of a nurse is this that you sent me? I open the door for the woman and she faints. She falls down. She puts her head back and hollers something crazy, and then she faints. My God, she's too *old* to be a nurse. She's –'

Kinderman waved her into silence. The woman looked innocently into his eyes. 'Is it bedtime?' she asked him.

The detective slowly sat at the table. He slipped off his hat and put it softly on a chair. 'Yes, it's almost bedtime,' he said to her gently.

'I'm so tired.'

Kinderman probed her eyes. They were honest and mild. He looked up at Mary, who was standing by with confusion and annoyance mixed in her face. 'You said that she said something,' Kinderman told her.

'What?' frowned Mary.

'You said that she said something. What did she say?'

'I don't remember. Now what's going on?'

'Please try to remember. What did she say?'

'"Finished",' grunted Mary's mother from the stove.

'Yes, that's it,' said Mary. 'Now I remember. She screamed, "He's finished" and then she fainted.'

'"*He's* finished"? or "Finished"?' pressed Kinderman. 'Which?'

'"*He's* finished",' said Mary. 'God, she sounded like a

werewolf or something. What's wrong with this woman? Who is she?'

Kinderman's head was averted. '"He's finished",' he murmured reflectively.

Julie came into the kitchen. 'So what's happening?' she said. 'What's going on?'

'Bad company,' muttered Mary's mother.

The telephone rang again. Mary answered it immediately. 'Hello?'

'Is it for me?' asked Julie.

Mary held the telephone out to Kinderman. 'It's for you,' she said. 'I think I'll give the poor thing some soup.'

The detective spoke into the phone. He said, 'Kinderman.'

It was Atkins. 'Lieutenant, he's calling for you,' said the sergeant.

'Who?'

'Sunlight. He's yelling his head off. Just your name.'

'I'll come over right away,' said Kinderman. He quietly hung up the phone.

'Bill, what's this?' he heard Mary asking behind him. 'It was in her shopping bag. Was that the package?'

Kinderman turned and caught his breath. In Mary's hands was a large and gleaming pair of surgical dissection shears. 'Do we need this?' asked Mary.

'No.'

Kinderman called for another squad car and took the old woman back to the hospital where she was recognized as a patient in the Open Ward of Psychiatric. She was transferred immediately to the Disturbed Ward for observation. The injured nurse and attendant, learned Kinderman, had sustained no permanent damage and were expected back to duty some time the next week. Satisfied, Kinderman left that area and went to the isolation section where Atkins was waiting in the hall. He was opposite the door to Cell 12, which was open. His back against the wall, his arms folded, he silently watched the detective approaching. His eyes seemed troubled and far away. Kinderman stopped and met his gaze. 'What's wrong with you?' asked the detective. 'Is something wrong?'

Atkins shook his head. Kinderman studied him for a moment. 'He just said you were here,' said Atkins remotely.

'When?'

'Just a minute ago.'

Nurse Spencer emerged from the cell. 'Are you going in?' she asked the detective.

Kinderman nodded, then he turned and walked slowly into the cell. He quietly closed the door behind him, went to the straightbacked chair and sat down. Sunlight was watching him, his eyes gleaming. What was different about him? the detective wondered.

'Well, I simply had to see you,' said Sunlight. 'You've been lucky for me. I owe you something, Lieutenant. Besides, I want my story set down as it happened.'

'And how did it happen?' Kinderman asked him.

'Close call for Julie, wouldn't you say?'

Kinderman waited. He listened to the dripping sound in the basin.

Sunlight abruptly leaned his head back and chuckled, then fixed the detective with a shining stare. 'Haven't you guessed it, Lieutenant? Why, of course, you have. You've finally put it all together – how my precious little surrogates do my work, my dear, sweet, elderly empty vessels. Well, they're perfect hosts, of course. They aren't there. Their own personalities are shattered. And so in I slip. For a while. Just a while.'

Kinderman stared.

'Oh, yes. Yes, of course. About this body. Friend of yours, Lieutenant?' Sunlight leaned his head back in rippling laughter that flowed into the strident braying of an ass. Kinderman felt ice at the back of his neck. Abruptly Sunlight broke it off and stared blankly. 'Well, there I was, so awfully dead,' he said. 'I didn't like it. Would you? It's upsetting. Yes, I felt very poorly. You know – adrift. So much work left to do and no body. It wasn't fair. But then along came – well, a friend. You know.

237

One of *them*. He thought my work should continue. But in this body. This body in particular, in fact.'

The detective was mesmerized. He asked, 'Why?'

Sunlight shrugged. 'Let's call it spite. Revenge. A little joke. A certain matter of an exorcism, I think, in which your friend Father Karras had been a participant and – well – expelled certain parties from the body of a child. Certain parties were not pleased, to say the least. No, not happy.' For a moment Sunlight's gaze was far away and haunted. He gave a little shudder, then looked back at Kinderman. 'So he thought of this prank as a way of getting back: using this pious, heroic body as the instrument of –' Sunlight shrugged. 'Well, you know. My thing. My work. My friend was very sympathetic. He brought me to our mutual friend, Father Karras. Not too well at the time, I'm afraid. Passing on. In the dying mode, as we say. So as he was slipping out my helpful friend slipped me in. Ships that pass in the night and all of that. Oh, some confusion by the steps when the ambulance team pronounced Karras dead, of course. Well, he *was* dead, technically speaking. I mean, in the spiritual sense. He was out. But I was in. A little traumatized, true. And why not? His brain was jelly. Lack of oxygen. Disaster. Being dead isn't easy. But never mind. I managed. Yes, a maximum effort that at least got me out of that coffin. Then at the last a bit of slapstick and comic relief when that old Brother Fain saw me climbing out. That helped. Yes, it's the smiles that keep us going at times, the bits of unexpected cheer. But after that it was rather downhill for a time. A time? Twelve years. So much damage to the brain cells, you see. So many lost. But the brain has remarkable powers, Lieutenant. Ask your friend the good Doctor Amfortas. Oh. No, I suppose I should ask him for you.'

Sunlight was silent for a time. 'No reaction from the gallery,' he said at last. 'Don't you believe me, Lieutenant?'

'No.'

The mockery vanished and Sunlight looked stricken. In an instant his features had crumpled into helplessness. 'You don't?' he quavered.

'No.'

Sunlight's eyes were beseeching and fearful. 'Tommy says he won't forgive me unless you know the truth,' he said.

'What truth?'

Sunlight turned away. He said dully, 'They will punish me for this.' He seemed to be staring at a distant terror.

'What truth?' the detective asked him again.

Sunlight shivered and looked back at Kinderman. His face was an urgent plea. 'I am not Karras,' he whispered hoarsely. 'Tommy wants you to know that. *I am not Karras*! Please believe me. If you don't, Tommy says he won't leave. He'll just stay here. I can't leave my brother alone. Please help me. *I can't go without my brother*!'

Kinderman's eyebrows were gathered in a question. He angled his head to the side. 'Go where?'

'I'm so tired. I want to go on. There's no need for me to stay now. I want to go on. Your friend Karras had nothing to do with the murders.' When Sunlight leaned forward Kinderman was startled by the desperation in his eyes. 'Tell Tommy you believe that!' he pleaded. '*Tell him*!'

Kinderman held his breath. He had a sense of the momentous that he could not explain. What was it? Why did he have this feeling? Did he believe what Sunlight was saying? It didn't matter, he decided. He knew he must say it. 'I believe you,' he said firmly.

Sunlight slumped backwards against the wall and his eyes rolled upward as from his mouth came the stuttering sounds, that other voice: 'I l-l-l-love you, J-j-j-jimmy.' Sunlight's eyes grew heavy and somnolent and his head sagged onto his chest. Then the eyes were closed.

Kinderman quickly got up from the chair. Alarmed, he moved swiftly over to the cot and lowered his ear to Sunlight's mouth. But Sunlight said nothing more. Kinderman rushed towards the buzzer, pushed it, then hastily stepped out into the hall. He met Atkins' gaze and said, 'It's starting.'

Kinderman raced to a Charge Desk telephone. He called his home. Mary answered. 'Sweetheart, don't leave the house,' the detective said urgently. 'Don't let anyone leave the house! Lock

239

the windows and doors and don't let anyone in until I get there!'

When Mary protested, he repeated the instructions and then hung up the phone. He went back to the hallway outside Cell 12. 'I want men at my house right away,' he told Atkins. Nurse Spencer emerged from inside the cell. She looked at the detective and said, 'He's dead.'

Kinderman stared at her blankly. 'What?'

She said, 'He's dead. His heart just stopped.'

Kinderman looked past her. The door was open and Sunlight was lying on his back on the cot. 'Atkins, wait here,' the detective murmured. 'Don't call. Never mind. Just wait,' he said.

Kinderman slowly entered the cell. He could hear Nurse Spencer coming in behind him. Her footsteps halted but he moved a little farther, until he was standing close by the cot. He looked down at Sunlight. His restraints and straitjacket had been removed. His eyes were closed, and in death his features seemed to have softened: on his face was a look of something like peace, of a journey's end that was long awaited. Kinderman had seen that look once before. He tried to collect his thoughts for a time. Then he spoke without turning. 'He was asking for me earlier, Miss?' he said.

He heard Spencer behind him saying, 'Yes.'

'Only that?'

'I don't know what you mean,' answered Spencer. She came up beside him. Kinderman turned his head to her. 'Did you hear him say anything else?'

She had folded her arms. 'Well, not really.'

'Not really? What exactly do you mean?'

Her eyes looked dark in the dimness of the room. 'There was that stuttering thing,' she said. 'A funny voice that he uses sometimes. It stutters.'

'He said words?'

'I'm not sure.' The nurse shrugged. 'I don't know. It was just before he started calling for you. He was still unconscious, I thought. I'd come in to take his pulse. Then I heard that sort of stuttering thing. It was something – well, I'm not sure – but like "Father".'

'"Father"?'

She shrugged. 'Something close to that, I think.'

'And he was still unconscious at the time?'

She said, 'Yes. Then he seemed to come to and – Oh, yes, now I remember something else. He yelled, "He's finished".'

Kinderman blinked at her. '"He's finished"?'

'That was just before he started to shout your name.'

Kinderman stared for a time; then he turned and looked down at the body. '"He's finished",' he murmured.

'Funny thing,' said Nurse Spencer. 'He looked happy at the end. For a second he opened his eyes and looked happy. Almost like a child.' Her voice was strangely disconsolate. 'I felt sorry for him,' she said. 'What a terrible person, psychotic or not. But there was something about him that made me feel sorry.'

'He is part of the angel,' murmured Kinderman softly. His eyes were still on Sunlight's face.

'I didn't hear what you said.'

Kinderman listened to a drop from the faucet smacking the porcelain of the basin. 'You may go now, Miss Spencer,' he told her. 'Thank you.' He listened to her leaving and when she was gone he reached down a hand and touched Sunlight's face. He held it there gently for a moment; then he turned and walked slowly out to the hallway. Something seemed different, he thought. What was it? 'What is bothering you, Atkins?' he asked. 'Please tell me.' The sergeant's eyes had a haunted look. 'I don't know,' he said. He shrugged. 'But I have some information for you, Lieutenant. The Gemini's father,' he said. 'We found him.'

'You did?'

Atkins nodded.

'Where is he?' asked Kinderman.

Atkins eyes seemed greener than ever, unblinking and whirling around a pinpoint of iris. 'He's dead,' he said. 'He died of a stroke.'

'When?'

'This morning.'

Kinderman stared.

'What the hell is going on, Lieutenant?' asked Atkins.

Kinderman realized what was different. He looked up at the ceiling of the hallway. All of the lights were burning brightly. 'I think it's finished,' he murmured softly. He nodded his head. 'Yes. I think so.' Kinderman lowered his gaze to Atkins and said, 'It's over.' Then he paused. 'I believed him.' The next instant the terror and the loss flooded in, the relief and the pain, and his face began to crumple. He sagged against a wall and started sobbing uncontrollably. Atkins was caught by surprise and for a moment he didn't know what to do; then he took a step forward and held the detective in his arms. 'It's all right, sir,' he repeated over and over as the sobbing and weeping went on for minutes. Just when Atkins was afraid it might never stop, it began to subside; but the sergeant held on. 'I'm just tired,' whispered Kinderman at last. 'I'm sorry. There's no reason. No reason. I'm just tired.'

Atkins took him home.

SUNDAY, MARCH 22

Chapter Sixteen

Which was the real world, Kinderman wondered; the world beyond or the world in which he lived? They had interpenetrated each other. Silent suns collided in both.

'It must be quite a knock for you,' Healy murmured. The priest and the detective stood alone at the gravesite staring at the coffin of the man who might be Karras. The prayers had ended and the men stood together with the dawn and their thoughts and the quiet earth.

Kinderman lifted his gaze to Healy. The priest stood beside him. 'Why is that?'

'You've lost him twice.'

Kinderman stared for a silent moment, then slowly returned his gaze to the coffin. 'It wasn't him,' the detective said softly. He shook his head. 'It never was him.'

Healy looked up at him. 'Can I buy you a drink?'

'Couldn't hurt.'

EPILOGUE

Kinderman was standing at the curb-side directly in front of the Biograph Cinema. He was waiting for Sergeant Atkins. His hands in the pockets of his coat, he was sweating, anxiously glancing up and down 'M' Street. It was almost noon and the date was Sunday, June 14th.

On March 23rd it had been determined that fingerprints lifted at three of the crime scenes matched three patients in the Open Ward. All three were currently in the Disturbed Ward, pending the results of a close observation.

Early in the morning on March 25th, Kinderman had gone to the home of Amfortas along with Doctor Edward Coffey, a friend of Amfortas and a neurosurgeon at District Hospital; he had ordered the CAT-scan for Amfortas that had revealed the fatal lesion. At Coffey's insistence, the front door lock of the house had been picked and Amfortas was discovered dead in his living room. It was later to be classed as an 'accidental death', for Amfortas had died of subdural haematoma resulting from the blow to his head when he fell, although Coffey told Kinderman that, in any case, Amfortas would have died within two weeks because of the deliberately untreated lesion. When Kinderman had asked him why Amfortas would allow himself to die, Doctor Coffey's only answer was, 'I think it had something to do with love.' A black woollen windbreaker with a hood was found hanging in a closet in Amfortas's bedroom.

On April 3rd, Kinderman's only other suspect, Freeman Temple, suffered a mentally disabling stroke and was now a patient in the Open Ward.

For three weeks following the murder of Keating, police security and precautions had continued in force at Georgetown

General, then were gradually relaxed. No other murders took place in the District of Columbia involving the Gemini *modus operandi* and on June 11th the seemingly Gemini-related murders were placed on the Homicide inactive file, although classified as 'open' and still unsolved.

'I am dreaming,' said Kinderman. 'What are you doing?' He stared numbly at Atkins who was standing before him dressed in a pinstripe suit and tie. 'Is this some joke?'

'Well, I'm married now,' said Atkins. He'd returned from his honeymoon the day before.

Kinderman continued to look shellshocked. 'I cannot stand this, Atkins,' he said. 'It's strange. It's unnatural. Have mercy. Remove the tie.'

'I might be seen,' said Atkins inscrutably.

Kinderman grimaced in disbelief. 'You might be *seen?*' he echoed. 'By whom?'

'People.'

Kinderman silently stared for a moment, then he said, 'I give up. I am your prisoner, Atkins. Tell my family I'm okay and am being well treated. I will write to them as soon as my hands stop shaking. My guess is two months.' His gaze dropped lower. 'Who picked out the tie?' he asked in a hollow voice. It had a floral, Hawaiian motif.

'I picked it myself,' said Atkins.

'I thought so.'

'I could mention your hat,' said Atkins.

'Don't.' Kinderman leaned in closer. His eyes were probing. 'I had a friend from school who became a Trappist,' he said, 'a monk for eleven years. All he did was make cheese, and now and then pick grapes, although mostly he prayed for people in suits. Then he quit the monastery and you know what he bought? The first thing? A two-hundred dollar pair of shoes. Loafers with little tassels on top and in the arches new pennies all shiny and bright. Am I making you nauseous? Wait. I'm not finished. The shoes were coloured purple, Atkins. Lavender. Am I making a point or as usual talking only to a tree?'

245

'You are making a point,' said Atkins, though his tone conceded nothing.

'Better stay in the Navy.'

'We're going to miss the beginning of the movie.'

'Yes, we might be seen,' said Kinderman darkly.

They entered the theatre and took their seats. The film was *Gunga Din*, to be followed by another, *The Third Man*. At the end of *Gunga Din*, when Din stood atop the temple of gold blowing faltering notes of his warning bugle call after Thuggee bullets had struck him, a woman sitting one row back began to giggle and Kinderman turned around and glared. The venomous look had no effect and when Kinderman turned around to Atkins to tell him that they ought to move to other seats, he saw that the sergeant was crying. The detective glowed fondly. He stayed in his seat, content with the world, and wept himself when 'Auld Lang Syne' was played in the background at the burial of Din. 'What a film,' he breathed. 'Such *schmaltz*. I love it.'

When the double feature was over, they stood in the busy and sweltering street in front of the theatre. 'Now let's go and have a *nosh*,' said Kinderman eagerly. Neither man was working that day. 'I want to hear about the honeymoon, Atkins, and your wardrobe. I am feeling some need of preparation for the future. Where to go now? To "The Tombs"? No, no, wait. I have a notion.' He was thinking of Dyer. He hooked his arm through the sergeant's and led him off. 'Come. I know the absolutely perfect place.'

Soon they were sitting inside 'The White Tower' smelling hamburger grease and discussing the movies they had seen. They were the only customers there. The counterman was standing at the grill with his back to them. He was tall and powerfully built and his face had a raw-boned, rough-hewn look. His white uniform and cap were spattered with grease. 'You know, we talk about evil in this world and where it comes from,' said Kinderman. 'But how do we explain all the good? If we are nothing but molecules we would always be thinking of ourselves. So how comes it we are always having Gunga Dins, people giving up their lives for somebody else? And then even Harry Lime,' he said with animation, 'Harry Lime who is the opposite, an evil man, even he makes a point in that scene on the ferris wheel.' He was speaking of *The Third Man*. 'That part he says about the Swiss and how after all these many centuries of peace the biggest product they have given us to date is the cuckoo clock. This is true, Atkins. Yes. He has a point. It could be that the world cannot progress without *angst*. Incidentally, I am working on a burglary-homicide on "P" Street. It happened last week. We must get into that tomorrow.'

The counterman turned and gave him a silent, dour look, then went back to the burgers, beginning to build an even dozen on the small, square bottoms of the buns. Kinderman watched him placing a pickle slice on each patty, a faint look of wistful longing in his eyes. 'Could you maybe put an extra slice of pickle on them, please?'

'Too much pickle's gonna ruin 'em,' the counterman growled. He had a voice like a drill sergeant, low and rough. He was placing the tops of the buns on the burgers. 'You want Continental cookin', go to Beau Rivage. They got all of that saucy crap over there.'

Kinderman's eyelids drooped. 'I'll pay extra.'

The counterman turned and set six burgers on a paper plate in front of each of them. His face and his eyes were stone. 'What to drink?' he asked.

'A little hemlock, please,' said Kinderman.

'We're all out of it,' the counterman said tonelessly. 'Don't fuck with me, pal. My back hurts. Now whaddya want to drink?'

'Espresso,' said Atkins.

The counterman shifted his gaze to the sergeant. 'What was that, professor?'

'Two Pepsis,' said Kinderman quickly, pressing his hand down on Atkins' forearm. The counterman's breath blew a hair in his nostril. With a glower he turned to get the drinks. 'Every wiseass on "M" Street comes in here,' he muttered.

A large group of Georgetown students came in and soon the

place was alive with laughter and chatter. Kinderman paid for the burgers and the drinks and said, 'I'm tired from sitting.' He stood up and Atkins followed his lead. They took their food to a stand-up counter that was set in an opposite wall. Kinderman bit into a burger and chewed. 'Harry Lime was right,' he said. 'Out of turmoil comes a poem – this burger.'

Atkins nodded in agreement, contentedly chewing.

'It's all part of my theory,' Kinderman said.

'Lieutenant?' Atkins held up a forefinger, pausing to chew and then swallow a mouthful. He pulled a white paper napkin from its dispenser, wiped his lips, and then leaned his face closer into Kinderman's; the babble in the room had grown excited. 'Would you do me a favour, Lieutenant?'

'I am here but to serve, Mister Chips. I am eating and therefore expansive. Let me have your petition. Is it properly sealed?'

'Would you please explain your theory?'

'Impossible, Atkins. You will put me under house arrest.'

'You can't tell me?'

'Absolutely not.' Kinderman took another bite of a burger, washed it down with a swallow of Pepsi, and then turned to the sergeant. 'But since you insist. Are you insisting?'

'Yes.'

'I thought so. First take off the tie.'

Atkins smiled. He unknotted the tie and slipped it off.

'Good,' said Kinderman. 'I cannot tell this to a perfect stranger. It's so huge. It's so incredible.' His eyes were aglitter. 'You're familiar with *The Brothers Karamazov*?' he asked.

'No, I'm not,' Atkins lied. He wanted to sustain the detective's giving mood.

'Three brothers,' said Kinderman; 'Dmitri, Ivan and Alyosha. Dmitri is the body of man, Ivan represents his mind and Alyosha is his heart. At the end – the very end – Alyosha takes some very young boys to a cemetery and the grave of their classmate, Ilusha. This Ilusha they treated very meanly once because – well, he was strange, there was no doubt about it. But then later when he died they understood why he acted the way

248

he had and how truly brave and loving he was. So now Alyosha –
he's a monk, by the way – he makes a speech to the boys at the
gravesite and mainly he is telling them that when they're grown
up and face the evils of the world they should always reach back
and remember this day, remember the goodness of their childhood, Atkins; this goodness that is basic in all of them; this
goodness that hasn't been spoiled. Just one good memory in
their hearts, he says, can save their faith in the goodness of the
world. What's the line?' The detective's eyes rolled upward and
his fingertips touched his lips, which were smiling already in
anticipation. He looked down at Atkins. 'Yes, I have it!
"Perhaps that one memory may keep us from evil and we will
reflect and say: Yes, I was brave and good and honest then."
Then Alyosha tells them something that is vitally important.
"First, and above all, be kind," he says. And the boys – they all
love him – they all shout, "Hurrah for Karamazov!"' Kinderman felt himself choking up. 'I always weep when I think of
this,' he said. 'It's so beautiful, Atkins. So touching.'

The students were collecting their bags of hamburgers now
and Kinderman watched them leaving. 'This is what Christ
must have meant,' he reflected, 'about needing to become like
little children before we can enter the kingdom of heaven. I
don't know. It could be.' He watched the counterman lay out
some patties on the grill in preparation for another possible
influx, then sit on a chair and begin to read a newspaper.
Kinderman returned his attention to Atkins. 'I don't know how
to say this,' he said. 'I mean, the crazy, incredible part. But
nothing else makes sense, nothing else can explain things,
Atkins. Nothing. I'm convinced it's the truth. But getting back
to Karamazov for a moment. The main thing is Alyosha when
he says, "Be kind". Unless we do this evolution will not work;
we will not get there,' Kinderman said.

'Get where?' asked Atkins.

'The White Tower' was quiet now; there was only the sizzling
from the grill and the sound of the newspaper turning now and
then. Kinderman's stare was firm and even. 'The physicists
now are all certain,' he said, 'that all the known processes in

249

nature were once part of a single, unified force.' Kinderman paused and then spoke more quietly. 'I believe that this force was a person who long ago tore himself into pieces because of his longing to shape his own being. That was the Fall,' he said: 'the "Big Bang": the beginning of time and the material universe when the one became many – legion. And that is why God cannot interfere: evolution is this person growing back into himself.'

The sergeant's face was a crinkle of puzzlement. 'Who is this person?' he asked the detective.

'Can't you guess?' Kinderman's eyes were alive and smiling. 'I have given you most of the clues long before.'

Atkins shook his head and waited for the answer.

'We are The Fallen Angel,' said Kinderman. 'We are the Bearer of Light. We are Lucifer.'

Kinderman and Atkins held each other's gaze. When the door chime sounded they glanced to the door. A dishevelled derelict walked in. His clothing was shredded and thick with soil. He walked mutely towards the counterman, and then stood with his eyes upon him in a meek and silent plea. The counterman glowered at him over his newspaper, stood up, prepared some hamburgers, bagged them, and gave them to the bum who then silently shuffled out of the shop.

'Hurrah for Karamazov,' Kinderman murmured.

Ghost and Horror Stories from Fontana

The Fontana Books of Great Horror Stories

Edited by Christine Bernard and Mary Danby
Numbers 1 to 15 (£1·00 each)

The world's most chilling horror stories, including classics from the past, famous modern tales, and original stories by new writers.

The Fontana Books of Great Ghost Stories

Edited by Robert Aickman and R. Chetwynd-Hayes
Numbers 1 to 17 (£1·00 each)

Stories of the dead – and the not-quite-so-dead, by some of the most imaginative writers of occult stories.

FONTANA PAPERBACKS

Book Tokens

**Give them
the pleasure of choosing**

Book Tokens can be bought
and exchanged at most
bookshops.

Stephen Donaldson

The Chronicles of Thomas Covenant, the Unbeliever

'Comparable to Tolkien at his best . . . will certainly find a place on the small list of true classics.' *Washington Post*

'An irresistible epic.' *Chicago Daily News*

'The most original fantasy since *Lord of the Rings* and an outstanding novel to boot.' *Time Out*, London

'Intricate, absorbing, these volumes create a whole new world.' *Sunday Press*, Dublin

The First Chronicles of Thomas Covenant, the Unbeliever

LORD FOUL'S BANE   £2.50
THE ILLEARTH WAR   £2.50
THE POWER THAT PRESERVES   £2.50

The Second Chronicles of Thomas Covenant

THE WOUNDED LAND   £2.50
THE ONE TREE   £1.95
WHITE GOLD WIELDER   £2.50

FONTANA PAPERBACKS

Fontana Paperbacks: Fiction

Fontana is a leading paperback publisher of both non-fiction, popular and academic, and fiction. Below are some recent fiction titles.

- ☐ SEEDS OF YESTERDAY Virginia Andrews £1.95
- ☐ CAVALCADE Gwendoline Butler £1.95
- ☐ RETURN TO RHANNA Christine Marion Fraser £1.95
- ☐ JEDDER'S LAND Maureen O'Donoghue £1.95
- ☐ THE FINAL RUN Tommy Steele £1.50
- ☐ FOR LOVE OF A STRANGER Lily Devoe £1.75
- ☐ THE WARLORD Malcolm Bosse £2.95
- ☐ TREASON'S HARBOUR Patrick O'Brian £1.95
- ☐ FUTURES Freda Bright £1.95
- ☐ THE DEMON LOVER Victoria Holt £1.95
- ☐ THE UNRIPE GOLD Geoffrey Jenkins £1.75
- ☐ A CASE FOR CHARLEY John Spencer £1.50
- ☐ DEATH AND THE DANCING FOOTMAN Ngaio Marsh £1.75
- ☐ THE 'CAINE' MUTINY Herman Wouk £2.50
- ☐ THE TRANSFER Thomas Palmer £1.95
- ☐ LIVERPOOL DAISY Helen Forrester £1.75
- ☐ OUT OF A DREAM Diana Anthony £1.75
- ☐ SHARPE'S SWORD Bernard Cornwell £1.75

You can buy Fontana paperbacks at your local bookshop or newsagent. Or you can order them from Fontana Paperbacks, Cash Sales Department, Box 29, Douglas, Isle of Man. Please send a cheque, postal or money order (not currency) worth the purchase price plus 15p per book for postage (maximum postage required is £3).

NAME (Block letters) _____

ADDRESS _____

_____

_____